1/20

# Lucky Caller

# Lucky Caller

**Emma Mills**

Henry Holt and Company

New York

Henry Holt and Company, *Publishers since 1866*
Henry Holt® is a registered trademark of Macmillan Publishing Group, LLC
120 Broadway, New York, NY 10271 • fiercereads.com

Library of Congress Control Number: 2019941037
ISBN 9781250179654

Our books may be purchased in bulk for promotional, educational, or business
use. Please contact your local bookseller or the Macmillan Corporate and
Premium Sales Department at (800) 221-7945 ext. 5442 or by email at
MacmillanSpecialMarkets@macmillan.com.

First edition, 2020 / Designed by Mallory Grigg
Printed in the United States of America
10  9  8  7  6  5  4  3  2  1

*To Hannah, from your Little Excess*

# 1.

IT WAS CHRISTMAS, AND DAN was in the middle of pro-
posing to my mom when there was a knock at the door.

All five of us looked that way—me, Mom, Dan, my
sisters Rose and Sidney, all of our heads swiveled en
masse like something from one of those Golden Age
musicals that Sid made us watch sometimes. Like we
were a "five six seven eight" away from breaking into
a tap number.

"Is this . . . ?" Mom looked a little confused when I
glanced back her way. Confused but happy—she still
looked really happy.

"No." Dan frowned from where he was standing in
the middle of our apartment's living room/dining room
combo. My mom was in one of the chairs by the window, which we had pushed to the side to accommodate
our little artificial tree. "Not . . . part of it."

Mom let out a laugh, her hand flying up to her face.
"Uh-oh."

The knock sounded again, gentle but insistent.

"Should I—" Rose went to stand.

"Nina's closer," Sidney pointed out.

"Yes, Nina, please." Mom grinned at Dan. He looked flustered but grinned back anyway.

I stood and went to the door.

Until this moment, nothing about the engagement had come as a surprise. The truth was, Dan had—albeit awkwardly—asked for "permission" from Rose, Sidney, and me a few days prior. It was oddly endearing, putting aside the notion of my mom somehow *belonging* to us and needing our *approval* to remarry.

Though Mom, too, had asked for our permission in a way, without formally asking for it, even before Dan had. She had taken us to Lincoln Square, the breakfast place near our apartment building, to celebrate the start of Christmas vacation and had cut her pancakes into increasingly small pieces, fiddled around with her napkin for a while, and eventually said, apropos of nothing:

"Dan and I are thinking."

"Wow, I had no idea you guys had achieved telepathic communication," Rose had replied, because Dan wasn't out with us at the time, and also because, despite it being exactly the kind of thing that any one of us would say, as the oldest, Rose often got there first.

"Dan and I are *thinking*—" Mom repeated, really hitting the word to imply that the rest of the thought would be coming momentarily, "—about our future together. About all of our futures together. And we were thinking—we've been talking—about . . ." Historically, Mom would get more and more measured the more uncertain she was of how to approach something. By this point, each word was treated to its own sentence: "The. Idea. Of. Us. Getting. Married."

Sidney looked up from her southwest scramble. "Married?"

"Yes."

"Like, in a church?"

"Probably not."

"Like, white dress, something borrowed, the Dantist is our stepdad now?"

"You know how I feel about that nickname."

"There's nothing mean about it," Rose said. "It's a portmanteau. His name is Dan, and he's a dentist. If anything, it's efficient."

"Why does Dan have to be defined by his career?"

"Why does his career have to fit so seamlessly with his name?" was my contribution.

"Nina."

"Mom."

She sighed. Picked up her fork and speared one of the minuscule pancake pieces. Rose's phone was on the table, and it vibrated once, and then again, in the silence. A freshman in college, Rose's semester had ended a week earlier than mine and Sidney's, and she had gotten a flurry of texts from high school friends over the last few days, people coming back into town for break. She looked like she wanted to reach for the phone, but she didn't. Mom had a *forks up, phones down* policy. The fact that it was even on the table was a direct violation, but I think Mom must've been too distracted to really care. Now I knew why.

"How do we feel?" she said eventually.

"Sleepy," Sidney replied.

Mom looked toward the ceiling. "How do we feel *about Dan and me*?"

"Oh, that," Sidney said, and then grinned at me. At thirteen, she was the baby of the family. We let her get away with too much.

"We feel . . ." Rose paused. She could be measured like Mom sometimes. "Okay. Right?" She looked from me to Sidney. "We feel okay? About Mom and the"—Mom opened her mouth to speak—"*Dan* making it official?"

The Dantist, or Dr. Dan Hubler, DDS, was twelve years older than Mom. He always wore khakis. He made his own almond milk. He and my mom had met online just over a year ago.

It wasn't the first time she'd dated since our parents split up—it had been almost ten years since they divorced. But it was the first time that it seemed like . . . something substantial, I guess. It was the first time that she seemed settled, and not in a bad way. Just in a way where she never acted any different around Dan than she did around us. She still seemed completely herself with him—still laughed as loud, still got just as exasperated sometimes.

Rose looked pointedly at me and Sidney when we didn't answer, and Sidney bobbed her head and said, "Sure, I guess," around a mouthful of eggs and bell peppers. I didn't respond. Just divided a piece of pancake in half with my fork and then halved it again. I guess I came by it naturally.

Truthfully, I wasn't exactly sure how I felt. I knew that Mom would be happy. I knew that I liked Dan well enough. But it had seemed abstract there in the booth at Lincoln Square, and even still when Dan had asked us afterward. Like something hypothetical.

But now here we were, in the middle of the afternoon on Christmas. Mom had found the box that "Santa" snuck under the tree after lunch, and it was right in the middle of happening—of becoming something entirely . . . *thetical*—when I swung open our front door to see who had unknowingly interrupted the start of this very real engagement.

It turned out to be Mrs. Russell, an older lady who lived a couple floors down. She used to babysit us after school when we were younger. Her grandson, Jamie, was in my class at school, and he lived with her and Mr. Russell.

She was holding a loaf of something wrapped in red cellophane with a silver bow stuck on top, and she smiled at me, eyes crinkling at the edges behind plastic lilac-colored frames.

"Hello, Nina! Merry Christmas!"

"Hi . . ." Saying *Mrs. Russell* out loud felt weird. We used to call her *Gram* like Jamie did when we were kids, *Grammy* when we were even younger. "Merry Christmas."

"Our mom's getting engaged!" Sidney called.

"Oh my!" Mrs. Russell said. "Congratulations!"

"Technically, it's still in progress," Sidney added.

"I'm sorry?"

Mom jumped up and joined us at the door just as Mr. Russell appeared next to Gram in the hallway, leaning on Jamie's arm.

My heart rate ratcheted up a little.

"Eleanor, Paul, Jamie, hi. Merry Christmas!" Mom said, and Mrs. Russell's eyes widened, clocking the box in Mom's hand.

"We are so sorry to interrupt—" she began, but Mom shook her head, and behind her, Dan said:

"Please, join us. This is the kind of thing that's even better among friends," though I wasn't sure if he had ever even met the Russells before.

"We couldn't intrude—" Mrs. Russell said, and there was a fair bit of back-and-forth before we all cleared out of the doorway and the Russells finally entered, Gram still looking apologetic, Mr. Russell (*Papa,* I thought absently) and Jamie shuffling in behind. Dan greeted Mrs. Russell, clasped hands with Mr. Russell and Jamie, and ushered everyone to sit, offering coffee or cider or hot chocolate or champagne.

"We don't have—" Mom started to say, but Dan winked, and when everyone was situated, he turned to my mom and said, "Michelle."

Mom's eyes shone. "Daniel."

"About . . . what I was saying before . . ."

"Yes," Mom said. "Yes. Obviously."

Mrs. Russell burst into applause, and we all joined in while Mom moved in to kiss Dan.

"Jamie, take a picture," Mrs. Russell said, and Jamie pulled a phone out of his back pocket. "In front of the tree!" she added, and I recalled all at once her gentle forcefulness. Camouflaged in a cheerful demeanor was Gram's iron will. "Arms around each other!"

Jamie took some pictures of Dan and Mom posing in front of the tree while the rest of us looked on like we were the crew of a Christmas catalog shoot. Afterward, Mom went to cut up the zucchini bread that Mrs. Russell had brought, and make a platter with some Christmas cookies. Dan and Mr. Russell started talking, which left Rose and me on the couch, Sidney on the floor looking through a new book, and Jamie hovering awkwardly nearby, still holding his phone.

I could see part of his screen from where I sat. He was thumbing back through the pictures he had just taken, my mom and Dan in nearly identical shots, faces pressed close, smiling wide. Past those pictures were a few of what must have been Jamie's Christmas morning with Gram and Papa. He paused on one of Papa with an array of shiny plastic bows stuck to the front of his sweater.

Rose cleared her throat in a way that wouldn't draw Jamie's attention but that I knew from seventeen years as Rose's sister was meant specifically for me. In confirmation, she looked from Jamie to me and back again, widening her eyes as if to make a point.

I blinked at her like I didn't understand. She blinked back like she knew exactly what I was doing. I turned away from her exasperated face, glancing in Jamie's direction again.

He had always been cute in a goofy sort of way, with brown eyes that could be by turns serious enough to make you feel guilty about whatever ridiculous childhood scheme you had tried to rope him into, or mischievous enough to get you into the scheme in the first place. His face had always communicated his feelings all too plainly—we used to call it the Jamietron, like a Jumbotron at a basketball game or something.

It was hard to read him now. He looked taller than the last time I had seen him, though the red-and-white-striped sweater he was currently wearing was approximately three sizes too big. The sleeves trailed way past his fingers. It still had the tag on the collar.

"New sweater, James?" Rose asked eventually. I guess she had given up on me.

Jamie looked up from his phone with something like surprise. "Oh. Yeah. How'd you know?"

"You got, uh—" Rose gestured to the back of her neck.

Jamie reached up and felt the tag, chagrin flashing across his face—there was the Jamietron of old. He gave the tag a yank, crumpling it and shoving it in his pocket. "Gram got it for me. I'm . . . supposed to grow into it."

"Did she also give you a vat of radioactive waste? 'Cause that might help things along," Sidney said. I nudged her with my foot, but Jamie just huffed a laugh, and then it was quiet again among the four of us.

"How's . . . stuff?" he said eventually, looking at Rose. She was always the default.

"Stuff is good," Rose replied.

He shifted a bit closer to where we were sitting. He really did seem taller. And broader, maybe? I would go down to the gym with Rose to use the ellipticals sometimes, but I never saw him down there.

"Still working at Bagels?" Rose said with a smile.

Bagels was a shop in the big strip mall by the Target uptown, sandwiched between a UPS store and a kids' clothing store. It technically had a real name—The Bagel Company or something like that—but the sign hanging above the place simply said BAGELS in bright red letters. So we just called it *Bagels* and left it at that. You had to say it like there was an exclamation point after it, though, like jazz hands were implied: *BAGELS!*

"I am," Jamie said.

Sidney looked up from her book. "Can you get us free bagels?"

"They usually sell out, but I could bring you a bag of leftovers sometime if they have any. It helps if you like pumpernickel or jalapeño though because those are usually the only kinds left."

Sidney wrinkled her nose.

Jamie looked back at Rose. "So . . . Do you like college so far?"

She shrugged noncommittally.

"How about eighth grade?" he asked Sidney.

"No one likes eighth grade," Sidney replied.

One corner of Jamie's mouth ticked up. "That's fair."

"How about you?" Rose said. "One more semester, and then you guys are done. Got big plans? Anything fun coming up?"

"Not really." He shifted from one foot to the other for a moment, and then: "Oh—I'm, uh, taking that radio class."

"Oh! So is Nina."

He glanced at me. "Yeah?"

"Yeah," I said. Meridian North High School's radio broadcasting class was open only to seniors and was reportedly one of the most fun electives you could take.

"Cool." A pause. "Hey, you'll probably be great at it. You know, because of your dad and stuff."

My dad hosted a breakfast radio show in San Diego—*Conrad and Co.*, KPMR 100.2, mornings from six to ten thirty.

"I mean, I don't think it's . . . genetic or anything," I said.

Jamie bobbed his head, smiled tightly. "True."

Silence.

Mom crossed into the living room with the cookie platter, and Rose hopped up to join her as she placed it on the dining room table.

"Sorry," Jamie said after a moment. "For just showing up in the middle of . . . an important thing." He grimaced a little. "I told Gram we shouldn't bother you guys, but . . ." He trailed off.

"It's not like it was a surprise," I said. "I mean. You were a surprise. You guys. Coming here. But we basically knew already about . . ." I waved a hand.

"Good." He nodded. "That's good."

It would never not be awkward around Jamie. The trick was to spend as little time with him as possible.

So when Rose came back with cookies, I got up to get some too. He didn't follow.

---

That night I stared up into the dark recesses of the ceiling in the room I shared with Rose and Sidney and knew deep down that I should've tried harder with Jamie. Like asked him what he was up to besides working at *BAGELS!*, or if he had picked out a college yet. Was he even planning to go to college? I didn't know, and peeling back the layers on why that was baffling and sad was too much for this time of night.

There's something a little sad already about going to bed on Christmas. You know it'll be 364 days until the next one. And Christmas at our apartment building, the Eastman, was one of my favorite times of year. They piped Christmas music into the lobby 24/7. There was a massive white tree decorated in gold and silver with a sprawling pile of gold-and-silver-wrapped boxes underneath it. White poinsettias everywhere. It was a historical building—more than a hundred years old— and it felt at its most authentic at Christmas, I think.

We had lived there for years. I had some early memories of the house we had shared with our dad before, a one-story place on the east side of Indianapolis, but the bulk of my life thus far had taken place in our two-bedroom at the Eastman. My mom took the smaller room—it was barely big enough for a bed and a dresser. The three of us shared the other room, which was larger due to a small bump-out in the back where the room abutted the elevator and the laundry room. I remember fighting Rose for that space when we were little—she was ultimately triumphant, but more fool her, because she had to learn to sleep through the sounds of the washer and dryer (at the far wall) and the sounds of the elevator (immediately adjacent). The elevator dinged when the doors opened, and we could hear the whir of it going up and down the eleven floors of the Eastman all hours of the day.

It dinged once faintly now, and I could hear the shift of the doors opening on our floor. People getting back late after an extended family Christmas, maybe, laden with gift bags and leftovers.

It had been a good Christmas overall. It was our second one with the Dantist. Last year, he gave us each a Polaroid camera and all the fixings—packages of film, photo albums, kits for decorating. We had since dedicated a portion of our wall to Polaroids—the first one was a blurry shot of the five of us, Sidney's face the only one entirely in frame, everyone else just a chin or an eye or a corner of forehead.

I guess it was our first family photo. Since we were going to be a family now, apparently.

We had visited my dad over the past summer, and there were Polaroids from that trip too: the beach, my dad's house, elaborate ice cream sundaes. Sidney posing in front of a display at the zoo. My dad and Rose on rented bikes, making funny faces.

He had called earlier—of course he had. Outside of

major holidays, he usually called every Sunday night. We always talked to him in turns, Sidney first, then me, then Rose, and my mom would round out the call sometimes, but not often. He had sent us money for Christmas, because "I never know what to get you," he said on the phone to me tonight. "I feel like you're all always changing what you like. I can't keep up. Is it makeup this year? Do we hate makeup? Are sneakers in? Is green cool?"

"Was green ever, like, especially cool?"

"Is it uncool?"

"I mean, I don't have strong feelings about it either way?"

"We'll ask Rose, she's the artist," he said, and Rose later said it depended on the hue, and intensity, and saturation. There were too many parameters to make a definitive call.

This year, the Dantist had given us each a piece of jewelry—his mother's jewelry, specifically. She had passed several years ago, and Dan told us he couldn't bear to sell it.

It was the real deal. Rose got a necklace with a diamond pendant on it. Sidney got pearl earrings. I got a ring—a thin gold band with five small opals set into it in a row.

"I know it's all a little old-fashioned looking," Dan had said tentatively. "Not the most . . . current thing. But I thought maybe . . . well, I thought you might like it."

"It's really nice," Rose had replied. "Thank you."

"Thanks," I said, and Sidney chimed in too, throwing her hair back and gesturing to one ear.

"Do I look *glaaaamorous*?"

"Very glamorous," Dan replied with a smile.

I was still wearing my ring that night, and I rubbed at the stones absently as I lay in bed. The light filtering through the curtains from the street below caught the gold a little, glinted.

Sidney must have been watching me through the dimness, because she spoke:

"The Dantist's presents were like something from Kingdom. Like he gave us magical relics. Gems with special properties. Mine would be for invisibility."

Kingdom was a make-believe game we invented when we were younger. Rose and I were ten and eleven, and Sidney was just six. Only Sidney still mentioned it from time to time—I think she had the fondest memories of it, being the youngest. It was very involved and deeply embarrassing, as childhood make-believe games often are.

"Mine would be for making people quiet when other people are trying to sleep," Rose said from her side of the room.

"The pendant of tranquility," Sidney replied, and after a beat: "Say what yours is, Nina."

"The ring of silence."

"We can't have overlap in our powers."

"You can't have earrings of invisibility."

"Why not?"

"How would that even work? You have two earrings and two earring backs. Does it only work if you have both earrings? What if you only have one earring in? Are you half invisible? Which half? Top to bottom, or like, left side, right side? And it's not even efficient anyway, like, what if you needed to go invisible really quickly? Like, gee, wait while I get both of these attached. Let me just fumble around with the earrings and the backs and like try to punch one through the closed-over skin if I haven't worn earrings in a while—"

"Okay, fine, they're not earrings of invisibility, they're logic shields. They're immune to your dumb logic. Invisibility is just a bonus side effect."

"That doesn't even make—"

"Rose!" Sidney squawked.

"Pendant of tranquility," Rose said.

"You're not even wearing it," Sidney muttered. It was quiet for a little while, and I thought maybe Sidney had fallen asleep until she spoke again. "Why did we stop hanging out with Jamie?"

"Yeah, Nina, why is that?" Rose asked.

"Ring of silence," I replied.

"No overlap!"

"Ohhhhhh my god."

It was quiet for a moment. Maybe the ring actually worked.

"Do you guys feel weird?" Sidney said eventually. "About the whole . . . engagement thing?"

"Define *weird*," I said, just as Rose replied:

"It's okay to feel . . ." She didn't finish. "It's okay to feel. Whatever you want to feel."

"I know that. But what do *you* feel?"

I swallowed. Rose didn't answer, so I did.

"When there was that knock at the door . . . did you have like a split second, like, totally stupid moment where you thought that maybe it was Dad?"

"What, like busting in to stop it from happening?" Rose said.

"I don't know." A pause. "I said it was stupid."

Neither of them replied.

"I'm happy for Mom," Rose said eventually. "But also, yeah, it's a little weird. Things are going to be different."

"How?"

"I mean, we'll definitely have to move."

I sat up in bed. "Wait, what?"

# 2.

Conrad: This is Pete Conrad. You're listening to 100.2 The Heat, and we're about to, uh, do the resolution thing.

Will: Yeah?

Conrad: Yeah, yeah, yeah. New year, new you, all that crap. Nikki, what's your resolution?

Nikki: I mean, it's always the same, isn't it? Go to the gym more, eat better, blah blah blah.

Conrad: How'd that go last year?

Nikki: How do you think?

Conrad: Well, I think you look great. You look great all year long.

Will: Awwww.

Nikki: No, I don't like when you're nice. It makes me suspicious.

Conrad: What? Why? I'm always nice.

Tina: Uh-huh. Yeah, right.

Conrad: I am! Tina, don't pile on with them. You guys always gang up on me. It's always three against one.

Nikki: You're a lot of things, Conrad, but nice isn't one of them.

Conrad: I am . . . offended. That's what I am. Truly. I think we'll find a lot of support out there for me, lotta people on my side. Call in if you think that I'm nice and these other three are full of—

Tina: Probably not helping your case.

Conrad: We're gonna put it to the listeners. You guys'll see. And call in if you've already given up on your resolutions. God knows I have.

Will: It's January third.

Conrad: I know—it's my longest record yet. 555-1002, give us a shout.

**TOP 40 MUSIC TOOK OVER,** and I paused the show.

I was always a day behind on my dad's show—with the time difference between Indianapolis and San Diego, I rarely ever caught it when it actually aired. Luckily, they archived them online.

It was the first day back to school after break. Everything had gone by quickly after Christmas. Rose still had another week off, but it was back to business for me and Sidney. No more sleeping in, lying around, eating cereal for lunch, and listening to Mom and Dan doing the crossword puzzle.

I had asked my mom the day after Christmas if the

engagement meant we were going to move. I don't know why I hadn't thought about it before except that I never really thought too deeply about much of anything if I didn't have to.

Mom answered in the affirmative.

"Sidney's finishing up middle school this year, so she can transition into high school anywhere. Rose has graduated, and you're almost done. Our lease is up in the summer. It just makes sense. The timing is right."

"So that's why you guys decided to get married now? For, like, the sake of convenient timing?"

"It was a factor," she said, "but obviously a marriage isn't founded purely on timing alone."

"Are we gonna move into Dan's house?"

She shrugged. "We might find a new place. Some place between Dan's job and mine. We've also been talking about . . ." She paused, considering. "Well, I'm thinking about going back to school."

My mom worked in a core facility at the School of Medicine downtown. A core was a place with shared machines that a bunch of research labs used since the machines were too expensive to buy individually. Mom's core did flow cytometry, which was a technique used to separate cells into different populations. I remember her explaining it once with M&M's when we were kids—pouring a bag out on the tabletop, all the different colors mixed together, and then separating them out into yellows and reds and blues. Flow cytometry used lasers to separate the cells out by different properties, just like you could separate M&M's by color.

She had mentioned going back to school to get her PhD before, but I didn't know it was an actual thing that was actually becoming real, like the marriage and the apparent move.

"So I'd still be working downtown," she continued. "If that were to happen. But we can find a place that will fit all of us if we want. If you want to keep staying with us for college, like Rose is."

"*Staying with us?*" I said to Rose later. "Can you believe she said it like that? Like it won't even be our home. Like we'll be *strangers* or something. Seriously?"

Rose just shrugged and said, "I mean . . ." and then she turned back to her sketchbook like she had expressed a complete thought.

I thought of her response to Mom at Lincoln Square: *We feel . . . Okay. Right? We feel okay?*

I felt okay with it only so long as nothing changed. That's what I should have said, but stuff like that never came in the moment. The perfect comeback only comes to you way after the offending incident, most especially when you're alone in the shower with no one but the shampoo bottle to tell it to.

When I reached my locker the first day back at school, Alexis Larsson was already there. She was someone who had probably never shared searing rejoinders with her shower products. Truthfully, she was the kind of person who probably warranted those comebacks herself, but she was something like my closest friend at school now that Rose had graduated.

Alexis had appeared in seventh grade, a transfer from some fancy junior high on the north side. None of those new-kid-is-an-outsider tropes applied. No, Alexis instantly became the coolest person in our grade. It was like on a reality show when they introduce someone new and controversial midseason for ratings.

The mystique and hype surrounding Alexis had mellowed out by now—there were so many more people at Meridian North High School to dilute it—but I still had that feeling every now and then of being twelve and completely awed by her. Hoping she would like me despite the fact that she must have, or we wouldn't still be friends.

"One more semester," she said by way of a greeting, holding one hand up for a high five and adding in an ominous voice: "*The beginning of the end.*"

"Hooray." I slapped her palm and then set about getting into my locker.

"How was your break?" We had texted a little, but she was gone for the bulk of it on a family ski trip to Colorado. All the Larssons got together at Grandpa Larsson's cabin in Breckenridge—it was an annual tradition. I caught the pictures and videos Alexis posted throughout, seated on a ski lift or posing in front of a massive fireplace or holding up a snowball with a devilish grin. Alexis didn't know I knew this, but one time she handed me her phone to look something up, and there was already a page open on the browser titled

"Become Instagram Famous in Eight Easy Steps!" I couldn't say what step she was on currently, but she had a couple thousand followers, so she must have been doing something right.

I shrugged. "Pretty good." I didn't feel like going into it. "How was skiing?"

"I snowboarded, mainly," she replied. "But it was everything."

One of Alexis's favorite phrases—things were often *everything* or *nothing*. She left very little room for the in between.

"What do you have this afternoon?" she said.

"Radio broadcasting."

"Ah." She grinned. "Ready for your big debut?"

I made a face. "No?"

"You'll do great. Shit, I'm gonna be late. Text me after," she said, and then quickly strode away.

---

I didn't care what Jamie said—the fact that my dad worked in radio didn't give me much of an advantage in radio broadcasting class. It didn't mean I automatically knew everything there was to know any more than Josh Epson's mom being our sophomore English teacher meant he inherently understood symbolism in *The Scarlet Letter* better than the rest of us.

Although since my mom worked in science, we always did have pretty great science fair projects growing up. So maybe we did have a bit of a leg up on that one.

The radio broadcasting course had a lot of components—learning about the history of radio, learning how to work with editing software, producing promos and stuff, and most importantly, creating and producing a weekly radio show for the student station.

"And keep in mind, a lot of these skills will be transferrable to podcasting," the teacher, Mr. Tucker, told us that first afternoon of class. He was a youngish guy with a beard and thick locks that he pulled back with a headband. "If you happen to be, uh, somewhat more interested in that medium." He went through the syllabus with us and gave a brief intro presentation. In the last part of class, we would need to divide up into groups of four for our radio shows.

"I'm good with however you guys want to do it, but you're going to spend a lot of time with your group over the course of the semester, so choose . . . mindfully, that's how I'll put it. Maybe your friend is here, but maybe working closely with them is going to drive you up the wall or get in the way of your productivity. Definitely keep that in mind."

The thing about Meridian North was that it was so massive, you could definitely get put in a class without any of your friends whatsoever. I knew some of the people here for sure. There was this girl Sammy—we had French together sophomore year—and her boyfriend who played on the soccer (baseball?) team. A kid named Fletcher who I knew from when I disastrously tried debate club in ninth grade (Prompt: "Does technology make us more alone?" Me: "Uhhh . . . I mean, yeah? But if you think about it . . . no?"). But there was no one I was an instant lock with, unlike the group of girls turning to each other at the front of the room or Sammy immediately grabbing her boyfriend's arm.

The girl sitting in front of me turned around. She had deep brown skin, tight curls cut short, and extra long legs stretched out into the aisle. I realized that I knew her—she was in the team sports class I took junior year. Her name was Sasha, and she played on the volleyball team. She had picked me for one of our class matches once even though my volleyball skills were about on par with my debate skills.

So maybe we weren't exactly friends, but we were friendly at least. "Want to be in a group?" she asked.

I shrugged like I wasn't supremely grateful to her for initiating, like I wasn't just sitting there hoping someone would. "Sure."

"We need two more."

We scanned the room, but groups of four were rapidly materializing.

"Uh, maybe . . ." Sasha began, but then a guy sidled up to us from the back. He was wearing a T-shirt with giant neon letters that said "GREATEST OF ALL TIME" on it, but in weird typography, stacked up into a column in chunks like GREA/TEST/OF/ALL/TIME.

"*Grea test* of all time?" Sasha read as the guy opened his mouth to address us.

He looked caught off guard. "No, it says—"

"What kind of test is that?" I asked, because I couldn't help it. "Like a diagnostic kind of thing?"

"All right, how are we doing?" Mr. Tucker called. "All grouped up?"

GREA/TEST/OF/ALL/TIME looked back at us, hesitating like maybe he had changed his mind, but then he plowed ahead. "Group? Us three?"

"Sure," Sasha replied, glancing at me. I nodded.

"Cool," the guy said, but a bit flat like it really wasn't cool, like maybe he didn't want to partner with people who pretended not to understand his T-shirt. "He's with us too." He gestured toward the back of the room, and a few rows behind us, Jamie Russell—wearing the same red-and-white-striped sweater he had worn on Christmas—gave us a little wave.

There seemed to be no way out of it.

"Works for me," Sasha said, and I echoed it weakly: "Yeah. Great."

The Greatest of All Time was named Joydeep Mitra. He gestured Sasha and me to where Jamie was sitting in the back. As we followed him, he looked up at Sasha appraisingly.

"You're really tall."

"Thanks, I hadn't noticed."

"No, but for real. Is the atmosphere, like, different up there?"

Sasha's expression was unwaveringly placid. "I don't know, what's the gravity like down there?"

A smile flickered across his face, but he didn't respond, just plopped down at the desk next to Jamie's.

"You guys know Jamie?" Joydeep said, and I nodded. Jamie nodded back, but not without a flash of that same kind of embarrassment he had worn on Christmas. *I told Gram we shouldn't bother you guys . . .*

Sasha greeted Jamie too, and then we were a group, I guess, officially. Mr. Tucker told us we needed to brainstorm the concept for our show—we would have a proposal due at the end of the week, and then we'd get our time slot. Once we officially started broadcasting, we would be on the hook for one show a week for most of the semester.

"The live broadcasts are a large portion of your final grade," Mr. Tucker told us after everyone had rearranged into their groups. "Since I obviously can't listen live to every single time slot, you'll be responsible for archiving each show as an audio file. Think of these audio files as assignments—failing to archive means a zero for that assignment for the whole group. No exceptions." He leaned on his desk, his pants riding up on one leg to reveal socks that were a shock of neon stripes. "I want you to be creative with your concepts. And I want you to have fun. And"—he smiled—"to make it a little more interesting, we're going to have bonus points for the group that has the highest average listenership at the end of the semester."

When we were turned loose for brainstorming, Joydeep said with no preamble, "Who here is just so fucking psyched about radio? Anyone? No one? Good. Because my brother Vikrant took this class three years ago, and he told me the secret."

"There's a secret?" Jamie said.

"Of course there is. There's a secret to everything."

"Okay," I said. "What is it?"

"Are you ready?"

I looked at Sasha, who just raised an eyebrow skeptically. "Pretty ready?"

Joydeep held his hands up like he was framing it in the air: "The nineties."

"What about them?"

"That's our theme."

"But why?"

"The station's catalog is full of nineties music. The school doesn't have access to a lot of the current stuff, but they do have permission for a shit-ton of stuff from the nineties. So if you pick the nineties as the theme for your show, you have a ton of music to choose from. All you gotta do is queue it up and do a few breaks where you say what the songs are, and that's it. Coast on by for the rest of the semester."

Jamie was frowning. "What do you mean by *nineties* though?"

Joydeep frowned back. "Music that was released between the years 1990 and 1999?"

"No, I just mean—that could be anything. Gin Blossoms or Boyz II Men or Chumbawamba or Nirvana or Biggie—"

"That's a lot of dudes on your list," Sasha said.

"Britney Spears or Aaliyah or Celine Dion or Lauryn Hill," Jamie amended.

Joydeep frowned. "What the fuck, did you *study* nineties artists?"

"I just like music," Jamie mumbled. "All I'm saying is, I think nineties is too broad."

"So you want us to narrow it down to, like, hip-hop recorded in a basement in February of '92?"

"That's kind of an extreme way to put it, but we could at least . . . pick a genre or something."

Joydeep shook his head. "No. Come on. The point is that there's a bunch of stuff to pick from. If we limit ourselves too much, we'll have to do actual work. If we say we're only doing hip-hop or whatever, we'll have to actively search out hip-hop in the catalog. Too much work. I'm telling you, all we need to do is search the year and queue up songs at random."

Jamie didn't look convinced.

"How about this: If you want, you can be music guy. Do you want to be music guy? Do our programming?"

Jamie looked to me and Sasha. "What roles do you want?"

"I don't care about being music guy," I said.

"Me neither," Sasha said. "And I don't want to be the host."

"Me neither," I echoed.

"I'll do that part," Joydeep offered.

"For real?" Jamie said.

Joydeep shrugged. "Sure. That's like the easiest part. All you have to do is talk."

"I mean, I don't think it's as easy as that," I said.

"Why not? I'm talking right now. Putting words together one after another. Still at it. Little to no effort involved on my part."

"Great audition," Sasha muttered.

"So we're decided?"

"Wait, no." I peered at the syllabus. "Someone has to be the producer. And someone needs to . . ." I scanned the requirements. "Do publicity and prepare on-air features."

"What's that?"

"Like weather, or news and stuff."

"That's fine for me," Sasha said. "Running the equipment would freak me out."

"Yeah, okay," I said. "I'll produce." It mainly involved pressing buttons. Sometimes modulating volume. I could do that.

"So in summary," Joydeep said, "I'm the host. Wonder Woman's gonna do publicity and shit. Where's Waldo over here will do music." Jamie looked down at his sweater, frowned. "And, uh . . ." Joydeep waved in my direction. "You . . . are the producer."

"I don't get a nickname?"

"Let me chill on it," he said with a grin. Then he slapped his hands on his thighs. "Great. It's decided. Nineties it is."

"Shouldn't we . . . vote or something?" Jamie said.

"Anybody else got any great ideas?"

We shared a look. The truth was, no. Like every other class I was taking this semester, I just wanted to get this done as painlessly as possible. I was willing to be a nineties power hour (or two hours, as the case may be). *Maybe Dad will have some recommendations*, I thought absently, before shaking that thought away.

I glanced over at Jamie. He met my eyes but just as quickly looked away.

"Excellent," Joydeep declared. "Get ready to party like it's—"

"Please don't," Sasha said.

## 3.

**IN NO WAY DID I** want to be in charge of our radio show. But technically, I was the producer, and technically, we needed to submit the show proposal by Friday. So we had to meet up outside of class to discuss more details.

It was Joydeep who suggested we meet in the student art gallery. We couldn't talk in the library, and he claimed the cafeteria was too "exposed."

*We don't want anyone taking our idea*, he texted in the chat we had started for our group.

*We already talked about it in class*, Jamie replied. *Any other group could've heard us.*

*I know. Wasn't thinking. Won't make that mistake again.*

The student art gallery was off the main hall, next to the lobby outside the auditorium. It was smaller than the average classroom, with gray carpet and white walls lit by fluorescents, and tracks of gallery lighting throwing additional light on the art. There were two doors facing the hall, I guess to facilitate traffic flow should there be an incredible stream of people coming through.

The truth was, though, no one really went in there except during parents' nights and stuff. The wall facing the hallway was made of windows, so it wasn't really a place where students could get up to any kind of shenanigans since you were visible to everyone in the hall. A bench inside ran along that glass wall, a round table was pushed up to it, and a couple of chairs sat around the other side. There were signs on both doors that read: WHEN THE DOORS ARE OPEN AND LIGHTS ARE ON, PLEASE COME IN AND ENJOY THE ART.

I had been in the gallery more often than most, probably, since Rose had always had something up in there, and her group of friends—my friends too—liked to hang out there at free period sometimes.

Paintings, drawings, prints, photographs, and paper cuttings lined the walls. A long glass case held items made by the Intro to Jewelry Making class (an actual course offered in Meridian North's extensive catalog), and there were a few big rectangular stands with pottery pieces on top of them. Rose had taken all of these classes and aced them. She was *Visual Arts Student of the Month* half a dozen times.

When we were all gathered there after school on Tuesday, I flipped open my notebook and pulled out the handout with the requirements for the proposal.

"So we need a name for the show."

"Okay, well, Joydeep is hosting," Sasha said, "so how about . . . *Into the Deep*?"

Joydeep made a face. "No, god, why are we going *into* me?"

"It's wordplay."

"I hate it."

There was a pause. "*Nice to Mitra*," Jamie suggested.

"No! Veto. Veto times a thousand," Joydeep replied.

It was quiet again. Sasha tapped her fingers against the table. Jamie had a bottle of water out on the table, and he ran one finger under the seam of the label, slowly tearing it up.

I absolutely did not want to take the lead on this. I was definitely not putting myself in charge. But "How about something to do with the theme?" came out of my mouth, seemingly of its own volition. "*Nineties Jam? Sounds of the Nineties?*"

Joydeep snapped his fingers. "*Grab Your Joystick*."

Jamie was taking a draw from his bottle of water and choked.

"You just said you hated wordplay!" Sasha said.

"That was before I thought of a good one."

Jamie was still coughing.

"Does that mean you like it?" Joydeep asked, slapping him on the back.

Jamie caught his breath. "Wouldn't say it's an endorsement."

"*Into the Deep* is good, though," Sasha insisted.

"It's garbage," Joydeep said definitively.

"I'm putting *Sounds of the Nineties* in the proposal unless someone thinks of something better," I said.

"I did," Joydeep said.

"No," Sasha replied.

"This is a democracy!" Joydeep looked out into the room as if the art was going to back him up. "We need a vote."

"All opposed, raise your hand," Jamie said, and three of us raised our hands.

"*Sounds of the Nineties* is fine, Nina," Sasha said. Joydeep crossed his arms, face sunk into a pout.

"You guys suck."

---

By the end of our meeting, it was official.

The show would be called *Sounds of the Nineties*. And Joydeep had solved what he called Jamie's "it's all too broad" problem.

"It wasn't my *problem*," Jamie replied, "I was just pointing out—"

"Each week is a different year of the nineties," Joydeep said. "That way, we narrow it down a little, but not so much that it's any more complicated than just searching 1994 or whatever in the catalog."

Jamie frowned. "We have to do more than ten shows, though. What happens when we run out of years?"

"We start over again," Joydeep said. "Or you can play all of Britney Spears's albums back to back, fuck if I care."

"That would take way longer than two hours. She has a ton of studio albums," Jamie said.

I cracked a smile.

"Not that I'm saying we should do that," Jamie continued, glancing between us. "Not that I'm *not* saying that, if people are into it—"

"One year a week sounds good to me," Sasha said, and it was decided.

# 4.

WE USUALLY WENT TO DAN'S house on Sundays for an early dinner.

He lived in Carmel, on the north side of Indianapolis, an area rife with yoga studios and car dealerships and traffic circles. *To rid us of the horror of unsightly traffic lights*, Rose joked, and Dan replied, *You know, they really have been proven to help with traffic flow.*

He had a house there, smallish but still way bigger than our apartment, with white siding, black shutters, and a plush green lawn. I knew from my mom that he had lived there for about eight years, ever since he and his wife got divorced. They never had any kids.

He had a lot of hobbies, though, the most curious being his YouTube channel. It was called *The Artful Heart*, and he did paint-by-numbers tutorials, with tips and suggestions for the beginning painter (paint-by-number-er?). His most recent video was titled "COLOR-INVERTED LIGHTHOUSE!!!" (All the dark values were swapped for light ones, and vice versa.) It had almost ten thousand views.

That was the strangest part—Dan was something of a sensation. I don't know how much of a market there really was for paint-by-numbers instructional videos specifically, but among the comments here and there from people thanking him for the tips or sharing their own suggestions were things like "this is so pure" and "why is this wholesome as fUCK????" and "i dont know him but id trust him with my life." Something about Dan—his quiet demeanor, his calm but enthusiastic advice—had made people on the internet like him.

He even had an online persona—worried about online safety, Dan went by the pseudonym of Mr. Paint.

So we found ourselves at Mr. Paint's house on Sunday, as per usual.

Rose had cried off, out for one last hurrah before her semester started again. "Tell Dan I'm gonna send him the updated design," she told Mom before we left. She was into screen printing and had agreed to make T-shirts for *The Artful Heart* after enough of Dan's viewers (fans?) had requested it.

We talked about the shirts over dinner, among other things, including the new equipment at Dan's dental practice and Sidney's upcoming audition for the Meridian North Middle School spring musical. It was "kind of a huge deal," she had stressed to us, since the spring musical got to be in the high school auditorium, "on the *actual* mainstage."

"As opposed to the imaginary mainstage," I said, and she rolled her eyes at me.

Sidney and I cleaned up in the kitchen after dinner.

Whoever didn't cook had to clean, and neither of us had cooked, nor did we usually. We were restricted to only the simplest of meal prep since the frozen pizza debacle of some years ago. (We tried to bake the thing whole, with the plastic on, cardboard, everything—Sidney had convinced me it was like making a microwave meal, where all you have to do is poke holes in the plastic wrap across the top. The smoke from it triggered the fire alarm, and the entire building had to evacuate.)

This evening, as Sidney halfheartedly stuck the dinner plates under the faucet before loading them in the dishwasher, I couldn't help but ask:

"What if we move in with the Dantist?"

I had been staring at one of the many completed paint-by-numbers paintings that hung in Dan's house. This one hung by the fridge—it depicted a small cabin nestled among some thick-trunked trees.

"You'll have to go to Carmel High School instead of Meridian North," I continued.

"So?"

"Sooo . . . doesn't that suck?"

Sidney shrugged. "School is school. Doesn't really matter to me."

*How could she be so chill about this?*

"What about all your friends?" I said.

She took her phone from her back pocket and held it to her chest. "They're right here."

"Broadway soundtracks are not your friends, Sidney."

"Okay, number one, you're wrong. Two, I meant I can *reach them* through here. We don't have to be in the same place all the time to be friends. We *transcend* just, like, being in the same class together."

She said this with the implication that I couldn't possibly understand, and maybe she was right. Alexis was probably my closest friend at school now that Rose had graduated, but it was a casual kind of friendship. We'd text, grab lunch together, hang out occasionally on the weekends, but I wouldn't necessarily say we *transcended* anything.

I scraped a plate vigorously into the trash. Too much wisdom coming from Sidney made me feel untethered. I was older. I was supposed to be wiser. I was supposed to be the one *transcending*. Then again, I was the one who went along with the frozen pizza plan way back when.

"I just feel like everyone's being really okay with everything," I said eventually.

"That's bad?"

"I don't know."

She gave me a skeptical look.

"I mean obviously it's not *bad*, it's just . . ." *Unsettling.*

I didn't finish. Just shrugged and kept on scraping.

# 5.

**BASED ON EVERYONE'S AVAILABILITY, OUR** radio time slot was to be Thursdays from 5–7 p.m. Sasha volunteered as a tutor a couple of days a week, and her Thursday session knocked us out of a 3–5 block. Jamie initially floated the idea of going for a morning time slot, but it was resoundingly vetoed by the rest of us.

"I'm not getting up earlier than I have to," Joydeep said. "And anyway, we can't stomp on *Maddie in the Morning*'s turf. She's a certified legend."

The student radio station was populated with not only shows from the radio broadcasting class, but also from student volunteers who were just, as Joydeep put it during our first class, "so fucking psyched about radio." Maddie, of *Maddie in the Morning*, was one such volunteer. She was Meridian North's equivalent of a breakfast show host: On Mondays, Wednesdays, and Fridays, Maddie was on-air from 6–8 a.m. Evidently, she was the only person who wanted that time slot, which is how she somehow acquired three of them.

Maddie had a remarkable ability to talk about

nothing—it was almost hypnotic. Even though it was terrible, you couldn't stop listening. A typical link or break, as Mr. Tucker told us the on-air bits were called, was something like:

*Homecoming. Everyone's got an opinion on it. E-ver-y-one. My opinion? I'm okay with it. I didn't always feel that way. But I think I feel that way now. [long pause] But if you think about it . . . it's not that great. Actually. Now that I think about it. Anyway, here's Wham!*

One rumor was that for music programming, she just put the catalog on shuffle and let it ride. She played the most random things: Norwegian rap followed by The Beatles followed by Shania Twain, followed by Maddie's opinions on electric vs. manual toothbrushes. (*Should we call it a manual toothbrush? You call it a manual car, and there are electric cars too, but also automatic cars. So should we call it an automatic toothbrush? Let me know what you think. Anyway, here's the third movement from Beethoven's fifth symphony.*)

A 5–7 p.m. time slot meant that I had two hours to hang around and do nothing after school since it didn't make sense to get the bus home, turn around, and take it right back. So I hung out in the library watching videos online, wasting perfectly good time I could've used doing homework in favor of doing it later and complaining about not having enough time to finish it.

The evening of our first show, we met in the studio. We were given a code from Mr. Tucker to get in since it was an after-hours show.

He had taken us all on a tour of the station during

class, showed everyone the booth where we would do our shows and the editing bays where we would work on promos and stuff. Everything was carpeted and a little run-down looking. Shelves of CDs lined the walls of the sound booth, and there were even racks that must have held tapes at one point, but now sat empty. An L-shaped table was set up with the soundboard, three computer monitors, and a few mics. There were also several rolling chairs, and a beat-up looking black leather loveseat shoved in one corner.

When I arrived, Jamie was already there, browsing one of the CD racks.

"What do you think the point of the CDs are?" I said. Jamie looked up, startled. "I mean, it's all digital anyway, right?"

"Oh. Yeah. I guess it's just like . . . set dressing."

"To really nail down the authentic radio feel?"

He smiled a little. "Exactly." He nodded toward the loveseat. "I was more trying to figure out why this was here. Kind of unexpectedly chilled out."

"I guess that's the vibe we're going for?"

Sasha arrived then, Joydeep just behind her.

"I already got the playlist queued up," Jamie told us as we all got into position: Joydeep and I sat in rolling chairs, side-by-side at the soundboard so that I could operate the controls and he could see which songs were coming up on the monitor. Sasha sat across from us, on the other side of the bend in the table near one of the guest mics, with her laptop open. Jamie settled in on the couch.

"Way to go, Waldo," Joydeep said. He took out some headphones and plugged them in, and then swiped at his phone for a moment before holding it out to Sasha. "Take my picture?"

"Sorry?"

"The public needs to see how cool I look," he said, putting on the headphones and pulling the mic on its holder toward himself. He posed with several approximations of a smolder and then spent the next few minutes on his phone, selecting, filtering, and posting the best one.

(I would later follow him—username deepz715—and discover the caption for that very first studio pic: *First time catching those waaaaves.*

"What waves?" I would ask, and he'd look at me like it was the most obvious thing in the world.

"Airwaves. For real?" A scoff. "*What kind of waves.*")

At five o'clock on the dot, I faded out the music and cued Joydeep.

He took a deep breath and then leaned into the mic.

What happened next was . . . unexpected.

"I am Joydeep," he said, and for some reason, it came out . . . incredibly weird. "You're listening to . . . the radio. This station, on the radio." His voice spiked by turns an octave lower or higher than usual, like a scrambled audio file. "You know the one, because . . . you chose to listen to it. Anyway. This is us. The *Sounds of the Nineties*. You're about to hear a song, and . . . this is that song."

He pointed at me, and I hurried to switch off his mic and switch on the music.

Joydeep pulled his headphones off and flashed a thumbs-up.

I blinked. "What was that?"

"Link number one! We did it!"

We all stared.

"Why was your voice like that?" Sasha asked.

"Like what?"

"Like you were . . . slowly melting," Jamie said.

"What?" Joydeep looked genuinely confused.

"Also, did you forget the name of the radio station?" Sasha said.

He threw his hands up in the air. "I'm doing my best! It's not like it's real radio anyway. Nobody's even listening!"

"It's definitely real, though," Jamie said.

"You know what I mean."

"There are three people listening right now," I supplied.

"What? You can tell?"

"There's a counter, remember?" I pointed to one of the monitors. Mr. Tucker had highlighted it in our "radio operations crash course" lecture—*You can track your audience in real time!*

Sasha and Jamie gathered behind me and Joydeep rolled closer in his chair and we all peered at the little box in the corner of the screen that contained a numeral 3. As we watched, 3 changed to 4 momentarily and then dropped back to 3.

"Someone just noped out of this song," Sasha said.

"We should write that down," Joydeep said. "They

hate whatever band this is. We shouldn't play them any-more."

"We can't be a nineties station that doesn't play Green Day," Jamie said.

"We could be if we wanted," Sasha murmured, and I grinned up at her.

Joydeep leaned back in his seat. "So what am I sup-posed to do different? I was just talking."

"No, you're just talking now. That was more like . . . awkwardly giving a presentation that you didn't prepare for," Sasha said.

"Being more specific might help," I added. "Also, yeah, maybe try talking in a more . . . conventional sort of way."

"I was!"

"No," I replied.

He looked exasperated.

"Just talk like you're talking now," Jamie said. "Like, conversationally. 'Hey, this is Joydeep. You're listening to 98.9 The Jam.' Like that."

"Be punchier," Sasha said.

"Punchier?"

"More excited. Radio deejays are always, like, hyped about shit."

"Normal or punchy? Which one am I going for?"

"Normal," I said, at the same time Sasha said, "Punchy."

"Tiebreaker?" Joydeep looked Jamie's way.

"Normal," Jamie said.

"I'll thread the needle."

"It's two to one!" I replied.

"Hey, you guys decided this isn't a democracy when you vetoed *Grab Your Joystick* without the slightest consideration."

"Okay, we actually did vote on that, in a very democratic manner, and anyway, why ask for a tiebreaker if you're just going to ignore it?"

Joydeep gestured to his throat. "I'm sorry. I think I should be saving my voice." We sank into silence until the next air break.

"Hey, this is Joydeep, and you're listening to . . . the radio."

He looked my way, and I waved my hand to indicate more.

"That song was . . . something, right?" He paused as if someone was going to answer. "This is our show, and you're listening to it. Which is cool, so. Thank you. Here is another song, and . . . hope you're having a great day. Okay, bye."

"You're not ending a phone call!" Jamie squawked as I started the next song.

"And *why* are you talking like that?" Sasha said.

"Like what?"

She made a face. "I'm JoyDEEP, and this is the RADIO. Here is A SONG."

"I was threading the needle!" he cried.

"You have to give like actual information, though," I said. "You have to be, like, specific about stuff."

"I was!"

Sasha raised her eyebrows. "That was specific? God, I hope you never witness a crime."

46

Joydeep folded his arms. "Tell me, why is it 'gang up on Joydeep' day? Why is that what we've all decided to do today instead of having a very nice and fun time doing radio?"

"You were the one who said you wanted to host!" I said. "And that it was *the easiest part* of this whole thing!"

"Well, I'm doing my best," he replied.

"It's not personal," Jamie said, in his reasonable Jamie tone of voice. "We all just want to do well. Plus Nina has, like, a legacy to uphold."

Sasha frowned. "What's that supposed to mean?"

"Nothing," I replied quickly, shooting Jamie a look. "It means nothing."

---

We parted ways in the hall after our show wrapped up for the night: ("This has been Joydeep and *Sounds from the Nineties*—uh, *of the Nineties*. Thanks for listening, and uh . . . yeah. Bye!"). Joydeep and Sasha headed toward the west entrance, but I followed Jamie in the opposite direction.

"Hey."

He turned and looked mildly surprised, like we hadn't just been sitting in a small room together for the last two hours. "Hey."

"So. About . . . all that." He didn't jump in—though I don't know why he would've—so there was an awkward beat before I continued. "Maybe, like . . . lay off the radio stuff?"

Jamie frowned. "The stuff that we were just doing? Where we do radio?"

I squeezed my eyes shut briefly. "I mean, like . . . the stuff about my dad."

"Oh."

"The whole . . . *legacy* . . . thing," I continued. "I just . . . I kind of just want to leave him and everything out of it. I don't want it to be about that. I just want to take this class and be done with it."

He nodded. "Yeah, sorry." He scratched the back of his head. "I shouldn't have mentioned it. I just think it's cool."

"It's really not."

He nodded again, and it was quiet.

"Are you taking the bus?" he said after a moment.

"Rose is picking me up." I paused. I couldn't not ask. We were going to the same place, after all. "Do you . . . want a ride?"

Surprise flashed across his face again. "Uh . . . sure. Yeah, that would be great."

———————————

Rose pulled up to the front of the school in Mom's car, exhaust billowing out the back tailpipe, plumes of white in the cold January air.

Jamie and I piled in.

"Well, what a surprise," Rose said, glancing back at him. "I charge by the quarter mile, you know."

Jamie looked like he wasn't sure if this was a joke.

"I'm kidding," she said after a moment, and Jamie huffed a laugh.

Rose had some kind of indie band playing, soft bleating with acoustic backing. It was a far cry from the "Best of 1990"—or at least the "Best of 1990" according to Jamie—playlist we had just broadcast.

"What were you still doing at school this late, James?" she said as we pulled through the parking lot.

"Our radio show," Jamie said.

"Oh." Rose cut a glance at me. "That's right. You guys are in the same group."

I hadn't mentioned it to her.

"How was work?" I said. A very subtle and nuanced change of subject.

"It was fine," Rose replied. She worked at the fancy mall on Eighty-Sixth Street, at a store that specialized in weird, boho kind of clothes. *That macramé stuff*, my mom always joked. Rose was dressed in some of it now, thick fringe spilling out the bottom of her winter coat. *I figure I'd better just lean into the whole art student thing*, she had said when she first started working there. *Just fully embrace it.*

Rose was now in her second semester at IUPUI, at the Herron School of Art + Design. (The "+" was a very deliberate stylistic choice: "Did they workshop that plus?" Dad had asked. "I've been in meetings like that, and lemme tell you, they make you want to off yourself. Should we put an exclamation mark after 'Summer Slam'? Let's talk about it for forty-five minutes. Make sure we consider every conceivable consequence of the exclamation mark.") She was studying visual com-munication design—something I wasn't entirely sure I understood.

The secret was: She wasn't entirely sure she under-stood it either.

I was the only one who knew it, but Rose had been struggling in her classes in the fall. She had almost failed a couple of them but just managed to squeak by with grades high enough to keep her scholarship. She played it off to Mom and said it was because she had been doing too much—working and all that. Mom tried to get her to cut back on her hours, and she had a bit, but I knew that wasn't the real reason.

We never talked about it, though. It was kind of our thing, Rose and me. We could pretend with each other, and that was okay.

At least most of the time. "So how did the show go?" she said, not quite as accepting of my subject change as I would have hoped.

Unconsciously, my eyes flicked up to the mirror. I could see Jamie looking out of the window in the back.

"It was . . . something," I replied.

Rose snorted. "Enthusiastic."

Alexis had texted me partway through the show: *Listening right now and I need to know if you're holding your host at gunpoint or like what the situation is in-studio that's making him sound like that*

*No offense lolol*

*But seriously though*

"Nah, we just need a little . . . practice," Jamie said. "Just gotta iron out a couple wrinkles."

That was being generous, but that was Jamie in general. I flashed suddenly on him in second grade, when we were in the same class at Garfield Elementary. We were growing seeds once as a class project—everyone got a little Styrofoam cup full of dirt, got to press their fingers in to create divots and plant the seeds. We left them along the window ledge, everyone's cups printed with their names. It's wild looking back how something that sounds so boring now can be so exciting to you as a little kid, but it was. I guess when you haven't experienced very many things, lots of mundane stuff becomes exciting simply because you've never done it before.

One boy in our class, Ethan Lowe, was really sad because everyone's seeds had sprouted but his. One day, when the teacher was occupied on the other side of the classroom with Ethan and some other kids, I caught Jamie hunched over two of the Styrofoam cups, quickly but carefully digging several of the thin green shoots out of the one labeled JAMIE and transferring them to the one labeled ETHAN.

"You're gonna get in trouble," I hissed.

Jamie didn't reply, just continued his covert transplant. Ethan was ecstatic when he later noticed that his plants had finally grown.

That was something I liked about Jamie—he was an optimist, but the kind who knew that optimism alone wasn't enough to make Ethan Lowe's radish seeds sprout. He was willing to take matters into his own hands.

"No, the show'll be great," Jamie continued now as we waited at a traffic light. "We'll get there," he said in a way that, despite all evidence to the contrary, made you think we just might.

# 6.

JAMIE PARTED WAYS WITH US in the elevator at the Eastman, thanking Rose for the ride and ducking off when the doors opened at the seventh floor.

Rose turned to me when the doors had shut once more.

"You never said Jamie was part of your radio group."

"Didn't seem relevant." I fixed my eyes on the floor numbers, watching the light switch from seven to eight.

Rose looked unimpressed. "Really?"

I gave her a look that said I wanted to pretend right now, and she didn't press further.

We reached the ninth floor and trekked to our apartment. Sidney jumped up from the couch when we got in.

"Guess what?" She was bouncing up and down.

Rose looked her over. "Haircut?"

"New shoes," I said, even though she wasn't wearing shoes.

"You've mastered the power of flight," Rose said.

"Your organs have been swapped out with someone

else's organs. It was the first-ever total organ transplant, and they did it in less than eight hours. It was truly a feat of modern medicine."

Sidney looked exasperated, nearly vibrating with the power of her news. "No! Stop it!"

"You said *guess what*, though," Rose pointed out. "We're *guessing what*."

I gasped. "You were adopted! Actually we're all adopted! We're all in the royal family! We're all in *different royal families*!"

"I GOT IN THE MUSICAL!" Sidney burst out.

Sidney loved theater the way other people loved sports or boy bands or video games. She followed the careers of Broadway actors like they were Hollywood celebrities. She memorized both parts of elaborate duets. Her friends got together to dream cast their favorite shows.

She had practiced her audition relentlessly over Christmas break—although not required, she had memorized the monologue and the brief song, and then rehearsed them to the point that they would probably be fixed in all of our memories for the rest of our lives. If any of us ever had grandchildren, they would likely remember Sidney's audition pieces too, such was the extent that they were seared into our collective consciousness.

But now, apparently, all of her hard work had paid off.

"I'm Miranda!" she said, jumping up and down, and we jumped up and down too.

"Is this good? Is Miranda good?"

"She's in like at least half the scenes! And she gets her own ballad! *I get a ballad!*"

"Who is this that gets a ballad?" Mom said, appearing from the hallway.

"It's me!" Sidney screeched. We were still jumping.

"She didn't tell you?" Rose said.

"She did—I just like hearing it again." Mom flung her arms in the air, started jumping too. "My daughter gets a ballad!"

"I am the most talented sister!" Sidney bellowed.

"Do we have to endorse that?" I asked.

"Today is Sidney's day," Mom replied with a grin.

"Today, you are the most talented sister!" Rose chanted, and we all chanted it back.

# 7.

Conrad: 100.2 The Heat. Got some news this morning of a personal nature.

Will: Oh my god, Conrad . . . are you dying?

Conrad: It's about my family. Geez.

Will: Ah. Got it. Boring, but let's hear it.

Conrad: My little girl is gonna be a star. Or, star of the junior high musical, at least.

Nikki: Awww, that's awesome! What show are they doing?

Conrad: Some millennial thing that one of the teachers wrote. It's about bullying, or the environment, or something like that. They basically, like, Weird Al'ed a bunch of fair use songs for some theme . . . Don't do drugs. Stop at stoplights. That kind of thing. Anyway, bottom line: Sid is starring in it. She will be singing her own ballad—

All: Ooooooh.

Conrad: Appropriate group reaction—thank you. Yeah, so she's got the ballad, she'll be doing her thing, and I'm just, uh, so psyched. I'm gonna be there in the front row.

Nikki: Are you?

Conrad: Absolutely. Just booked the time off. So if you're just tuning in and you hate my guts, you can look forward to at least one Conrad-free show in April. You're welcome.

Will: Conrad's gonna be that dad standing in the aisle with the video camera.

Conrad: You bet I am. I'm totally going to be that guy, like, shushing everyone and taking a thousand pictures. Huge bouquet of roses—like so big you can't see over it. Just so obnoxious.

Tina: Sounds about right.

Conrad: Heyyy!

Nikki: Did you guys ever do school plays?

Tina: No, I was way too self-conscious for that.

Nikki: Will?

Will: Nah. That stuff's for the geeks, right?

Conrad: And my daughter?

Will: Oh yeah. Forgot that part. [laughter]

# 8.

**NEXT WEEK BROUGHT OUR 1991** episode. Joydeep's hosting hadn't altered much from our first show—it was still wooden and awkward.

"You know, you could try actually talking about stuff when you get on there," I suggested after our second *You are listening to the* Sounds of the Nineties, *and here is a song* type of break.

"Like what?"

"I don't know, just like . . . conversational stuff. About your life."

"Conversational how? I'm just talking to myself."

"You're talking to the listener."

"I don't think the listener cares about, like, what I had for breakfast or where I'm going for college and all that."

Sasha looked up from her laptop. "Do you know where you're going?"

Joydeep nodded. "Pomona."

"Where's that?"

"It's one of the Claremont Colleges in California. My

brother Vikrant goes to Harvey Mudd. They're, like, incredibly selective."

"And you already got in?"

"Early decision."

"Why'd you pick it?"

"'Cause my brother's there," he said, like it was obvious. "My uncle lives out there too, there's this whole West Coast branch of the Mitra family. They're in Anaheim, though, so close but like, not too close, you know?"

"You could talk about that on-air," I said.

"The West Coast Mitras? That would be weird. And why do you care anyway?"

"About the West Coast Mitras?"

"About the show. Why does it matter what I talk about?"

"I'm the producer," I said. "I'm just . . . trying to produce." Though the question was apt—why did I care? The bare minimum would carry us through this. But for some reason I had a weird feeling of wanting to *iron out the wrinkles*, as Jamie had put it. And he was doing his part, putting the playlists together and in a thoughtful way, not in a random, *just search the year and press shuffle* kind of way that Joydeep originally suggested. And Sasha had come in today and shown us the social media accounts she had started for *Sounds of the Nineties*, all of them branded with a logo that she designed herself. They looked pretty legit—substantially more so than the actual show seemed to warrant at the moment.

"Let's just go with the flow," Joydeep replied, and that was annoyingly hard to respond to. Like, what can you say to that? *Disagree, let's go against it. Let's walk this thing upstream.*

It was quiet after that. In between links, everyone did their own thing. Sasha worked on content to post. Jamie sat on the couch, a notebook open in his lap, working on next week's playlist. Next to me, Joydeep was on his phone, typing furiously. Every couple of minutes he would pause, shake his head, tap the screen a couple times, and then begin typing again.

"What are you doing?" I asked finally, because it looked like just the kind of work that was begging to be inquired after.

He looked up at me with a gleam in his eye.

"You know *Cat Chat?*"

"Yeah . . ." We had all shared our show themes in class by this point. In honor of the Meridian North Bobcats, one of the groups had titled its show *Cat Chat: Judgment-Free Advice for the Bobcat in Need.* It was that girl Sammy I had French with sophomore year, her boyfriend Colby, and a couple of other girls. They billed it as a "write-in advice show for students and the community at large." Joydeep had quietly scoffed when they presented their idea.

"Way to set themselves up to fail," he had said later.

"I don't know. It could be fun," I had replied with a shrug. They were the only group in our class not doing a music-based show. The upside of doing an all-talk show was that you only had to do one hour instead of two. The downside was that you had to talk for basically the whole hour—a couple music breaks were allowed, but the majority of the time had to be talk-based.

Joydeep had just made a face in response, a healthy mix of disgust and contempt.

Right now he said, without a moment's hesitation, "I'm sending them bogus questions."

"Why?"

"Because of their mission statement to be *totally nonjudgmental*. That is bullshit. I will get them to judge something. Also, Colby is my bro. We're on the soccer team together. We do this kind of thing all the time. Here, listen to this." He cleared his throat and began reading in an official-sounding voice: "Dear *Cat Chat colon Judgment-Free Advice for the Bobcat in Need*. I can't stop eating plastic wrap."

Sasha let out a snort, and Joydeep's lips quirked.

"There's more. From the top: Dear *Cat Chat*, etc. I can't stop eating plastic wrap. Sometimes I make food just to wrap it in plastic wrap, so then I can eat the plastic wrap with the food sauce and flavors already on there. I just love it. I call it plastic flavor." He paused, frowning. "Clear flavor?"

"*Invisible* flavor," Sasha said, and Joydeep nodded. I shot Sasha a look and she just shrugged and gave a sheepish smile.

"Perfect. Invisible flavor. I find the texture of the plastic wrap to be . . ." He made a chef's-kiss motion with his hand. "Intoxicating. Is this weird? What do you think? Would you ever give it a try? Do you think I should be concerned about the long-term effects on my intestines?"

Sasha let out a snort.

"Sincerely, Gladly Glad-Wrapped in Broad Ripple." He looked up at us. "What do you think? Should I send it as is? Does it need a little more sizzle?" He didn't wait for a response. "I'm gonna send it."

"How do you know they'll even answer it?" I asked.

"Because they're desperate for material. No one is sending in questions."

"Not true," Sasha said. "I heard part of their first show. They answered questions basically the whole time."

"Clarification: They answered *my* questions basically the whole time."

"You submitted all of those?"

"Sure did."

"They were normal, though! How to deal with a friend who moved away, what should I tell my little brother about our cat that died. Stuff like that."

"I had to lull them into a false sense of security. Then, bam! Invisible flavor." He looked way too pleased with himself. "You might say that I am the invisible component that gives their show flavor." Then his expression turned to one of disgust. "*No question left unanswered. A judgment-free zone.* What complete bullshit. I love Colby, but literally no one is more judgmental than him. He once gave Taylor Barnett shit for like two weeks for wearing red pants."

"What's wrong with red pants?" Jamie said.

"Nothing. Colby's just a prick."

"I thought you said he was your bro."

"He can't be both?" Joydeep replied.

I grinned.

# 9.

ON SATURDAY AFTERNOON I WAS heading downstairs to pick up a package for my mom when the elevator doors opened at the seventh floor, and there was Jamie.

I used to go months at a time without running into him at the Eastman. It was a big building, after all. We didn't live on the same floor. But I guess when it rains, it pours.

Today he was dressed in black pants and a black dress shirt, an apron slung over one shoulder. His hair still looked as messy as usual, but a little like he had attempted to corral it.

"So what are you . . . some kind of waiter?" I said with a delivery like it was an actual joke, despite it not being one at all, not even a little bit.

He flashed a quick smile anyway, stepping into the elevator and pressing the "door close" button.

"I work for Pipers. The catering place?"

The Eastman was a historic building, and part of its history was as a wedding venue. There were three ballrooms of varying sizes located off of the lobby—they had formal names, but as kids, we always called them Papa Bear, Mama Bear, and Baby Bear—and a big, glass-roofed atrium, where the ceremonies were usually held.

There was also an in-house wedding planning and catering company called Pipers, which apparently Jamie worked for.

"I thought you worked at that bagel place, though?" I tried sounding casual, like I didn't know exactly what *BAGELS!* was, like our mom didn't used to take us up there on weekends for breakfast when we were younger.

"Yeah, the weekend hours there are just mornings, so I can do both."

The elevator doors opened then, and we stepped off into the lobby. Next to the elevator was the Mama Bear ballroom, which was already set up with tables covered in purple cloths. A few people also dressed in black moved around laying place settings.

Jamie paused in front of the ballroom, so I paused too. "It's good money, if you ever want to . . ." He trailed off, scratching his head. "Just . . . They're usually looking for extra people, especially for spring and summer, so you know . . . If you're looking."

I nodded. "Cool."

"It's also kind of fun," he said. "Seeing the weddings and stuff. Like, it's cool seeing . . ."

"What?"

He looked a little embarrassed. "Just . . . seeing people happy like that." A shrug. "Anyway, I should . . ." He gestured to the room.

"Yeah, no. Me too. See you."

"See you," he said, and headed off into the ballroom.

I watched the line of his shoulders as he retreated, and was seized suddenly with the memory of him sitting across from me on the school bus in middle school. We used to take up our own row on the ride home after school, sitting with our backs to the windows, facing the aisle and each other. Rose usually sat in the row in front of us, headphones on. Sometimes she'd join in whatever we were talking about, but oftentimes, she kept to herself. *You and Jamie are in your own world*, she'd say. *Seriously, the things you guys talk about sometimes . . .*

And we did talk about all manner of things, dissecting movies and shows we'd both seen, talking about teachers and school stuff, trying to think up the weirdest hypothetical situations.

"Would you rather be a clown or marry a clown?" I asked one afternoon. Jamie had pondered this as the bus rolled to a stop and a kid near the front headed off.

"Clowns make people happy," he replied eventually. "I would be the clown."

"Clowns are terrifying, though."

"Maybe it's like fifty-fifty, happy to terrifying."

"Like terrifying half the time, or terrifying to half of all people?"

"Second one," he said. "I guess I'd try to avoid the terrified half, and stick to the happy half. What about you?"

"Neither."

"You can't *neither* this, that's not allowed."

"I guess I'd be the clown? But I don't like the idea that half of all people would hate me. And I feel like it's *at least* half. Maybe more like seventy-thirty."

"Then maybe you should marry the clown."

"Oh, I couldn't do that. They're terrifying," I replied, and Jamie had grinned.

# *10.*

WE WENT TO THE DANTIST'S for a movie night that evening, me and Mom and Sidney. Sidney and I went downstairs to the basement "media room" after dinner to check out Dan's collection of DVDs and pick one for us all to watch. Dan was fairly behind-the-times with respect to streaming services.

The DVDs sat on shelves lining the far wall. On the opposite side of the room was Dan's video-making setup. He had an easel where his latest project was displayed (a bouquet of flowers in a glass vase) and a little table with paints and brushes and stuff on it. There was a camera set up on a tripod and one of those lights with a white umbrella behind it, like a real photographer might have.

"There's a lot of weird stuff in here," Sidney murmured, running her fingers along the titles on the shelf. She sputtered a shocked laugh. "*The Big Easy*? Ew. Ach. Blech. Yuck."

"It's a nickname for New Orleans," I said.

She pulled out the case. "Why does the cover look like that, then?"

I shrugged. "It's probably about people having a bunch of sex. In New Orleans."

Sidney recoiled, shoving the DVD back in the case. "I don't wanna watch Dan's sex movie."

"It's not really a sex movie. I just said that."

"We can't risk it."

"If it were bad, Mom wouldn't let us watch it."

"Should we bring it up there and see what happens?"

"No. Pick something normal."

"You're supposed to be picking too."

"I trust your judgment," I said, though that was patently absurd. Sidney did have her wise moments, but once when she was younger, she ate half a bottle of tropical fruit Tums because she thought they were candy.

I wandered over to the easel while Sidney reviewed our options. I peered at the half-finished painting, the little squiggles and segments with tiny sky-blue numbers inside them. It was actually really detailed. I wondered how long it took Dan to do one of these things, how long it took to get a video together.

I stepped over to the camera. For as much as Dan eschewed Netflix and the like, he seemed pretty cutting edge when it came to his video technology. The camera looked totally professional. I reached for it to get a better look, but it was attached to the top of the tripod. A little lever was positioned to the left, and I tried to slide it to release the camera. It was stuck, though, so I had to give it a good bit of force.

But I didn't know the lever would release the top of the tripod attached to the camera, and that with the jolt of force, both pieces would shift and fall . . .

I fumbled for the camera, but it was too late. It hit the ground—the concrete underflooring—with a loud crack.

"What'd you do?" Sidney looked up sharply, a copy of *WALL-E* in one hand, *The Da Vinci Code* in the other.

My stomach sank as I crouched down to pick up the camera. The back screen was cracked, and the lens had popped off.

Sidney came over, still holding the DVDs.

"Oh, bummer," she said in that sort of sibling way that's part aggrieved for you, part relieved that they're not the one who did the thing.

"Yeah." I wondered dully if I should leave it exactly where it was, undisturbed like a crime scene, so the damage could be assessed in full.

But I just straightened up with the parts in hand.

When I emerged from the basement into the kitchen, Mom and Dan were loading the dishwasher. They were mid-conversation, and Dan turned to us with a smile on his face, which slipped when he saw the camera.

"Oh, Nina," Mom said. A familiar chorus.

"Sorry," I said weakly. "There was . . . kind of an accident."

"Nina didn't mean to break it," Sidney said helpfully, really cementing that she had nothing to do with it.

Dan just took the pieces, inspected the damage to the screen and the lens, and then nodded thoughtfully.

"Well, you know, these things happen, don't they? I'll send it back to the company, get a quote for repairs."

"What about your videos?" Mom said. "You're right in the middle of one."

"Oh, that'll be all right. I used to shoot them on my laptop, you know. I can just set it up on the table—it has the camera built right in. The film quality might not be as nice, but I think it'll be just fine. Helps to have the footage right there in the program. Don't have to mess around with importing and all that. That DSLR footage takes ages to get onto the computer."

"Sorry," I said again. "I can help to . . . I'll pay. To fix it."

"Don't worry about that." Dan waved a hand. "We'll get it all sorted out." He then turned to Sidney, who was still holding the DVDs. "*WALL-E* or *Da Vinci*?" he said brightly. "What'll it be?"

---

"Those cameras aren't cheap," Mom said on the way home.

"I know."

I already felt terrible. Guilty and also, like, irrationally annoyed at Dan's niceness? It made no sense, but it grated, that I could be shitty and careless and he could be so nice about it. Maybe that's why I felt compelled to add, "I didn't do it on purpose," even though picking an argument with Mom was not a super reasonable thing to be doing.

"I didn't say you did," Mom said. "I just . . . wish you would be a little more careful sometimes."

Snapping *I am careful!* didn't seem to be the kind of thing that a truly careful person would do, so I held back and instead kept silent the rest of the ride, even as Sidney tried to spark a discussion about the movie.

I googled it later anyway, even though I knew Mom was right—those cameras were expensive, and it wouldn't be cheap to fix.

I felt another irrational surge of annoyance at Dan, seeing the prices online. Why did he have to have such a nice camera in the first place? More to the point, who told him to be a fifty-something-year-old YouTuber anyway?

I shut the top of Rose's laptop and fell back against my pillows. Rose was still out—sans computer, clearly—and Sidney was showering, so our room was empty for a moment, silent in the way that it could never really be silent at the Eastman—the sound of the shower, the TV on low in the next room, the *thump* of the dryer, and the *whoosh* of the elevator.

I reached for my phone. Opened up a text and added Jamie.

We had all already texted for *Sounds of the Nineties* planning purposes anyway. So this wasn't that weird, just texting him. And anyway, he told me I should let him know if I was interested:

*Hey who would I talk to for a job at Pipers?*

# 11.

*PARIS AT NIGHT: VALUE SWAP!!!! Published by TheArtfulHeart, January 30*

*. . . So now that we've got our colors arranged, it's time to start in on our foundational work. My apologies for the lower film quality today . . . Hopefully you can still catch all the details here.*

*You know, this reminds me of when we first started on this journey together, before I got my, uh, recording setup upgraded, if you've been watching since then. If you have, I sure do appreciate you. If you've just popped by, well, I sure appreciate you too. Any length of time you've chosen to spend with me is meaningful to me. It's about the art, but it's also about the human connection, isn't it? We wouldn't be here without that.*

# 12.

THURSDAY ROLLED AROUND, AND I made my way to
the studio for our 1992 broadcast. Jamie was programming the playlist when I arrived.

"Hey," he said, glancing up as I dropped down into
one of the rolling chairs.

"Hi." I started riffling through my backpack for my
headphones.

It was quiet, just the click of the mouse as Jamie
added songs. "So, uh, did you hear back from Michelle?"

I had met with the catering manager from Pipers the
afternoon before. I was to be hired on a kind of second-
string basis for "this stage" of the wedding season—
after initial training, I would get called in when one of
the normal waitstaff couldn't make it in or when it was
a particularly big wedding (according to the website,
the Meridian Room could seat up to three hundred).
Then when "rush season" started, I would be included
more often if things were going well.

"Interviewed yesterday."

"And?"

"I'm supposed to train this weekend."

"Nice." His expression was neutral, so I wasn't sure how to interpret that "nice." I needed more data to draw a conclusion.

"I guess we're gonna be coworkers," I said.

"Guess so," he replied, with a smile that was indeed a little more conclusive—maybe he didn't hate the idea.

The others arrived then, and Jamie moved to his usual spot on the loveseat. Joydeep flopped down into his chair and pulled out his headphones.

"How are we feeling tonight, party people?" he asked, and Sasha gave a smile that looked like it was against her better judgment.

"Fine. You?"

"Fired up. Ready to go. Let's do this."

The first link went as follows:

"This is 98.9 The Jam. My name is Joydeep. You're listening to *Sounds of the Nineties*. Thank you for joining us. For *Sounds of the Nineties*. Tonight we are playing songs from the year 1992. A great year. I wasn't there, but . . . I'm sure cool stuff happened. Here is a song, and that song is 'Rhythm Is a Dancer' by SNAP!"

He pointed to me. I switched on the music, and by all rights, the music should have started then. It was usually kept at a low volume in the studio, but we should have been able to hear it.

Instead: silence.

I fumbled with the dial, thinking the studio volume might've been turned down. I couldn't remember what was playing—if anything was playing at all—when I first arrived.

Jamie peered over at me. "What's going on?"

I twisted the studio dial up and down again. Nothing. Shifted the slider on the board that controlled the music. Still nothing.

"Check outside," I said, and Jamie jumped up and hurried out of the sound booth. Music should have been playing out there as well, in the small hallway leading to the editing bays.

I thought back to class with Mr. Tucker:

*Something we* absolutely *do not want is dead air. Dead air is any silence that lasts for more than a few seconds when you're broadcasting. Got that? We're talking* seconds *here. Now I'm not saying you can't take a pause when you're having a discussion or making a point on-air. But it's really important that when you're speaking or having a conversation during a broadcast, you keep the ball rolling. And it's even more important that if there's some kind of technical malfunction, you act quickly, and you get something on as fast as you can.*

Jamie came back in. "There's nothing."

"Are we not broadcasting?" Sasha asked, looking concerned. I wondered if she was recalling Mr. Tucker's words as well. *Say it with me now: No dead air. It's the cardinal rule of radio. No. Dead. Air.*

"Try another break," Jamie suggested. "We'll go out and see if it's playing."

I went to pause the playlist, but Joydeep shook his head.

"Wait, what am I supposed to say?"

"I don't know. Read a PSA or something."

"Got it."

I switched on his mic as Jamie and Sasha both stepped out.

"Hey, Joydeep back here. From before. A little . . . earlier than anticipated. Just wanted to read you a PSA. A very important . . . notice . . . that is right here. On my desk. Um."

He hadn't called up a PSA before I cued him, which, as the producer, was my fault. I mimed drinking.

Joydeep frowned. "Water?"

Shook my head, mimed more forcefully.

"Drink. Drinking!"

I did a steering wheel motion.

"Driving."

I made a slashing motion through the air.

"Don't," Joydeep added.

Frantically, I pushed my hands together in an *all together* kind of move. "Don't drink and drive!" Joydeep burst out, triumphant. I gestured to continue. "It will kill people. Dead. It will make them dead. If you do that. So don't do it."

Sasha stuck her head back in and gave us a thumbs-up.

"Here's another song," Joydeep said.

I switched over to the music. Sasha ducked back out.

"You need to work on your charades skills," Joydeep said.

"I got you to say it!"

Sasha came back in shaking her head, followed by Jamie, looking perplexed.

"Nothing?"

"It works when Joydeep's on, but something's wrong with the music," Sasha said. "It's not broadcasting."

"Try one of the PSA tracks or a station ID or something," Jamie said. There weren't really commercials on 98.9 The Jam, but there were a ton of prerecorded PSAs for things like cyberbullying and sexting and a whole host of other "teen-targeted" issues. (*If you WOULDN'T say it to their FACE, then WHY would you SAY it ONLINE?* was a particularly ominous one. "Way too much echo," Joydeep commented the first time we played it. "Did they record it from inside a toilet?"

"Why would a toilet make it sound like that?" Sasha had asked, baffled.)

I clicked on the panel for that particular PSA. Nothing came on.

"So all we can do is broadcast live?" Joydeep looked panicked. "What are we supposed to do? I can't talk the whole time!"

"I don't know. Just get back on the air for now, and we'll try to figure it out," Jamie said.

Joydeep got back on while we inspected the cables and wires at the back of the board and checked the computer.

"Should we restart it?" Jamie mouthed to me, and I shrugged. Meanwhile, Joydeep continued:

"So to expand on the thing I said before, drinking and driving is terrible. If you're gonna drink, go ahead and do that, but don't plan to drive afterward, because that is just. Irresponsible. Drink responsibly. Or don't drink. That is up to you. That's a life choice. Me? I don't. Because it would be illegal. And you know me. Joydeep Mitra. A man of the law. And this man of the law . . . is hopefully going to have a song for you on the air . . . very soon. A song from the year 1992. Or really, at this point, a song from any era. Just some cool, good music. Coming at you. From our studio. Out . . . into the environment . . ."

He started signaling to me somewhat desperately, a *How long do I have to keep this up for?* kind of look on his face.

Sasha noticed and mouthed "WEATHER" to him, holding up her phone.

"And in the meantime . . ." Joydeep scrunched up his face. "Wet Thorpe?"

"Noooooo," Sasha whispered, waving her arms frantically.

"In the meantime, enjoy the silence and we'll be right back." Joydeep pushed his mic away, and I scrambled for the mic control as he said, "What the fuck is *Wet Thorpe*?"

It was definitely broadcast.

"Oh my god, Joydeep," Jamie exclaimed as Sasha shouted, "WEATHER!" and then my fingers finally found the button.

It was not looking good for us.

# 13.

**IT WAS NO SHOCK WHEN** we were called to stay after class on Friday.

Mr. Tucker sat on the edge of his desk. A chant of *No! Dead! Air!* played on a loop in my mind, fueled by anxiety and the sober expression on Mr. Tucker's face. His voice was measured when he spoke: "So. About your last show . . ."

Our solution to the music problem hadn't been particularly elegant. We were too afraid to turn the system off and then back on again in case we messed up something even more spectacularly. So basically, we just played through the playlist and did the links like usual, as if the music was actually being broadcast. As if we weren't violating No Dead Air at all.

*Nobody's listening anyway*, Joydeep had said, and he was right. The counter fluctuated between one and zero most of the night—it topped out at two for a moment there and then dipped back down when whoever it was realized that between Joydeep's lengthier-than-usual links and PSAs, there was absolutely nothing being broadcast.

"You actually listen to the shows?" Joydeep asked.

"Everything's archived, remember?" Mr. Tucker said gently.

"Yeah, but that's like . . . sixteen hours of radio a week."

"Fifteen," he corrected. "We've got the talk show, remember?"

"How could I forget *Cat Chat?*" Joydeep said blandly, and I shot him a look.

Mr. Tucker didn't acknowledge it, just continued: "I will admit, I do fast-forward through the music a lot of the time, but I try to listen to at least a couple links for each show, your intros and sign-offs. You know, during my commute, at the gym and stuff, it fills up the time. And I like hearing you guys. Plus I need to be able to give you feedback, right?"

We all nodded.

"So about your show last night. It seemed like there were some . . . technical difficulties?"

"We're sorry," Jamie jumped in. "There was a problem with the music. It was my fault." It patently wasn't. "We tried to fix it, but we couldn't figure it out."

"I went ahead and restarted the system this morning, checked the equipment and the software, and everything seemed to be in order, so it seems like something that got resolved by the restart. We're broadcasting fine now. But if something like this happens again, I want you guys to shoot me an email as soon as you know that something's not right with the equipment. I know there's no one on after you guys, so you have the responsibility of closing up shop for the night. And that includes letting me or someone else at the station know if things aren't running correctly."

We all nodded.

"Definitely," Jamie said. "We will. We're sorry."

And I thought maybe that would be it, until Mr. Tucker spoke again, a wry expression on his face.

"And about the language . . ."

"It won't happen again," Joydeep said quickly. "Scout's honor."

Mr. Tucker nodded and then dismissed us.

Joydeep let out a breath when we got in the hallway. "Good thing I'm not a Boy Scout."

# 14.

I FOLLOWED JAMIE WHILE SASHA and Joydeep headed their separate ways. It seemed like we were making a habit of this.

"I didn't need you to cover for me."

"I wasn't."

"You were," I said as we made our way down the hall. "I was running the board. I should've been able to figure it out."

"We were all at fault. Or . . ." Jamie scrunched up his face. "None of us were, actually. It was a freak malfunction. We were just unlucky."

Maybe that was true. But either way: First it was the job at Pipers, and now he was taking the blame for this. I didn't want to owe Jamie anything. It wasn't specific to him—I didn't want to owe anyone anything. But something about it being him specifically made it worse.

"I don't need anyone . . . *rescuing* me, or whatever," I said after a moment.

"I know." He glanced over at me with a hint of a smile. "Believe me, I remember."

I was reminded all at once of our childhood game of Kingdom, and there was no way Jamie wasn't thinking of it too. Kingdom had always had a rescue component, but it was very rarely a rescue of my sisters or me. Instead, we focused our efforts on saving Jamie.

Kingdom was invented out of boredom, as most childhood games are. It was one of those weird sorts of imaginary games that you get into at nine or ten, when you're old enough to think up some truly ghoulish things but young enough to still want to play pretend.

My sisters and I were obsessed with fairy tales at the time, and we wanted to make our own. We decided being princesses or whatever was too played-out, so we took on different roles: Rose was a rogue bounty hunter named Iliana. Sidney, only six at the time, was a troll, because she was obsessed with the trolls in *Frozen*. I remember her glaring up at us when she declared that she wanted her name to be "Quad."

"Why?" Rose looked baffled.

"Because that's the name I want!"

"But—"

"Quad! Quad! Quad!" she chanted, her little fists beating in time against her thighs.

We were forced to relent eventually and decided that Quad the Troll had very specific powers—camouflage, communication with animals, and super strength.

I established an intricate backstory for my character, Aurelie. She worked in a bakery by day, but by night she practiced all manner of magic—predicting futures, making potions, casting spells. I remember tying dental floss around a rock we found outside and holding it over a map that Rose had drawn, shushing the others while I *focused my energies*. I liked the idea of a seemingly normal person with hidden powers that they only revealed at incredibly crucial moments. I liked, I suppose, the idea of being underestimated and then exceeding people's expectations.

Jamie joined our game since Gram watched us pretty regularly after school. We gave him little choice in the matter, but Jamie usually went along with whatever we wanted to do anyway. It was no fun having Jamie rescue us, so we decided we would rescue him—the errant prince always getting himself into scrapes with dragons that were after his gold, or sorcerers who gave him poisoned fruit, or witches who put him into trances. We dubbed him Prince Hapless, after one of Rose's vocabulary words. Hapless meant *unlucky*.

Jamie's portrayal of Prince Hapless was amazing. He seemed every inch the charming, funny, completely brainless prince. The kind who'd accidentally fall in thrall to a witch because he'd stopped to help her fix a wagon wheel or something and didn't realize he was being hexed.

Prince Hapless would frequently slip into a coma, or a trance, and sometimes it was a counter-spell that brought him out of it, or the breaking of a cursed relic. Sometimes it was a kiss.

I was the only one willing to "kiss" Jamie—I would rest my hand over his mouth and peck the back of it, making an overexaggerated smacking sound. His eyes would spring open. For a second, as I hovered there, still close, they would be all I could see.

I liked that second.

Maybe it was nostalgia or spending more time with him lately, maybe it was the weirdly potent memory of Jamie wearing one of Papa's white dress shirts with a scarf for a sash. Whatever the reason, as we walked past the auditorium, then the administrative offices, I couldn't help but ask: "So . . . What's Prince Hapless up to these days?"

Jamie smiled almost reflexively, but it faded after a moment. "He's dead," he said.

"Dead?" I repeated.

"Mm. He's entombed in a majestic field next to this, like, super clear lake. The flowers growing around his grave bloom for just one day every spring, and it's an official day of mourning for all his people. And then after that, they throw like a really dope music festival there."

A pause. "Sorry to hear that. That he died. The music festival sounds cool, though."

He grinned.

"What about, uh . . ." Jamie's expression shifted to more of a grimace, some embarrassment tingeing it, like maybe he didn't want to acknowledge my fake fantasy character name even though I just acknowledged his fake fantasy character name. Or maybe he didn't remember it. Maybe he had forgotten Aurelie, the baker by day, enchantress by night. "Your person."

"Oh, you know. Probably just . . . baking bread. Hustling people at magic pool. That kind of stuff."

"Nice." It was quiet. Jamie cleared his throat eventually. "So." He looked around as we reached the end of the hallway, and stopped at the doors to the parking lot. "Where are you headed?"

I blinked. "I thought you were headed somewhere."

"I was following you."

"Oh."

"I actually have class back in the gym," he said.

"Oh," I said again.

He smiled a little, still awkward. "So . . . I should probably—"

"Yeah. Okay."

"See you."

"Bye."

My class was back in that direction too, but it was too awkward to announce that, to have just said goodbye and then walk together in the same direction.

So I lingered and looked at the school directory like I hadn't been wandering the halls of Meridian North for the last three and a half years, like I wasn't acutely aware of the location of my next class, and I listened to Jamie's footsteps shuffling away.

# 15.

Conrad: This is 100.2 The Heat. We're giving away tickets to our Birthday Bash in just about ten minutes here, so stay tuned. We're going to play one of our favorite games, which is . . .

Will: Ancestry Quarrel. [pause] Because Family Feud is, you know, copyrighted or whatever.

Conrad: Yeah, no, that one doesn't get better with age. But anyway, we're going to get a couple people on the line here in a minute, but in the meantime, we're talking about—what are we talking about?

Nikki: Do you ever pay even a little bit of attention to what's going on here?

Conrad: You know, I have faith that my amazing team will keep me informed.

Tina: We're talking about first love.

Conrad: Oh. Blech.

Nikki: What? Why?

Conrad: Why what?

Nikki: That, like, disgusted sound.

Conrad: It wasn't disgusted, it was just—why are we talking about that?

Nikki: Because of Tina's news segment earlier! You weren't even listening!

Tina: The story of the woman with the locket from her first boyfriend? She saved it all that time? They got together again twenty years later?

Conrad: I was checking Twitter.

Nikki: Conrad!

Will: Booooooo.

Conrad: Will, you were on Twitter too!

Will: Uh, yeah, reading through all the stories of first love from our listeners.

Conrad: Yeah, right.

Nikki: I can vouch for him. I can see his screen from here.

Conrad: You never vouch for me, Nik.

Nikki: You never give me anything to vouch for.

Tina: Tell us about your first love, Conrad.

Conrad: Nah, I don't believe in all that.

All: Booooooo.

Nikki: How can you not believe in first love? It's not like ghosts or something, I think it's generally accepted as being a real thing. If you've been in love even one time, that's your first love.

Conrad: I just don't believe that it's, like, this huge thing. Like, where do you even count it from? I thought I was in love with Jennifer Watts in first grade. I loved this girl Kelsey . . . Valenti? Valencia? Kelsey Valencia—that was it—from math class in seventh grade. I loved Alicia Silverstone in high school. Got nowhere with her, FYI.

Tina: Shocking.

Conrad: So which one's the first one? What makes it first love?

Nikki: It's the first one where they actually love you back.

Conrad: Well, then. Maybe I'm still waiting on it.

Tina: You've got three kids, Conrad!

Conrad: [sputters a laugh] That's true. How about that, then? They're the loves of my life. My little girls.

Will: Aren't they in college?

Conrad: Excuse you. Only Rosie is in college. Nina is a senior, and Sid is in eighth grade.

Tina: Wow, you're like really old.

Conrad: Yeah, you guys don't remind me of that nearly enough.

Will: Gotta keep you grounded.

Conrad: Excuse me, who is the show named after?

Will: See, that's exactly why.

Conrad: All right, all right. We're going to get some folks on the line for our game, so give us a call now. In the meantime, here's one from Megan whatsit—the country crossover one. What's her name?

Tina: Megan Pleasant.

Nikki: You'd know that if you weren't so old.

Conrad: 555-1002. Give us a call if you want to play. Or if you want to work for me. I'm currently hiring an entirely new team.

# 16.

**THAT WEEKEND BROUGHT MY FIRST** official night of training with Pipers at the Eastman. There was a wedding in the Mama Bear ballroom (the Crystal Room, if we're being technical)—the midsized of the three reception spaces.

The wedding was pretty formal—along with the usual dress shirt and slacks, we had to wear vests and black ties. I had tied mine really poorly, even after watching a variety of YouTube videos on the subject, before Rose got home and tied it perfectly.

All of the other catering staff members were older than Jamie and me—a few college students, some actual adults. Jamie seemed to fit right in with everyone, though—talking animatedly with one of the guys as they filled water glasses, pausing at the bar stand to say something to the bartender that she responded to with a wide smile.

I shadowed a woman named Celeste, who showed me the staging areas where the food was kept (there were no event kitchens at the Eastman, apparently, so the food was prepared offsite and trucked in; I had never thought of it much except for the big signs at the back of the building that said DO NOT BLOCK PIPERS LOADING ZONE), and outlined the general tasks for the evening. We weren't always responsible for setup (it was often done the day before, for the first wedding of the weekend), but were instrumental in cleanup both throughout and after the event. We would have to deliver food, fill drinks—general waitstaff-type stuff, I think, though I'd never done any of it before.

I followed Celeste around for the whole evening— plates of salads in each hand, clearing dishes as she dictated—and meanwhile, a wedding happened around us.

It was kind of an odd feeling, to witness an event like that but be so peripheral to it. I couldn't help but glance toward the head table now and then throughout dinner, to where the flower girl—maybe five or six—sat with the bride and groom. She appeared to be the bride's daughter, and wore a crown of flowers that matched the bride's bouquet. The little girl kept turning excitedly to the groom to point things out to him over the course of the meal. When it came time to cut the cake later that evening—three figurines sitting atop it—the three of them held the cake cutter together. The little girl got the first bite, and beamed up at the couple. They beamed right back.

I kept catching glimpses of Jamie across the room over the course of the evening too, murmuring something to one of the other waiters, both of them laughing quietly. Running his hands through his untidy hair.

Retrieving fallen napkins. Offering an arm to an elderly woman as she made her way out of her seat.

It wasn't until the end of the night—the guests having cleared out, the wedding party having packed up the gifts and gone—that Jamie approached me. We were finally done cleaning up, and had been dismissed for the evening.

"What'd you think?" he said.

"Good," I replied, pausing to wave to Celeste as she headed out. Jamie turned and waved too. "It was good."

Truthfully, my feet ached. I had sweat through my shirt.

Still, I liked it.

"Should probably hit the road," Jamie said. "Long commute home."

He then made a face like he knew how cheesy that was, but I smiled.

As we waited for the elevator, he said, "So . . . Is your mom gonna have a wedding like this?"

I thought of the flower girl, the three figurines on top of the cake.

"Nah." I watched the numbers above the doors track downward. "I think it'll be pretty . . . informal."

According to Mom, all she and Dan needed was an officiant; Rose, Sidney, and I would be the only guests. Their main stipulation was just to wait for warmer weather so they could have the ceremony out by the canal that ran through downtown. It was picturesque—sloping green lawns, arched bridges crossing at certain points. Mom had always wanted an outdoor ceremony.

"It's fine, I'm not trying to be a bridesmaid or anything," I added after a moment.

"You'd have to make a speech."

The maid of honor tonight had stood up, un-crinkled her speech, and then promptly burst into tears.

"Rose would definitely be maid of honor," I said. "She's the favorite."

"Parents don't have favorites."

We stepped into the elevator. "See, you can think that 'cause you're an only child."

It was a careless thing to say, and I felt instantly guilty about it. I actually didn't know for sure that Jamie was an only child. Maybe he had siblings somewhere, or half-siblings. The truth was, I had no idea what the situation was with his parents. I didn't even know if Gram and Papa were his maternal or paternal grandparents. He never talked about it, and Gram and Papa had never offered. He had lived with them at the Eastman for at least as long as we had been there.

I asked my mom once, when I was eight or so, and she'd said, "It's not our business. Okay? That's their business."

"When does someone else's business become your business?"

"It doesn't," she had replied. "Unless *they* choose to make it that way."

But in this moment, Jamie just shrugged good-naturedly. "Fair. No one to compete with. But if there really are favorites, then that means I have to be the favorite *and* the least favorite."

"There's no least favorite," I said. "It's just favorite and then everyone else."

"Ah."

The elevator dinged, opening at the seventh floor, and with a good night, Jamie headed off. The doors closed, and I was alone. I leaned against the back wall of the elevator, exhausted.

# 17.

DURING MONDAY'S RADIO CLASS, WE split up into our groups and dispersed to "conceptualize" station IDs, which were just the short clips that played before songs or in between commercials to remind people what station they were listening to. One that got played a lot on the station started with the sound of thunder, and then an echoey voice filtered in: *Storms ahead? Keep it switched to 98.9 The Jam—hot student radio for nothing but blue skies.*

"We can do better," Joydeep stage-whispered after Mr. Tucker played us a few examples.

But now the four of us were in one of the editing bays at the station scrolling through sound effect options, and Joydeep didn't seem to be paying any attention. He was hunched over his phone, an intent look on his face. Every so often he would huff a laugh to himself, tap back a few times, tap away, laugh again.

"What've you got?" I said eventually.

"Hm?" he said.

"For *Cat Chat*."

Joydeep flashed me a grin. "I feel like this could be my best work yet."

"Let's hear it."

He held up his phone and cleared his throat. "Dear *Cat Chat colon Judgment-Free Advice for the Bobcat in Need*." He paused. "Can you even believe that's real life, though? Can you believe that four people sat down and thought that was a good idea?"

"You thought *Grab Your Joystick* was a good idea."

"Because it is. But Cat Chat? *Cat Chat*? Jesus Christ, it makes my ears nauseated."

I snorted. "Go on, then."

"Okay. Dear *Cat Chat*, etc. etc. I really need your help. It's kind of a desperate situation. The thing is"—he paused for dramatic effect, and all of us, damn him, totally leaned into it—"my boyfriend thinks he's a tree."

"What?" Sasha said.

(*What?* Colby of *Cat Chat* would later say on-air.)

"Or at least, he wants to be a tree. He has taken to dressing almost exclusively in brown corduroys and green tops. That's fine with me. That's a fashion choice. But he is always referring to his legs as his 'trunk' and his arms as 'branches.' He has started referring to certain bodily fluids as 'sap' and others as 'phloem.'"

"Joydeep, this is . . . you're . . ."

(*PHLOEM!* Colby would burst out, letting out a choked sound. *PH-PHL-PH-PH-PH*—

*Get it together, Colby,* Sammy would hiss in response.)

"At first I thought maybe it was a coping mechanism. Or some kind of sex thing. But I'm worried that it goes deeper than that. I'm worried that my boyfriend really, truly thinks he's a tree. What should I do? Should I humor him when he asks me to prune his leaves? Remember what I said about the phloem?"

(*I can't. I can't. I'm sorry. I can't.* Colby would steadily increase in hysterics. *This is too—too much—too— PHLOEM—*

*Colby!*

*FUCKING PHLOEM, Sam!*)

"It's all becoming a bit much. But I want to be a supportive girlfriend." Joydeep looked up—"Gotta throw 'em off the scent"—and then back down at his phone. "Tell me, *Cat Chat* team . . . What should I do? Sincerely, Barking Up the Wrong Tree in Zionsville."

"You're not okay," Sasha said, but she was struggling to keep a straight face.

# 18.

*This is Maddie in the Morning here on 98.9 The Jam. Hey, did anyone else listen to that one show yesterday? Does anyone listen to the radio at all anymore? Believe me, that's something I wonder sometimes. I know my Nona listens. She's probably listening right now—good morning, Nona! I don't really listen that much, to be honest, but my mom had it on in the car yesterday when she picked me up, and this weird talk show was on, did you guys hear it? Where the guy totally lost it talking about tree sap? [beginning to laugh] Honestly, that was amazing. It was . . . AMAZING. He totally like nuclear-level lost it right there on-air. And the other girl got so mad at him. Like, SO MAD. She was all, "Get it together, Cappy!" Was that his name? Cappy? Cadby. "Get it together, Cadby!" And he was just totally gone, just completely out in space. It was the worst thing I've ever heard. I loved it. [happy sigh] Anyway, here's "Wonderwall." [pause] I'm kidding. That was a joke. Like that thing, where people say . . . Can you imagine, though? If I was serious? [pause] Actually, you know what? Screw it. Here's "Wonderwall."*

# 19.

**"TELL ME YOU GUYS HEARD** it, though," Joydeep said with satisfaction. All of us were gathered in the studio on Thursday for 1993 night. We had already done the first link. "I got them. I broke Colby."

"Congratulations?" I said, and he held his hand up for a high five. I sighed and high-fived him back.

"Now I just gotta get Sammy."

"Can we maybe not focus on wrecking someone else's show?" Jamie said.

"I'm not trying to *wreck* anything. I'm just proving a point."

"Which is?"

Joydeep contemplated it for a moment and then shrugged. "How easy it is to mess with something that stupid."

"Seriously?" Jamie didn't look happy.

Joydeep frowned. "What's your problem?"

Jamie's face softened. "Sorry." He shook his head. "I just . . ."

"What is it?"

"I just want our show to be good."

"Fucking with their show and improving our show don't have to be mutually exclusive," Joydeep replied.

"Then I just . . . think it's mean."

"You gotta toughen up, Waldo. The world is mean."

"We don't have to be."

Joydeep didn't reply.

We were pretty deep into the show—a few breaks, a lot of songs from 1993, and some off-air conversation between us here and there—when Jamie circled back around to Joydeep.

"So . . . where did we end up on the no more prank questions to *Cat Chat* thing? We're all in favor, right?"

"I don't remember agreeing to that," Joydeep said.

"I listened to their last show, though," Sasha said. "It was funny as hell."

"Not on purpose."

"So? Funny's funny. They should hire Joydeep."

Joydeep did a 360 in his rolling chair. "See? The people love my stuff."

"Maybe you can bring some of that to our show," I said.

"That's not our format, though. Our format is nineties music and chill. That's our wheelhouse. That's where we live. We don't want to move away from that."

"Oh, so that's why you host the way you do—it's a conscious choice to *not* be funny and interesting," I said. For some reason, I was weirdly annoyed on Jamie's behalf.

"Okay." Joydeep feigned surprise. "Is it 'pick on Joydeep' night again? Did I miss that notification?"

"I'm just saying," I replied. "You can be funny and interesting in real life. Like, you have the capacity. But you become all weird and wooden whenever the light goes on."

"Technically, it's whenever the light goes off," Sasha said.

"Sorry?"

"On the soundboard. When the light is off, it's broadcasting. Remember Mr. Tucker said it's like the opposite of what you'd think?"

*Running the audio control board is not difficult*, Mr. Tucker had told us. *It looks like there's a lot going on, but really there are only a couple of things you need to worry about. You've got sliders for volume—the music and the mics all have their own sliders—and the buttons underneath that broadcast them. The sliders? No big deal. Slide up to increase volume, slide down to decrease. The buttons, though, you've got to keep in mind. Look here all the way on the left of the board—this is the slider for the main mic. See how the button underneath is lit up right now? Press it down, and it's not lit—this means your mic is on. When you're done talking, slide the dial down, press the button again, it lights back up. It's now off. You have to keep this in mind, okay, because it's the opposite of the big old sign outside the studio that says ON-AIR. That sign's lit? You're broadcasting. This button is lit? You're not broadcasting. The sign outside is not what puts your voice on-air, okay, that just indicates what's going on inside the studio to people outside the studio. It's this button right here that tells the tale.*

"That's what I meant," I said.

Sasha just looked at me, and then we both looked at the soundboard.

The button for Joydeep's mic was not lit. Not even a little bit. Not that a partially lit button was even an option; it was very much a binary. *Press it down, and it's not lit—this means your mic is on.*

The horror on Sasha's face was probably reflected right back on mine.

"Uh-oh," I said weakly.

---

*I got them. I broke Colby.*

We all stood staring at the monitor as our archive file played back.

*Congratulations?*

*Now I just gotta get Sammy.*

"Is that what I sound like on the radio?" Joydeep murmured.

"No," Sasha murmured back. "You sound like a robot whose motherboard is slowly melting."

"How did this happen?" Joydeep said.

"I got switched up," I said, like that somehow justified it.

"You weren't switched up before!"

"That's what switched up means—I knew what it was before but I just got it backward this time! I wasn't paying attention, okay?"

Jamie shook his head mournfully. "Tucker's gonna flunk us when he hears this."

"It's not *that* bad," Joydeep said.

"Every time we thought music was playing, it was just broadcasting us sitting here talking! And every time we thought we were broadcasting a link, it's just silence!"

"We could say we were . . . experimenting with a new format," Joydeep suggested.

"What about the part where you admitted to sending fake shit into *Cat Chat*?" Jamie replied.

"Ahh." Joydeep looked chagrined. "In that case, I guess it is that bad."

"Unless . . ." I said.

"What?"

Technically, it wasn't a good thing to do. But that didn't necessarily make it a bad idea. "We delete the file."

The three of them blinked at me.

"We'll get a zero for not archiving," Sasha said.

"We could get kicked off the air if he actually listens."

"She's right," Joydeep said.

Jamie's brow was wrinkled. "We shouldn't."

"Let's vote." Joydeep threw his hand in the air. "All for deleting?"

I raised my hand, studiously ignoring Jamie's gaze. Sasha looked between me and Jamie and then sighed, raising her hand too.

"Great."

"Wait. It should be unanimous," Jamie said, reaching out as I went for the mouse.

"We never specified that."

"We didn't *not* specify it either."

"That makes no sense," Sasha said.

Jamie squeezed his eyes shut. "Just . . . Let's vote again."

"Fine. Who doesn't care if it's unanimous?" Joydeep asked. The three of us raised our hands again.

"Sorry, Waldo," Joydeep said, and then to me: "Send it to hell."

# 20.

WE GOT THE NOD FROM Mr. Tucker at the end of class on Friday. The *stay where you are* nod. The *we have things to discuss* nod.

I could hear the hustle and bustle of the hallway, the footsteps and shouts of a midafternoon class commute, but it was quiet among the four of us as Mr. Tucker joined us in the back, where we had taken to sitting together since the first class. He settled atop one of the desks, the hem of his pants shifting up to reveal socks patterned with bottles of ketchup and mustard. His face belied the whimsy of the socks.

"So there seemed to be a problem with the file for your last show," he said. "I couldn't find it anywhere."

Joydeep was the quickest with a response. "Yeah, we must've . . . I think we, uh, probably . . . forgot to record."

"It's a good thing I caught part of it live."

Jamie sputtered, "What?"

Sasha, at the same time: "You did?"

Joydeep grimaced. "Soooo . . . Does that mean we get credit?"

"It won't happen again," Joydeep assured Mr. Tucker after a lecture that wasn't as long as it should've been, but definitely longer than I would've preferred. I would've preferred no lecture at all. "We'll be way more careful."

"I'll take you at your word," Mr. Tucker said, and I thought that was the end of it, but he didn't stand, didn't dismiss us. "There's something else I wanted to discuss with you while I have you here. A little . . . critique of your show."

"Here it comes," Joydeep murmured.

"I want to know about your decision to have just one on-air host."

We looked at each other. We couldn't say, *None of us wanted to talk except Joydeep*. I shrugged in hopes of pushing the answer off onto someone else.

"I know there are some single-host shows among the station volunteers—Maddie is a champ, if you've heard her stuff in the mornings—but since this is an elective class, it's often chosen by people who are interested in getting on-air. It's pretty rare to get a group where the majority of people want to stay behind-the-scenes. As it stands, you all are the only group with just one host."

Jamie responded for us. "Um, I guess we just thought it would be more . . . streamlined that way? I'm doing the music programming, Sasha is doing publicity and stuff, and Nina is running the board and producing. So we're all . . . contributing, just . . . in different ways. And all that stuff needs to get done anyway, right? We're just sort of . . . putting more emphasis on it . . . individually?"

"Hm" was Mr. Tucker's reply.

"It's been working out so far," Joydeep said.

"Has it?"

None of us spoke.

"I'm just saying, it's something to consider. I heard some interesting things—albeit things I wasn't supposed to be hearing—because of your misbroadcast. I heard some fun conversation. Stuff like that can get people to tune in. And as it stands . . . I'd say your show is in a bit of trouble at the moment."

"We have a plan, though," Joydeep said suddenly. "A . . . substantial plan. To make the show better."

I looked over at him, but he studiously ignored everyone's gaze.

"Really," Mr. Tucker said.

Joydeep nodded. "We're going to do something big. To boost listenership."

"Yeah?"

"Yeah." He was still bobbing his head. "Of course. Hence the . . . substantial plan."

"Care to let me in on that plan?"

"It still needs some . . . refinement. But we're gonna . . . We'll fix this. We're gonna get things . . . tightened up. And we're gonna get people listening. Like, so many people. You'll see."

"No more technical malfunctions?"

"No, sir," Joydeep said, and I shook my head.

"No. Sorry."

"Okay. Well, I'm looking forward to seeing this . . . *substantial plan* in action."

"Me too," Sasha muttered as Mr. Tucker headed away.

# 21.

WE ALL MET IN THE student gallery after last period for an emergency *Sounds of the Nineties* team meeting.

"So what can we do?" Joydeep paced back and forth, looping between the pottery stands. He touched each stand as he passed—blue vase, purple-and-white cup, green plate, and back again. "Something major to get people listening."

"We didn't have to do anything until you opened your big mouth and said that we had a plan," Sasha said. "Who even talks like that? We have a *substantial plan*? What is that? What's next?"

"Synergy," Jamie said. "Optics. Data streams. Fully optimized content."

Joydeep pointed at him. "I like all those words."

"You've both left the rails," Sasha said.

"How about we brainstorm?" Jamie suggested.

"How about Joydeep goes back to Mr. Tucker, tells him there is no plan, and we go on living our lives," I replied.

Now Sasha pointed my way. "I like her plan."

"Is it substantial enough for you?" I said.

"It's not insubstantial," she replied.

"We've gotta do something." Joydeep stopped abruptly at the blue vase. "We have to turn this shit around. Like, we *have* to." He began pacing again. "It won't be hard. We just have to, like, do some kind of big giveaway or interview someone famous or something." He nodded to himself, caught up in his own Joydeep energy stream. "That's good, though. How about we have a special guest? A celebrity or something?"

"Yeah, right," Sasha said. "Who here knows a celebrity?"

Jamie looked my way, and unfortunately, Joydeep clocked it.

"What?" Joydeep said.

Jamie just shook his head, looking apologetic, and I remembered our conversation about my dad: *I just want to leave him and everything out of it. I don't want it to be about that.*

"What?" Joydeep said again. "You guys are doing that thing."

"What thing?"

"That thing where you communicate with your eyes."

"We don't do that," Jamie said.

"You definitely do," Sasha replied, glancing at Joydeep. "I noticed it really early on."

"Same, and let's definitely circle back to that, but in the meantime, which celebrity do you know?"

"He's not—" I shook my head. Sighed. "It's my dad. But he's not a celebrity."

"He kind of is, though," Jamie said gently. "Here, at least."

"What? Why?" Joydeep looked between us, head swinging back and forth like he was watching a tennis match. "What's he do? Is he an actor? Does he do the news?" His eyes widened. "Is he a serial killer?"

"How are those your top three kinds of celebrities?" Sasha said.

"He's . . . I mean. Technically. He's . . ." I mumbled.

"Sorry?"

"A . . . radio host."

"*What?*" Joydeep said.

"A radio host," I repeated.

"No, I heard you, I just can't believe you have an actual radio host as your *literal next of kin* and our show is as shitty as it is."

"Hey!"

"It's flowing through your veins, Nina! You should be a goddamn ringer, but instead, after three complete shows you can't even keep track of the fact that 'light off' means broadcasting and 'light on' means *not broadcasting*!"

"Hey," Jamie said, suddenly stern.

"I'm sorry." Joydeep looked at me, eyes imploring. "I am. It's just . . . We have to do something."

"I thought you didn't care about the show," Sasha said.

Joydeep looked away. "I became . . . more invested."

"Because Tucker might flunk us?" Jamie said.

"Yes. For sure. I can't flunk, I need a good final transcript. But also . . ." Joydeep trailed off.

"Also what?"

He looked suddenly uncomfortable. "We kind of . . . put a wager on it."

"Who?"

"Me and Colby and a couple other guys in class," he said. "For most-listened show. We put a bet on it before the whole . . . *Cat Chat* breakdown this week. Whoever has the lowest listenership has to buy everyone else's tickets for prom. And I can't stress to you how much I *can't do that*, so we have to do well."

"Why did you agree to it if you can't do it?"

"That's the whole point of a bet. It has to hurt to lose," he said, like it was the most obvious thing in the world.

Jamie frowned. "But—"

"*But*," Joydeep continued, "it only hurts *if* you lose. So we can't lose."

"Is that why you were messing with their show?" Sasha asked. "Sabotage?"

"No, I did that because it was hilarious. It actually had the opposite effect. More people are listening to them than ever, which completely sucks."

"Maybe *we* should have a bogus advice section," Jamie said thoughtfully. "You're a lot funnier thinking up fake questions than you are trying to do the weather and stuff."

"Hey!"

"*Welcome to the show, this show, on the station you are*

114

*listening to*," Sasha replied in a wooden, not-inaccurate impression of Radio Joydeep.

"Point taken." Joydeep turned back to me. "What's your dad do on the radio, then?"

"He has a morning show. They just talk about random stuff, play music, do games and things." This morning they gave away concert tickets with a game called *Guess That Sound: Animal or Adult Video? Edition.* It was about as highbrow as you'd expect. "It's not even here, though. The show got bought a few years ago, and he moved to California."

"Do a lot of people listen?" Joydeep asked.

"I mean, I guess? It's a bigger market there, which is why he moved. But he's not, like, a *celebrity* celebrity." He had interviewed some famous singers and bands before, had hosted big concerts for the radio station and stuff. But it wasn't like he was out there getting recognized on a daily basis—that was kind of a main feature of radio fame.

"He used to be on-air here, though?" Joydeep said.

"Yeah. 99.5, in the mornings."

Joydeep nodded slowly, wheels turning. "We can say he's a local celebrity. A hometown hero back on the airwaves."

"He's not even local anymore, though, is kind of the main point," I said, but Joydeep wasn't listening.

"A hometown hero *returning triumphant!*"

I looked to Jamie and Sasha for help. To my surprise, Jamie was nodding too. "We could interview him on-air. And maybe he could visit our class or something, give a talk about being in the business for real. That could score us some points with Tucker."

Joydeep pointed to Jamie. "Yes. Yeah. This is good."

"Sasha," I said, looking to her for reason.

But she just gave a small smile. "I don't hate the idea. It would be . . . kind of cool, actually. And we could even . . ." She paused.

"What?" Joydeep said. "Hit us with that magic, Wonder Woman. *Lasso us in truth.*"

"You're the worst."

"I'm the greatest of all time."

Sasha rolled her eyes, then took a breath. "What if at first, we bill it as an interview with a mystery guest? Like a *secret* celebrity interview. We can advertise for it, like dropping clues as to who it is. So part of the whole thing is in the buildup to it. Generating buzz and stuff. Getting people to guess who it's gonna be." She shook her head. "None of the other groups are doing anything like that. So even if no one really cares after the big reveal—sorry, Nina—" I waved a hand. "It'll show Tucker that we put effort into doing something different. And score us some points for doing, like, actual publicity."

"I like that," Jamie said. "There's only one issue." He glanced at me. "Do you think he'd do it?"

I took a deep breath. "Well . . . I mean, he's coming to town for my sister's school play in April. So . . . I think he could do it then?" In theory, if he came in on Thursday, he could do the show, talk to our class on Friday, and catch the opening night of the musical that evening. We weren't going out to California for spring break this year, so he said he'd make a trip out here.

"Perfect," Sasha said, and Joydeep punched his fist in the air.

"We're back on track!" he cried.

We were definitely something.

# 22.

**MY PHONE LIT UP WITH** a text from Joydeep a few days later.

*You should put together a list of fun facts about your dad*
*What? Why?* I replied.

*To build hype for the mystery guest. We've got to tease him*

*Ew,* I said.

*To the audience, gross!* he replied, and two more messages quickly followed.

*We gotta give them a little bit of FLAVOR, you know*
*Like of what's to come*

I didn't reply right away, and to my surprise, my phone buzzed once more.

*Look I get that everything up until this point has been kind of a clusterfuck. I'll admit that. So that's why we have to turn this thing around*

*You just don't want to lose your bet,* I said.

*I mean yes*
*But also I don't want to fail*
*And anyway, I think it's important to Jamie*

I frowned, my thumbs hovering above my phone screen, before typing:

*So?*

*He's my bro*, Joydeep replied.

I didn't respond right away, and my phone buzzed again after a moment or two.

*The mystery guest thing is going to be big for us. Nobody else is going to have that. It's super cool your dad is doing this*

*It's super cool you brought it up in the first place*

*So let's make the most of it, yeah?*

*Yeah okay*, I sent.

Joydeep replied with two thumbs-up.

# 23.

**FACTS ABOUT MY DAD.**

I tapped my fingers lightly against the keys of Mom's laptop, not pressing anything down. Just *tap tap tap tap*.

His favorite band was Pearl Jam. He was a terrible cook. He started in radio during college, interned at a station here in Indianapolis over summers, then got his first on-air job right out of college. It paid very little, so he also waited tables at TGI Fridays and deejayed at weddings and parties.

None of this was particularly helpful in terms of our show. Joydeep asked for *fun* facts.

My mom and dad technically met on the radio—that was a fun fact. Or it was, I guess? Until it all expired?

They got divorced when I was seven. We did two weekends a month at my dad's for the next six years.

He always woke up early, even on the weekends. Conditioned from years of doing morning radio, I guess. The show started at 6 a.m., so he would get up at four forty-five. "Sleeping in" meant sleeping until seven or so, and even then, he said he'd still catch sight of the clock and feel panic, like he was meant to be in the studio.

He traveled sometimes, doing stuff for the station. I remember him coming back one time with teddy bears for the three of us when we were little—each bear had a yellow-patterned dress and apron on, with bows attached to their little teddy bear heads.

I loved that bear. It was special in particular because Dad picked it out all on his own. He stopped at the airport gift shop or the drug store or wherever and saw those specific bears, and for whatever reason—they were cheapest, he thought they were cute, they would fit in his suitcase—he picked them out and bought them and traveled all the way back with them, just for us.

When my dad's show got bought and we found out that he would be leaving, I was in eighth grade, Rose was in ninth, and Sidney was in fourth. It was early fall, and my dad had taken us to Graeter's for ice cream. Crowded around one of the small round tables with our favorite too-big waffle bowls, he announced that he would be moving to California.

"This is a really big opportunity," he had said, "but it's not gonna—we'll still spend time together, and it doesn't mean that I don't . . ." He broke off a bit of cone, stuck it in the top of the mound of ice cream like he was planting a flag. "You can come for trips and stay longer—summer vacation, and Christmas—"

"I want to have Christmas with Mom," Sidney said flatly.

"Well, it's something we're working out now. We can definitely—"

"Mom knows?" Rose said.

"Of course she knows."

"Why didn't she tell us?"

"I wanted to be the one to tell you. I wanted you to hear it from me." He looked at the three of us. "This isn't going to change anything," he said.

Which was an absurd thing to say. That's what I remember thinking most clearly. That it was a complete and total lie—it was so obviously going to change everything. I think I understand a bit better now what he might have meant—that it wouldn't change how he felt about us. It wouldn't change the fact that he loved us and cared about us—things he should've said but didn't.

No one finished their ice cream that day. We pitched soggy, half-eaten waffle bowls with pools of melted ice cream in them. We rode home in silence.

Sidney took it hardest, I think. She sank into a terrible mood that lingered over the next few weeks. Finally, in a desperate attempt to cheer her up—after Sidney refused movies and games and dolls, even an offer to dive into Rose's makeup bag—Rose asked, "What do you want to do? Anything. Just . . . What'll make you feel happy right now? Tell us and we'll do it. Whatever it is."

Sidney had lifted her head, looked Rose right in the eye.

"I want to play Kingdom," she replied.

# 24.

JOYDEEP AMENDED HIS ORIGINAL REQUEST a couple hours after we chatted: *They have to be facts that are INTERESTING, but vague enough that people can't just google and find him right from it.*

*We need to CULTIVATE the MYSTERY*

*Okay I will KEEP THAT in MIND JoyDEEP*, I replied.

I ended up sending him a generic list. It was pretty bare bones. Joydeep didn't even look at it until the next time he got on-air—I could tell by the color commentary.

"So. There is something cool that we're going to do, that I am going to tell you about," he said. "On *Sounds of the Nineties*." Joydeep gave me a meaningful look, like he wanted credit for correctly ID'ing the program. "We're going to have a very special interview with a very special mystery guest in April. So. Because of that, we've got three facts here for you today, about him—or her. Them. The mystery guest." He cleared his throat and looked down at his phone, where he had my list pulled up. "Fact number one . . . Our mystery guest has lived in the state of Indiana. Hm. How about that.

Fact number two . . . Our mystery guest has a connection to the restaurant chain TGI Fridays. Huh. Cool. Fact number three . . . Our mystery guest's favorite color . . . is yellow." He cast me a truly exasperated look. "Cool stuff. Really intriguing. Here's a song by a person."

I scrambled to switch on the music.

"What?"

"*His favorite color is yellow*? That's the best you could do? That's a fun fact to you?"

"I don't know! You said to keep them vague."

"Not so vague that they could apply to any person who's lived here, eats cheesy potato skins, and likes yellow! That could be any of us!"

"Hey, if you care so much, *you* compile a list. Why do I have to be the one to do extra work?"

"It's your dad! If anyone knows him, it should be you! But fine, if you're gonna give me *his favorite color is yellow*, I'll make a list myself."

It was quiet after that while Joydeep rage-googled. I guess Sasha must have been looking too because her head snapped up a little while later.

"Your dad interviewed This Is Our Now?" she asked.

They were the boy band of the moment. Or of the last few moments, probably. "Yeah, before one of their concerts a couple years ago. They weren't as big then."

She grinned. "What'd he say about them? Did he have a favorite member?"

"Um . . . I can ask?"

"Do it."

♦

I texted him. Later that night he'd answer, *The one with the shaggy hair was the friendliest*, and we would identify him as Josh.

"Put it on the list," Joydeep said. "That's a fun fucking fact right there."

It was quiet in the studio for a bit after that, *Sounds of the Nineties* playing low, until Sasha suddenly burst out: "We got a notification!"

"Hm?" Jamie looked up.

"Online! Our account! Someone said something about us." A pause as she clicked. "bbright720 says, *Bless @soundsofthe90s for playing TB back to back. No one else out there giving him the respect he deserves on air.*"

"TB?"

Joydeep glanced at the monitor in front of him, scrolled through the playlist. "There's no TB."

"Are any two songs back-to-back by the same artist?" I said.

"Not on purpose," Jamie murmured.

"Ah." Joydeep made a face. "I copied one when I was messing around with the list earlier. Sorry."

"Who is it?" Jamie asked.

"Existential Dead," Joydeep read. "'Love Is a Blackened Lung,' 1994."

Sasha raised an eyebrow. "That weird grunge thing?"

"That weird grunge thing," Jamie confirmed. "The catalog has all their albums."

"I've never heard of them," I said.

"That's probably why they're in the catalog," Joydeep replied.

"Who's TB, though?" I looked to Jamie, but he just shrugged.

"I'm not super familiar with them either. I kind of threw that one in last minute."

Sasha did some clicking. "Tyler Bright. Lead singer." A pause. "Maybe we should play more."

"Why?"

"This bbright720 guy has like twelve thousand followers. If some of them like that band too, then maybe we'll get more listeners."

"That's a good idea," Jamie said, and went over to Joydeep's monitor. "I'll add a couple more to the list."

"Oh, great," Joydeep said with false brightness. "More gravelly moans and echo guitar."

"We should answer that bbright person," I said. "Tell them we'll put more on."

"Got it," Sasha replied.

*@bbright720 thanks for the love! Keep it tuned, more Existential Dead headed your way soon!*

It was quiet for a bit until a track started with a low, heavy guitar riff.

"This is them," Jamie informed us.

The singer's voice was deep and gruff as he started in on the verse.

"I can't even understand what he's saying," Sasha said after a moment or two.

"Check these lyrics," Joydeep said. "*Under the crushing weight of your gaze/Cannot breathe or see through unnumbered days/Choke me out, choke me out, choke me out.*" He grinned. "Then four more stanzas of *choke me out.*"

"There's no way he's actually saying that," Sasha said, just as the deep-voiced singer begin wailing something that sounded like *chah-me-ahhhhhhh* over and over again.

Joydeep held his phone out toward her so she could see the screen. "Deep stuff."

"Whatever it is, fourteen people are listening right now," I said.

"For real?" Jamie leapt up to look at the counter onscreen.

I nodded. "That's like our highest listenership so far."

"Check our account," he said, and Sasha clicked back over.

"bbright720 tweeted again! *Yooo thank you @sounds ofthe90s you are killing me tonight with these cuts from* Three Deep. *Can we get something from* Velvet Flycatcher *next?*"

"You sure as hell can," Jamie said with a grin.

---

We played five more Existential Dead songs that evening—all of them sounded pretty similar, with similarly bleak lyrics—and our listenership peaked at twenty-three people. We got three more tweets, and even though we had broken from our official 1994 theme by playing songs from Existential Dead's 1991 and 1992 albums (*Velvet Flycatcher* and *Cryptic Undertow*, respectively), it seemed worth it for the numbers.

"We should definitely mix some more of them into

the playlist," Joydeep said. "We might actually have a shot at best listenership."

"Colby said they're averaging fifty people a show,"

"Colby's full of shit. It's probably half that," Joydeep scoffed. "He's notoriously exaggerated the size of things in the past, if you know what I mean."

"I don't," I said, and Jamie shot me a look, clearly trying to suppress a grin. "What could you possibly be referring to?"

# 25.

Conrad: We're talking this morning about weird—well, not weird, we're not here to judge—let's just say, unusual things that people just can't let go of. Earlier we talked to Rick who has kept—

Nikki: And worn! Not just kept! Actually legitimately worn!

Conrad:—he's worn his same retainer, his original one from seventh grade, every night for the last thirty years.

Will: That's, I mean . . . I just don't know about that. The bacteria on that thing, ughhh . . . I don't even want to think about it.

Tina: Wouldn't it melt? Like, over time?

Nikki: What?

Tina: Like, wouldn't the heat of your mouth melt the retainer?

[silence]

Conrad: Tina, I'm not judging you, but that's the most cuckoo bananas thing that's come out of your mouth in a really long time.

Tina: What? Why?

Will: You think a temperature of 98.6 degrees Fahrenheit is sufficient to melt plastic?

Conrad: How would anyone use plastic forks and spoons if that was the case?

Tina: I meant like over time, like, wouldn't the constant exposure to—

Conrad: How would there have ever been plastic straws? Wouldn't we just liquefy our straws immediately?

Tina: I'm saying your body heat might wear it down over time—

Nikki: Couldn't drink out of a plastic bottle either. You might just melt that thing right down, according to Tina.

Tina: That's not what I'm—

Conrad: Okay, we're going to be taking more calls here in a moment, so let us know, is there something you've been holding on to for ages, a thing you just can't let go of, like Rick's retainer? Or Tina's troubling notion of thermodynamics? Give us a call.

Tina: I hate you guys.

# 26.

**I LISTENED TO MY DAD'S** show that night while I was doing homework. A woman called in and admitted she had kept all of her grown children's baby teeth. Another lady had saved the McDonald's bags from her first date with her ex-husband.

*Ex?* Dad exclaimed. *Ex-husband? Maybe it's time to ditch the bags, then?*

*It's bonfire time! Light 'em up, Kristy!* Will bellowed.

Sidney was definitely a packrat like that—she kept all manner of old drawings and notebooks and assignments, like her sixth grade pre-algebra homework was really going to come in handy someday.

I was kind of the opposite most of the time. But I did have a shelf above my bed with a few random trinkets—a couple Polaroids of me and Alexis, making faces at the camera, a wooden duck, a plastic tiara Sidney had given me, a jar of tinfoil gum wrappers. I always took the foil and folded it back into its original shape, then folded it again into a thicker, smaller rectangle. I started when I was a kid, but it was mostly out of habit now. The gum that comes in little plastic compartments arguably tastes better, but I still got the strips sometimes, still stuck the wrappers in the jar.

Rose had a shelf over her bed too—it held an art print from a show she went to last year, a little enamel box she kept jewelry in, and some glass figurines. A teddy bear sat up there too, one of the honey-colored ones my dad had gotten for each of us, with its yellow-checkered dress and apron and bow. We used to refer to them as the Honey Bears, and had decided that they were sisters like us.

I had no idea where my bear was. And for some reason, sitting there that evening, I was seized with a sudden and powerful urge to locate it. A quick search under my bed and in my part of the closet revealed nothing.

Rose was sitting on her bed, working on something.

"Have you seen my Honey Bear?" I said.

Rose looked up from her sketchbook, pulled out her earbuds. "What?"

"Honey Bear." I pointed to the shelf above her bed. "Mine. Have you seen it?"

"Uh, no. Ask Sid."

I went to Sidney, who was in the living room holding her script, one sheet of paper covering the page, her face screwed up in thought.

"Can't talk. Memorizing," she said.

"Have you seen my Honey Bear?"

"No."

"Where's yours?"

"Under my bed, in the blue Tupperware." With that, she went back to memorizing. Sidney was a packrat, sure, but an organized packrat.

I could've given up then, but maybe I wanted a reason to procrastinate on finishing my calculus homework. I went to my mom, who was sitting at the dining room table leafing through a catalog. Dan was the only person I had ever met who ordered clothes through catalogs and not online.

"Mom, have you—"

She had heard me ask Sidney, of course, because our living room and dining room were in fact the same room.

"Maybe in the storage closet?" she said.

---

Each floor of the Eastman had a storage area—a gray-walled room that was portioned off into "closets" with chain-link fencing.

Ours was packed with Christmas decorations and plastic bins full of old stuff.

I pulled out a couple of the most easily accessible bins and started digging through them. I hadn't been at it very long when something caught my eye—not my Honey Bear, but a small container full of cassette tapes. I extricated it from the rest of the clutter and opened it up.

The tape on top had red writing on the label. CONRAD AND MICKEY: THE SUPERCUT, it read in handwritten letters.

I pocketed the tape and kept looking.

# 27.

*This is Joydeep here on* Sounds of the Nineties. *It's time for some more facts about our mystery guest. So. We have learned a few things about this mystery person. He—they?—she?—lived in Indiana. They are associated with the restaurant TGI Fridays in some secret capacity. They like the color yellow better than any other color. Those were our original facts. And owing to those facts being, just . . . so super interesting, we've got some new facts for you tonight. So let's get started.*

*First of all, this mystery guy—person—has a connection to the band This Is Our Now. Can you believe that? We have it on good authority that this person's favorite member is Josh. Next up, this mystery person . . .*

# 28.

WE MADE A DECISION, THE evening of our 1995 episode, to officially depart from the "one year an episode" format. The demand for more Existential Dead songs was just too high, meaning at least seven people had tweeted at us about it, which was six more people than were tweeting at us before.

Existential Dead only had three albums, the last having come out in 1994. So if we wanted to keep them in rotation, we had to switch up the theme.

"We can still do songs from the featured year each week," Jamie said, "but it definitely seems worth it to mix some more Existential Dead in."

He even went through the playlist and added songs that were suggested via online algorithm, "For Fans of '90s Cult Grunge."

We were sitting around the studio that evening while a track from Existential Dead's 1992 album *Cryptic Undertow* was playing when Sasha looked over at me.

"So do you think your dad will be able to stay for the whole show when he comes, or just part of it?"

"Uh . . . not sure. Why?"

"I'm making some more posts to tease the interview and I wonder if it sounds better if we say it's an interview with the mystery guest *and* they'll be co-hosting that night, if he can stay the whole time."

The truth was, I hadn't exactly mentioned the interview thing to my dad yet. But he was for sure coming in April for Sidney's show. He was definitely taking time off for it. So it would be fine. It wasn't a big deal. I just had to get around to asking.

"Yeah, I don't know," I said. "I'll check with him." Then I pivoted to Joydeep. "Hey, so what kind of stuff are you planning to ask in the interview anyway?"

"Hm?" Joydeep was doing something on his phone.

"We're reading facts and stuff now, but what about the actual thing? What kind of topics are you thinking?"

We had told Mr. Tucker about the details of our *substantial plan*—he was really enthusiastic about it, especially the idea of Dad coming to talk to our class about his career in radio.

"This is great initiative," he had said. "I'm really impressed."

Right now Joydeep just shrugged. "I'll probably wing it. It's just asking questions, how hard can it be?"

"It's not *just* asking questions. There has to be some back-and-forth."

"There is back-and-forth. There's a question and an answer."

"Yeah, but, like, you have to be able to adapt your questions based on the answers. Look—like, Sasha, do you like sports?"

She glanced up from her computer. "Yes."

"What's your favorite one?"

"Volleyball."

Silence.

I turned back to Joydeep. "See? You have to be able to, like, have a conversation with someone or else it goes nowhere. Just asking a question isn't enough. You have to . . . react."

Joydeep just blinked at me for a moment and then said, "I can do that."

"Maybe you should practice, though, is all I'm saying."

"I can do that too," he replied.

When it came time for the next link, Joydeep turned to me with a gleam in his eyes and then turned back to the mic.

"This is *Sounds of the Nineties*. That was a song called 'Fatalistic Wasteland' by the band Existential Dead. Hey, if you are listening right now, you're in luck, because we've got a guest in-studio today. Everyone, please welcome . . ."

I shook my head forcefully. "Don't," I mouthed.

At that last moment, Joydeep swiveled his chair, taking his mic with him. "Sasha!"

Sasha's eyes widened, and for a moment, it was totally silent in the studio.

There was nothing for me to do but stand and swing one of the guest mics toward her.

"Uh . . . hi," Sasha said, pulling her headphones on. "What a . . . surprising opportunity."

Joydeep was unabashed. "Sasha, tell us, what's your favorite sport?"

"Volleyball."

"Awesome. Volleyball is a really dynamic sport. Would you say it's your favorite one to play, to watch, or both?"

"Both, I guess, but I also like watching basketball," Sasha replied.

Joydeep nodded. "The girls' basketball team is really good this year. Did you ever play on the team here? Or want to?"

"I played in middle school, but in high school, I kind of wanted to . . . focus on one sport so I'd also have time for other stuff."

"Why'd you pick volleyball for your one sport?"

"Mm . . ." She considered for a moment. "I like the net."

"Okay, wasn't expecting that. What is it about the net that's so great?"

"I guess I like the fact that it keeps you and your team together. And there's no physical contact with anyone you're playing against, so you're not getting elbowed or knocked down or whatever. And I like that you're . . . like, it feels as if you're more part of a whole in volleyball. Like, you can definitely be a star in basketball, but with volleyball, it's more about functioning as a unit all together instead of as individuals, if that makes sense."

"Yeah, for sure," he said, and then looked toward me with a triumphant *See?* kind of expression.

"What's your favorite sport?" Sasha said loudly into the mic. Joydeep winced and then blinked over at her.

"Me?"

"Yeah, you. Who else would I be talking to?"

His lips twitched. "It's soccer."

"Good. Now that we've established both of our favorite sports, maybe we should play a song."

"You don't want to hear my, like, deep philosophy about soccer and teamwork and stuff?"

"No, I'd way rather hear"—she leaned over to peer at the monitor—"'Back for Good' by Take That. Keep it tuned to 98.9 The Jam for more *Sounds of the Nineties*. We'll be back with you soon."

I started the music, and Sasha slid her headphones off.

"What was that?" she said to Joydeep.

"What was *that*?" he replied. "Are your parents radio hosts too?"

"They're accountants. Hey, maybe next time, don't force me on-air without my permission just because you're annoyed at Nina."

"I'm sorry," he said, and he did look genuinely sorry. "I shouldn't have put you on the spot like that. I just knew Nina's answer to the favorite sports question would be really boring. That was good, though, right? As far as winging it goes?"

"It was good," I said. "It was actually really good."

"Don't sound so surprised," Joydeep replied.

"You sounded totally normal," Jamie said, and paused, considering. "Maybe your problem so far has been that you're talking to no one. As soon as someone else is there, you're good at it." He turned to Sasha. "And you're really, *really* good at it."

"At what? Answering questions?"

"Hosting. Being on-air. You're a total natural. Why didn't you want to host in the first place?"

Sasha shrugged. "I don't usually like that kind of thing. But . . . this was pretty okay."

"It was way better than okay," I said. "You know, Mr. Tucker did suggest we have a co-host."

Sasha and Joydeep shared a look.

"What do you say?" Joydeep said. "Will you take this audio journey with me?"

"I don't know how I feel about it when you put it like that," Sasha said, fighting a smile.

Joydeep adopted a serious expression—too serious, which turned it back into funny. "Sasha Reynolds . . . will you be my co-host?"

Sasha considered it for a moment.

"Yeah, okay," she said, a smile breaking out. "I'm in."

# 29.

ROSE PICKED JAMIE AND ME up after the show, and
when we were situated in the car, instead of heading
right off, she looked over at me.

"Mom's with Dan, and Sid is at rehearsal. Do you
guys want to get food?"

I glanced back at Jamie. "Okay with you?"

A look of surprise passed briefly across his face, and
he nodded.

We went to Sawasdee, a Thai place on the west side
that Mom loved. It had the best decor—colorful satin
tablecloths, flowers everywhere. The waiters wore
brightly patterned shirts, and the spicy soup you got
with every meal was Rose's favorite.

It was quiet after we ordered. Jamie was fumbling
with his napkin.

"How was the show?" Rose asked.

It wasn't terrible, in fact. Sasha joined Joydeep on-air
for the rest of the links. Jamie was right—she was a natural. And somehow, even when Joydeep was reading
PSAs or the weather or whatever, having Sasha there

to make offhand comments or to react to stuff made Joydeep sound way more relaxed.

"Surprisingly okay," I replied. "How was class?"

Rose shrugged. "It was fine."

That could mean anything. Rose was pretty tight-lipped about school these days. I never knew how to approach it. I was still the only one who knew how things had really gone last semester.

It was last November when I found Rose in our room going through her portfolio. Mom and Sidney were out at a movie with the Dantist.

Rose very rarely got upset—or at least she very rarely showed it. So when I walked in that night and she looked up, eyes red and ringed with mascara, I knew not only that something was wrong, but also that the *something* that was wrong had reached critical mass.

"What is it? What happened?"

She looked up from the portfolio, from the various scattered pages around her, and shook her head. "I'm just . . . not good at this."

"Are you kidding?" Rose had never seemed to suffer from a lack of self-confidence before. "You're great at art. You know that."

"I'm not good at studying it," she amended, voice hoarse. "I'm not good at being a student of it. Nothing is . . . It's not at all like it was in high school. It's not . . ." She shook her head. "It's not what I thought it was gonna be, and I'm not good at it." She swallowed. "I'm failing at it, actually."

"For real?" Rose failing a class was inconceivable.

Any of us failing a class was hard to imagine—I wasn't the best student in the world, but Mom hammered the importance of decent grades into us from *coloring outside the lines* age. We were all at least average or better in school, and Rose had always been the best.

But apparently that wasn't the case for Rose in college. She had nodded mournfully, looking back down at her portfolio. "I don't know what to do."

Right now, across the table at Sawasdee, Rose contemplated Jamie.

"Are you planning to go to school next year?" she said.

He nodded. "Yeah. I got into Butler."

"Nice." The waiter set down the soup in front of us, and Rose reached for her spoon. "Nina's going to IUPUI, has she mentioned?"

"I haven't gotten my acceptance yet," I clarified.

"You'll get in," Rose said.

"But there's still financial aid stuff," I replied. "If it doesn't work out, I might go to community college."

Jamie nodded. "Nice."

"What are you gonna major in?" Rose asked him.

Jamie shrugged, pulling his bowl closer. "I'm not sure yet. I don't really care what I do, to be honest. I just want to make a lot of money."

It was so un-Jamie-like. I looked over at him.

"For real? You? Cutthroat businessman fueled by capitalism?"

He shook his head. "Not for myself. Not for, like, cars and watches and stuff." He picked up his spoon. "I

144

just want to be able to take care of them. My grandma and grandpa. Like how they've taken care of me. I just want them to not have to worry about anything, ever. Like, something comes up, it's handled. Done. I got it." He nodded, more to himself than to us. "That's what I want."

Rose leaned back in her chair. "Maybe I need some kind of motivation like that," she said. "Maybe I'm too selfish."

"You're not selfish at all," Jamie replied.

"Thanks for that, but we haven't hung out in a while." Rose smiled wryly. "Maybe I've gotten way more selfish since then."

"I wouldn't believe that," Jamie said. "Just . . . based on your track record."

"Yeah? What's my track record?"

Jamie's eyes shone. "Well, Iliana was the most generous bounty-hunter-slash-assassin-slash-rogue in the land."

"That's it—I should be more like Iliana," Rose said. "She always had her shit together."

"She definitely saved my life a bunch of times," Jamie replied with a grin.

# 30.

FOR THAT FINAL GAME OF Kingdom in the autumn of
my eighth-grade year, Sidney insisted that Jamie join us.
And not only that, she made a big fuss about all of us
dressing up.

It was one thing to play a game like that when we
were in fourth or fifth grade like Sid was. Rose and I
were that age when we originally thought up Kingdom,
after all. But now I was in junior high—and Rose had
just started high school, for god's sake!—and Sidney
not only wanted us to play a make-believe game, but
she also wanted us to do so while wearing *costumes*.

That was our hard line. Rose refused to dress up,
which meant that I refused too.

"It's enough just to play," Rose said. "We don't have
to . . . wear special outfits for it or anything."

"Jamie will dress up!"

"He won't."

Sid was adamant: "He will!"

He had answered neutrally enough to my text
when I invited him to join us. That was a minefield in
itself, figuring out how to even ask. I tried to explain

that it was an important thing to Sidney, tried to make it sound like she dragged us into it, to convey that it was definitely embarrassing. But Jamie just texted back promptly: *Sure. Let me know when.* No reservations, no further questions.

We picked a weekday afternoon purposefully so the game wouldn't drag on. Mom was still at work, but Rose was in charge of us after school at this point. There was a short stretch of time between us arriving home on the bus and Mom getting back from work, and that's the time we picked to play.

A knock sounded at the door that afternoon, and when I opened it, Jamie was standing there in the hallway wearing jeans, a white button-down, a scarf tied into a belt, and snow boots. A worn plaid throw hung over his shoulders, fashioned like a hooded cape.

"Where's your outfit?" he said, frowning.

Something in my chest seized uncomfortably, like my heart was temporarily too big for my rib cage.

Sidney appeared at my side and jumped up and down, knocking me on the arm. "I told you! I told you he would dress up!"

Rose appeared too, saw Jamie's outfit, and her lips curved into a small smile. "Okay, Hapless. I guess we're really doing this."

---

Rose put on a pair of Mom's old cargo pants and a bomber jacket. She took a belt and attached some stuff to it with hair ties—a ruler, a protractor, a TV remote, and a hairbrush.

"Hairbrush?" Jamie said.

"The bristles are blow darts."

"Nice."

I wore Rose's eighth-grade formal dress—it was puffy and gold, with layers of tulle—with a pair of boots and threw her middle school graduation gown over it like some kind of wizard robe. Back in the day, Sidney's Quad outfit had been made out of an old pillowcase, like some kind of bootleg Dobby. But this time she took one of Rose's shirts, a long, dark plaid thing with rips in it, and wore it like a tunic, along with the knee, elbow, and wrist pads my mom insisted on after our dad got us skates for Christmas one year.

"Armor," she informed me. "In case we go into battle!"

"So what's our backstory?" Jamie said when we were all dressed and assembled in the living room. "Where have we been the last few years?"

"Adventuring," Rose said, at the same time that I said, "Counting our riches," because even though the last game of Kingdom never had a definitive ending—it kind of just faded away—that's where I would've wanted us to end up.

"Who cares where we were?" Sidney said. "We're back together now because Hapless has been put under a spell."

"What kind of spell?" Jamie said.

"A witch cast a curse on you that makes you forget everything good in your life and in the world. You'll forget things one by one until only the worst, most terrible memories and things remain, and it'll drive you into a deep despair."

Rose and I blinked at each other. Sidney was ten. What did she know about deep despair?

"That's kinda dark, Sid," Jamie said.

She shrugged.

"How long have I got?"

"Until you've forgotten all the good stuff?" She paused to consider. "A few days, maybe."

"What do I lose first?"

"Cake," she said. "You forget about cake. All cake, in order, starting with the best kind of cake and ending with the worst kind of cake."

"What's the worst kind?"

"Fruitcake, at Christmas."

"And the best?"

"Chocolate."

"No." I frowned. "The best are those ones you see online where you cut them open and the inside is hollow and a bunch of M&M's pour out."

"You're both wrong. The best is vanilla with rainbow sprinkles, and the worst is carrot," Rose said. "Regardless, you've lost every kind of cake."

"And your favorite book when you were a kid," Sidney added. "And your best friend from school."

"Geez," Jamie said. "How long until I lose mac and cheese?"

"You just did," she replied, and Jamie's face split into a grin.

"Ruthless. Okay." He looked between the three of us. "What do we do first?"

---

The Eastman consisted of two towers joined together by a central lobby that housed the front desk, the leasing office, and the three ballrooms. There was also a small indoor pool on the west side of the building and the offices of a few businesses, all connected by a main hallway. It was a pretty nice building in terms of amenities, but parts of it were definitely wearing down a bit. My mom complained occasionally about the lack of upkeep, particularly in the units—paint peeling away on the ceiling, appliances wearing down. A screen on one of the windows in our bedroom had had a hole in it for ages. We hadn't opened that window in years.

Still, the rent was affordable, and it was either way nicer or way cheaper than a lot of other places around here—not too close, but not too far of a drive to the School of Medicine, where Mom worked.

For Kingdom, we designated different areas of the Eastman as different parts of the kingdom. The pool was a swamp, and the mail area was a magical vault. Certain parts of the parking lot had their own designations—the area by the trees where the barbecue stood was a sacred glen, the concrete parts without shade were the Wilds. Even employees of the Eastman, albeit unknowingly, took part in our game.

The front desk attendant had to walk the perimeter

of the building every couple of hours. ("Expressly whenever I need to get a package," Mom would say. "Somehow they always know, and they choose that exact moment to leave.") We made that person— whoever it happened to be—into a member of the Evil King's Watch. We would run and hide from them, track their movements, create plans to infiltrate their guard.

For this particular game, this resurrected game, we entered the stairwell on our floor under Sidney's direction: "We're busting Hapless out of a tower," she said. "Go up there, and we'll come get you."

Jamie went ahead of us to the landing between the ninth and tenth floors.

"How do we know how to find him?" Rose asked.

"Magic intel."

"Do we know that he's under the curse?"

Sidney nodded.

"How?"

"Magic intel," she repeated more insistently.

"Who's our magic source? Where is the intel coming from?" I said.

Sidney looked annoyed. "A frog told me. A magical talking frog. He jumped out of a pond and he told me. Is that okay with you?"

Rose hid a smile. "Lead the way."

When we started up the stairs from the ninth floor and found Jamie on the landing, he was sitting on the ground, slumped against the wall. With one look up at us—baffled, exhausted, confused—I remembered how good at pretend he was.

"What's happening?" he said. "What are you doing here?"

Sidney crouched by him. "You've been cursed, but everything will be okay if you do exactly what we say."

"You have my word," he replied, all princely dignity. But then his expression sank back into confusion. "I have to get back to my castle. There are things I need to do. I have to see to my people and feed my dog. His name is . . ." He trailed off, looking off into the distance with a puzzled look on his face.

"What?" Sidney prompted.

"Sorry?"

"His name is *what?*"

Jamie's brow scrunched. "Who?"

Sidney looked at me in delight.

"On your feet," Rose said. "Let's get out of here."

I extended a hand to Jamie and he clasped it, grinning at me. "Let's go."

# 31.

Sasha: This is *Sounds of the Nineties* here on 98.9 The Jam. I'm Sasha.

Joydeep: I'm Joydeep.

Sasha: And tonight we're highlighting songs from the year 1996.

Joydeep: Quite a year.

Sasha: Was it?

Joydeep: I don't know. I assume so?

Sasha: We've also got some music coming up from Existential Dead, so if you're a fan of them or of nineties music in general, keep it tuned.

Joydeep: Hey, Sasha?

Sasha: Hm?

Joydeep: What is the best piece of advice you've ever gotten?

Sasha: Are you trying to interview me right now?

Joydeep: Well, as the brand-new *Sounds of the Nineties* co-host, I feel like we should, uh, give the listeners an opportunity to get to know you better.

Sasha: Yeah, because they've learned so much about you so far.

Joydeep: Well, I guess it's an opportunity to get to know both of us, then.

Sasha: You just want to practice for the interview with our mystery guest.

Joydeep: Nah, I think we established I don't really need practice, as our producer would probably agree. Can't I be genuinely curious?

Sasha: Oh my god. You have an article open called "Thirty-Three Interesting Conversation Starters."

Joydeep: I do not!

Sasha: You do too. You do. I can see it. Everyone in the studio can see it.

Joydeep: Okay, well, even the greats need inspiration sometimes. So what is it? The best advice you've ever gotten?

Sasha: Umm . . . Probably something from my mom. She's really smart.

Joydeep: Hit us with that mom knowledge.

Sasha: Well . . . uh, okay, there's this one. When I was younger, I used to get really sad about stuff ending. Like . . . I would go to camp in the summers—like different camps each year, usually—and I'd make friends and stuff over the weeks or whatever, and when it was over, I'd be so sad because I wouldn't see any of the people again.

Joydeep: Camp sadness. Got it.

Sasha: I remember saying to my mom once, like, it's totally pointless making friends at camp because even if you go back to the same one the next summer, they might not even be there, and you're not going to see them the rest of the year anyway. They're not going to be like your real-life friends. And my mom told me that part of growing up is just . . . learning that people come in and out of your life, and that there are all kinds of levels of friendship, all different types. And maybe you'll make a friend, and you won't see them again, but it doesn't devalue what you had with them or the time you spent together. That's still valid, even if it wasn't built to last. It's not any less . . . significant, you know?

Joydeep: Damn. Mama Reynolds swooping in with the sage wisdom.

Sasha: What about you? Best advice?

Joydeep: Uhh . . . My brother Vikrant told me that the thing on the end of a shoelace is called an aglet.

Sasha: That's not even advice.

Joydeep: I know. I panicked. Yours was really good. Here's a song, and that song is "Upturned Sunset" by Existential Dead . . .

# 32.

**MY SEARCH OF THE STORAGE** room closet for my Honey Bear had turned up fruitless, but I still had the *Conrad and Mickey: The Supercut* tape. What I didn't have was anything to play it on. And what I didn't know was why I actually cared to hear it, but I did.

I knew the editing bays at the station had tape players, but it was hard to get in there when no one else was around. I could try to stay late after our show, but I didn't want anyone finding out why, for some reason. I didn't want anyone asking about this.

I ended up texting Alexis:

*Do you have a tape player?*

Alexis had most things. And I knew she wouldn't ask why. She was pretty easygoing, pretty carefree about stuff like that.

*Mmm no but Tate might?*

Alexis's brother Tate was in his early twenties. He had finished up college at Duke and moved back home to work at their dad's company for a bit. According to Alexis, he was "hipster to a fault." He liked mushroom lattes and artisanal beef jerky. *He'd ride one of those bikes with giant front wheels if he could*, she told me once. *No, scratch that— he'd go full horse-and-buggy if that was an option.*

*I'll ask him*, she texted.

She appeared at my locker the next day with a small, rectangular tape player. I thanked her and shoved it in my coat pocket.

Alexis smiled. "You just need some big Jamie Russell style headphones to go with it. You remember those jank ones he used to have in junior high? The cord was like six feet long?"

I did remember. Jamie always had those headphones with him back then, an old, bulky pair with a long cord stretching into his pocket. One day in particular sprang to mind—Jamie walking by the lunch table where Alexis and I and a group of other girls sat, those head-phones around his neck. It was the fall of eighth grade, around the same time that our final game of Kingdom was underway.

He had glanced my way as he passed, a smile break-ing his face. "Hi, Nina."

"Jamie Russell!" Alexis had said, eyes alight. "Come sit with us."

Jamie had hesitated, but Alexis gestured to one of the other girls to scoot over, and Jamie slipped onto the bench next to me.

"How's it going?" Alexis said as Jamie began to unpack his lunch. That was another thing about him—he always brought lunch to school in a Velcro lunch bag.

"Good," he replied, unwrapping aluminum foil from a sandwich. He glanced over at me, eyebrows flicking up a little in a way that said, *This is weird, right?* Jamie and I were friends, but he and Alexis weren't.

"Hey, do you know Kieran Cooke?" Alexis asked, as if this was not weird at all. "He's in your homeroom, right?"

"He is, and no, not really."

"You don't know anything about his girlfriend at Yeatman, do you? The one on the debate team?"

"You seem like you know more about her than I do," Jamie replied simply.

"She definitely exists, though," Alexis said—not a question but a statement seeking confirmation.

Jamie was good-natured as always, but under the table his leg bounced up and down. "I don't know. You'd have to ask him."

Alexis cut a look over at Natalie Fisher, seated to my left.

"See, I just don't think Kieran's a good Kiss Cam candidate, Nat."

"Sorry?" Jamie said.

"Nothing," Alexis replied, and a couple of the other girls at our table giggled.

I had felt supremely uncomfortable during this exchange, except for the fact that every time Jamie bounced his knee, his leg brushed against mine, and somehow that single, fleeting point of contact made me feel like there was molten hot lava at my core, radiating outward.

They had gone on talking about something else, and

Jamie ate his sandwich and jiggled his leg and then the warning bell rang, signaling the end of lunch and the end of any more possible discussion of the Kieran Cooke strategy.

Jamie only asked me when we got off the bus at the Eastman that afternoon. We had spent the ride debating a hypothetical: Would you rather have a hit song that everyone knows but most people hate, or an album that a few people love but most people haven't heard of? "Hey, what was Alexis talking about at lunch? What's Kiss Cam?" A pause. "Besides that thing at basketball games. I figure they're not, like, taking Kieran to a game just for that."

"It's a game Alexis invented," I said, and for some reason I felt really embarrassed saying it out loud.

"What kind of game?"

"A kissing game. Sometimes they'll play it at free period or lunch or whatever. She'll, like, hold her hands up"—I made a rectangle with my fingers, held it in front of me, and scanned around like a camera panning across a crowd—"and pick someone random, and you have to go kiss them."

Jamie didn't speak, frowning down at the ground as we reached the front of the Eastman.

"Or, you know, get them to kiss you," I added. "But you don't just do it without their permission, that would be bad."

"Sounds kinda bad anyway," Jamie said. "Like kinda mean, right?"

"Why?"

He shrugged. "Just, like . . . the idea of kissing some-one because someone else told you to. How is that sup-posed to make the other person feel?"

"Happy that they get kissed, I guess?" It came out sounding defensive, and I had no idea why. Alexis wasn't mean. She was just . . . her. "Or they don't kiss you if they don't want to. You can ask or whatever, but it doesn't mean they have to say yes. And sometimes she does research, you know, like with Kieran. She wouldn't pick him for Nat if he had a girlfriend."

Jamie just nodded, but didn't speak further.

Right now, back in the hallway at Meridian North with Alexis's brother's tape player in my pocket, I won-dered if Alexis ever thought of Kiss Cam anymore. She'd had a boyfriend for the past couple of years, but they had broken up at the beginning of senior year. What would she do if I held up my hands, scanned the hall, and picked someone? Knowing Alexis, she'd probably go right up and see if they wanted to kiss her. She was fearless sometimes. But it wasn't just fearless-ness—it was a disregard for consequences that I both envied and disparaged.

She smiled at me now, gestured to my coat pocket where I'd crammed the tape player. "Hope that does the trick for whatever weird retro thing you've got going. It might need batteries, though."

"Got it. Thanks."

# 33.

THAT NIGHT, I CLOSED MYSELF in our room and popped *Conrad and Mickey: The Supercut* into the tape player, plugged in my headphones, and pressed play.

It took me . . . a while to realize the tape needed to be rewound. But once I figured that out, a voice—familiar but slightly altered—filtered through. It was my dad.

"This is Z 99-5, and we've got someone on the line here . . . What's her name, Producer Shoebox?"

"Michelle."

"Okay, Michelle. Are you there? What's up? Or should I say, wazzup?"

[chorus of *wazzups*]

"Don't do that," the caller said. "No one likes that. Everyone is sick of it."

"So did you call just to give us feedback, Michelle?"

"I'm calling because we've got beef."

"You and me?"

"Yeah."

"Hey, Conrad, maybe Michelle wants some of your

beeeeeef." [siren sound] [cash register sound] [woman moaning]

"No one likes you either, Producer Shoebox. Okay? I listen to this show every day, and no one likes you, just so you know."

[sad foghorn] [high-pitched female voice saying *nya nya nya*]

"Do you realize how sexist your soundboard is? Like, where are the sounds for when men complain? Where are the male sex sounds?"

"I'm sorry, Michelle, Producer Shoebox can only express himself through the magic of sound and innuendo, but we will be sure to load up some male org— Can we say that, Shoebox? I'm gonna say we shouldn't. We will load up the male happy fun time sounds just for you, Michelle. So what's our beef about? Or did that pretty much cover it?"

"Oh, we've barely scratched the surface."

"Okay. Let's hear it. What's your main issue? The real, uh, heart of the beef."

"Whenever I call in for tickets, you always pick up, but then you just say *keep trying* and hang up on me."

[*nya nya nya*]

"I swear to god, if you don't knock that off—"

"Sorry, Michelle. Producer Shoebox, cool it, okay? For like one second?" [pause] "I see your finger on that button, and if you play a foghorn stinger, we're not friends anymore." [pause] "Steve." [pause] "If you press that button, you're leaving the booth. You won't be allowed in here anymore."

[pause]

[sad foghorn]

"Out. Right now. I'm not even kidding." [scrambling] "Sorry, you still there, Michelle?"

"Honestly, whatever they pay you guys, it's too much."

"We got you listening, didn't we?"

"I like the music. And the contests. Which takes me back to—"

"The beef, yes, right. Okay, but you know that's sort of how these call-in things work, right? You gotta keep trying if you want to be the lucky caller."

"I'm lucky enough that you pick up the phone, but not enough to be the winner! It's rigged!"

"Rigged specifically against you?"

"Why do you always pick up?"

"Maybe I like the sound of your voice."

"Then why don't I ever win the tickets?"

"I mean, I can't give tickets away to every girl whose voice I like."

My mom made a sound like *eughfhfh* and hung up.

# 34.

**I LISTENED TO THE TAPE** again the next day. And the day after that. It was just the one exchange—the *Supercut* in the title made me think maybe there would be more, but I fast-forwarded through, stopping to play periodically, and there was nothing but silence.

I was listening to it again in the library on Tuesday during my free period when my phone buzzed with a message from Sasha in the *Sounds of the Nineties* group chat.

*We need to meet up* was all it said.

So we met at the student gallery after school.

Sasha wore an odd expression as she sat down on the bench along the wall. "So . . . we kind of have a problem," she said.

"Is it Jamie's face?" Joydeep replied.

Jamie looked hurt. "Hey!"

"Sorry." Joydeep grimaced. "Instinct. Vikrant will get me if I don't get him first."

Sasha ignored the exchange. "Basically, they think that Existential Dead is our mystery guest."

"What? Why?" I said. "Who's *they*?"

"The Deadnoughts."

"The *what* now?"

"It's what their fans call themselves."

"*Dead not*? Like, not dead?"

"*Dead N-O-U-G-H-T*, like a ship, a dreadnought."

"It's like a play on words," Jamie said.

"Oh, great," Joydeep replied. "I know how horny you guys are for wordplay."

"Why would they think that?" I said, trying to focus on the matter at hand.

"Because we keep playing their songs, for one thing," Sasha said.

Jamie frowned. "That was a listenership strategy."

"Yeah, well, it worked. We got a bunch of people who love Existential Dead to listen, and now they think we're delivering them the band live on the air."

"Just because we played them a few times? That's stupid."

"Also, because there are some, uh . . . similarities, based on the facts that we gave about Nina's dad."

"What do you mean, *similarities*?"

"So I started looking into it once we started getting messages about it, and not a whole lot is known about these guys. Apparently they were really cryptic and under the radar or whatever back in the day, and that was a part of the appeal for their fandom. There aren't a *ton* of fans these days since they never really got huge in the first place, but they've had kind of a resurgence online in the last few years. Like, there are Tumblrs dedicated to Tyler Bright and stuff, all this *Oh, I was born in the wrong decade, heart eyes* kind of stan stuff. But anyway, he's originally from Indiana. Like your dad."

"So?" I said. "Lots of people are originally from Indiana. We're all originally from Indiana."

"Actually, I lived in Illinois until middle school," Sasha replied.

Jamie nodded. "I was born in Michigan."

"Really?" I said.

"And I was born in India, we moved here when I was three, thanks for asking," Joydeep said. "I win for traveling the farthest, and the prize is getting to tell Nina she's wrong."

"Okay, yes. Clearly we're not all from Indiana," I amended. "But I'm just saying—that's not proof of anything."

"Yes, but we also said your dad's favorite color is yellow," Sasha said.

"So?"

"One of their more popular songs—I mean, it's relative since they never got super popular in the first place, but still—anyway, it was called 'Truly Madly Yellow.'"

"Oh, we played that one!" Jamie said. "Remember?" He started mumble-grunting something that sounded like *Take my hat wabababa yellow flamajamaaaaaa.*

"Oh yeah!" Joydeep said. "*Flamajamaaaaaaaaaa eat my faaaaaaaaaaaace.*"

I shook my head. "That's not anything."

"It's not *eat my face*, it's *east of fate*," Jamie said.

"What's *flamajama*?" Sasha asked.

"I feel like we're getting off track?" I said.

"Right." Sasha turned back to me. "Also, we said that thing about how your dad's favorite member of TION is Josh."

"I will give you a hundred dollars if you can connect that shit together," Joydeep said.

Sasha raised an eyebrow. "Get ready to pay up. It's not confirmed or anything, but there's a rumor that the bassist from Existential Dead went on to become a music producer and that he was one of the people behind TION's first album."

"And he loves Josh?"

"I mean, it's less about Josh specifically, and more about how we said he had a connection to the band."

I shook my head. "This is ridiculous."

"Agreed," Joydeep said. "Except for one possibility."

"What?"

"Nina, is there literally *any chance* that your dad is the lead singer of Existential Dead?"

I couldn't help but sputter a laugh. "No. Literally no chance."

"But how do you know?"

Sasha blinked at me, deadpan. "Yeah, Nina, like how does anyone *really know* that their dad isn't an obscure cult nineties rocker?"

"He's not old enough," I replied. "Existential Dead's first album came out in 1991, right? He was like . . . a freshman in high school then."

"So?" Joydeep said. "Maybe it was like a . . . Bieber thing."

"You really think that voice is coming out of a fourteen-year-old?" Jamie said, and then in a deep rasp belted, "*Flamajamaaaaaaaaa!*"

"I mean, sure, maybe he's not the lead singer, but he could be one of the other guys."

Sasha pulled up a picture of the band online. It was black-and-white and grainy, and their faces were cast in shadow, but still—four long-haired, kind-of-young-but-definitely-not-fourteen-year-old guys.

"None of those people are my dad," I told Joydeep.

"Come on, they took that picture with a potato," he replied. "I could be in it."

"Why do you want it to be my dad?"

"Because it would be interesting! And anyway, what's our other option?"

"We squash this," Jamie said. "That's literally it. We just tell them straight up that Existential Dead is not coming here."

"Okay." Sasha nodded. "Okay, yeah. Obviously, that was my thought, but I just wanted to check with you guys before I blew our *secret guest* thing online."

"Well, hold on a sec," Joydeep said. "Pump the brakes, Diana."

"What?"

"We don't have to ruin the mystique of the secret guest. It's kind of the main thing we have going for us at the moment. Let's just put something out saying it's definitely not Existential Dead. Like, as long as we're super definitive, I don't know why we have to give the whole thing away yet."

We looked at each other.

Finally, Jamie shrugged. "Sure. Why not?"

We drafted a statement:

> *We have been promoting a special celebrity guest interview on our radio program for the last few weeks. There appears to be some confusion regarding the identity of this guest based on fun facts we have given. We would like to state, in no uncertain terms—*

"Capitalize it," Joydeep said.

> *IN NO UNCERTAIN TERMS, that the band Existential Dead is not—*

"Capitals," Joydeep prompted again.

> *NOT appearing on our show. Thank you. Signed, The Sounds of the Nineties Team.*

"Perfect," Jamie said.

# 35.

**"WE HAVE A PROBLEM," SASHA** said before we started our 1997 episode on Thursday evening.

"What?"

"The comments on our statement."

Blckndlng00 said: *They said the BAND will not be appearing. That could mean Tyler is coming ALONE. A solo session!*

TBheartsIN replied: *OR that theyre not just appearing—theyre performing!!!!*

"Uh-oh," Joydeep said.

"It's okay," Jamie said. "It's just some comments. We can totally fix this."

---

*We would like to state, IN NO UNCERTAIN TERMS, that the band Existential Dead is NOT appearing, performing, interviewing, or speaking in any capacity on our show, nor are any of the members of*

*Existential Dead doing so on an individual basis. We are in NO WAY affiliated with Existential Dead. Thank you. Signed, The Sounds of the Nineties Team.*

---

"Guys," Sasha said when Jamie dropped down into his seat in radio class on Friday. "It's not working."

"What?"

"The statement isn't working. The Deadnoughts won't buy it."

"How can they not buy it?" Joydeep said.

"They're saying it's misdirection. Apparently Tyler Bright used to cancel shit all the time back in the day and then show up at the last minute. They think that's what's happening. Like it's some conspiracy or something. Honestly, you should read some of the stuff they're saying."

"Fine," Joydeep said. "Fuck the mystique. Let's just tell them it's Nina's dad."

"Sounds good to me," Jamie said. "What do you guys think?"

"Let's do it." Sasha looked at me expectantly.

I looked away.

"Well . . ." A pause. "So the thing is . . ."

During our Sunday call, my dad had mentioned his trip to town for Sidney's show. And I could have brought it up then. I could have easily asked in that moment—or any number of moments before then, to be honest—but I just . . . hadn't.

They were all looking at me intently. I glanced at Jamie for a second, but he clearly already knew, and the flash of disappointment on his face was too much for me.

I took a deep breath. "My dad, at the moment, is not, like . . . one hundred percent totally confirmed."

Sasha's voice was calm. "What percent is he confirmed?"

"I haven't totally . . . completely . . . mentioned it to him. Yet."

Joydeep threw his hands up in the air. "Oh, great. So we've been hyping up something that might not even happen?"

"He's definitely coming for my sister's show, though. He'll be here in town, so there's no reason why he shouldn't be able to do it. It'll happen. Even if something comes up or whatever, he could call in, maybe . . ."

"Which is it?" Sasha said. "It'll happen, or he could call in, or *maybe* he could call in?"

"We already told Tucker about your dad visiting class, though. That's legit probably the only reason he's okay with us right now," Joydeep said.

"I know," I replied.

"So what are we supposed to do?" Sasha asked. "Should we announce it's him? Or not?"

I didn't speak.

"No," Jamie said finally. "Just let the Deadnoughts think what they think for now. It's not hurting anyone, and we literally said it wasn't happening, so if they want to keep on believing it, then that's their problem."

"What about the class session, though? What do we tell Tucker?" Joydeep said.

Jamie shrugged. "That's up to Nina."

"Don't put it all on me."

Something flashed across Jamie's face, a mix of disbelief and annoyance. "But it is on you! You said we had a guest!"

"I never said that exactly. I said I *thought* he'd do it." *Nina Conrad, hairsplitter extraordinaire.*

"So it's our fault for jumping to conclusions," Jamie said. "For believing you."

"Yes, Jamie, I think you of all people would know how super full of shit I am." It was the exact wrong thing to say. The wrong moment to be flippant. But that was what I did—I was an expert at picking wrong moments. Or maybe at picking the exact right moment for the exact wrong thing.

Jamie shook his head. The Jamietron shuttered, all the exasperation and annoyance shutting off into blankness.

Sasha and Joydeep were looking between the both of us, wide-eyed, and only when Jamie turned and started packing up his stuff did Joydeep say, "Hey, come on. We can totally figure this out."

Jamie didn't reply. He just left before class had even begun.

# 36.

OUR LAST GAME OF KINGDOM—the Kingdom revival, as it were—spanned some time. It wasn't the neat, single-afternoon, open-and-closed story that Rose and I were hoping for when we originally agreed to play.

It was Rose who pointed out that in order for Prince Hapless's curse to really be accurate, he would have to forget us eventually. And then he might not trust us, might not believe that we were really trying to help him when all he remembered was the worst of the world.

Ten-year-old Sidney had a response for that, as she did for everything:

"We have to be mean to you," she told Jamie. Our journey thus far had led us to the patch of grass next to the barbecue area by the parking lot. There were a few tall trees lining the lot that turned yellow this time of year. The leaves hadn't fallen yet—they formed a canopy of color above us. "If we want to keep you. If you want to remember us. You only forget the good memories, so we have to be mean to make sure we're not good memories anymore."

Distress flashed across the Jamietron. "I don't want that."

"It's the only way," she replied, eyes shining. "I'll go first." She cleared her throat. "You're stupid, and we don't need you."

Jamie blinked at her guilelessly—pure Hapless. "I don't believe you."

"It's the truth."

"Sidney—" Rose started.

"It's the only way," Sidney insisted, and Rose sighed. She turned to Hapless.

"Your . . . shoes . . . aren't shiny."

Jamie narrowed his eyes, looked toward Sidney. "Is that mean enough to make me not forget?"

"Nope."

"They are the least shiny shoes I've ever seen," Rose amended. "And they're ugly."

"That's better." Sidney looked to me. "Aurelie?"

"I don't wanna be mean to him."

"Then he'll forget you."

"Aurelie wouldn't do that though," I said. "She'd find a different way."

"Nope." Sidney was adamant. "It's the only way."

I looked at Jamie. He just shrugged and smiled a little in an *It's okay* kind of way.

"What if I waited?" I said. "What if I was only mean at the very last minute?"

Sidney considered this for a moment. "It's risky."

"I'll risk it."

She shrugged. "Your choice."

---

In the midst of the game—amid those autumn afternoons where we would meet for an hour or two after school, before my mom got home from work—came my birthday.

We never really had birthday parties with friends, only small, "just us" gatherings to celebrate, but I begged and begged my mom to at least let me invite Alexis over, and she relented. Alexis came with a silvery gift bag in hand containing a makeup set that I had no idea how to use and that Rose eventually co-opted. We used to try to do YouTube tutorials, and Rose's looks always turned out way better than mine.

Jamie came by too, with Gram, carrying a big cake. I looked over at Mom in surprise—I knew she had a store-bought one in the fridge—but she just smiled at me.

The cake had poorly piped lettering on it that said *Happy Birthday Nina*, and some decorative swirls.

"Cut a slice," Jamie said, and again I turned to my mom, the usual cutter of cakes. "No, you should do it," he insisted.

I cut into the cake and pulled out a slice, and a cascade of M&M's fell from the cake's center. Everyone *ooh*ed at once and then laughed and clapped, and when I looked over at Jamie, he was beaming.

"We looked up how to make it," he said. "The best kind of cake, right?"

I nodded. It was.

I didn't notice Alexis looking between the two of us. I didn't think of Alexis at all in that moment, in fact—just Jamie's bright eyes and his broad smile. Gram encouraged us all to grab a plate, take a slice. The cake was delicious.

It was at a sleepover at Alexis's house a couple weeks later—we were gathered in the family room watching some garbage slasher movie—when she turned to me and said, "It's your turn to play Kiss Cam, Nina."

I was a permanent bystander of Kiss Cam. An observer, but never a player. Alexis had never picked me, and I had never volunteered. Truthfully, I definitely wanted to kiss someone. Like, I wanted to know what it felt like, I wanted to be someone who had *been kissed*. But the actual idea of kissing a random person terrified more than it thrilled. "Right now?" I said.

"No, at school." Alexis's eyes lit up. "On the field trip." The whole eighth-grade class was supposed to go to the Indianapolis Museum of Art the following week. "You're gonna kiss Jamie."

My stomach swooped with some strange mix of anxiety and excitement.

"Or . . ." Alexis looked thoroughly pleased with herself. "You get bonus points if you get him to kiss you."

How did you get someone to kiss you? What were you supposed to do? I had to ask, and of course Alexis had an answer. She had an answer to everything.

Whether it was necessarily true or helpful or correct was another story.

"Look at his lips," she said. "Then at his eyes, then back to his lips. Like, back and forth." She leaned in. "Here—practice."

I looked at her eyes and her mouth and her eyes and her mouth, which split into a grin, and then let out a cackle.

"You're gonna sprain your eyes. Don't look that *fast*. You have to, like . . . *linger*. And, like, kind of lean into him." She shook her head. "You know him, though. He's your friend. Just say whatever will make him kiss you."

"I don't know what that is."

"Make something up."

"I don't know . . ."

"It'll be great," she said with a smile. "Trust me."

———

The day of the field trip arrived, and on the bus to the museum, Jamie sat up toward the front with some other guys. Alexis and I shared a seat closer to the back, and although I liked being her chosen person of the day, my stomach was roiling.

She knocked her shoulder into mine. "You ready?"

"I really don't know if—"

"You're the only one who hasn't played. And it's fun. You're going to have so much fun."

At the museum, we toured a new abstract exhibit

and made our way through the textiles gallery. It was in the contemporary art wing that we were turned loose to complete some worksheets—and it was there that Alexis winked largely at me, gesturing to where Jamie had wandered down a small hallway.

There was an art piece at the IMA I had always liked. It was called *Acton*, by an artist named James Turrell. It was a windowless room, totally empty, with two sets of track lights attached to the ceiling and pointing toward the walls on either side of the entrance. The lights were turned low so that the illumination was softened, the whole room dim. Along the back wall of the room there appeared to be a large, dark, rectangular canvas.

In the dimness it looked like a painting, but when you got close enough to it, you realized that it was really a hole cut out of the wall, that there was space behind it, a darkened room on the other side. You could reach right in.

When I was little, I remember being too scared to reach into the darkness but also unbelieving that there was space back there at all—until I finally stretched out my hand and felt no resistance as it moved through the space where something solid should have been.

I remember standing in there with Sidney and Rose and Mom once when I was a bit older. We were all quiet, contemplating the piece. We had all already reached into the space. Sidney was seven or so at the time and eventually broke the silence by announcing:

"I don't get it."

"That's okay," Mom said. "You don't have to get it. It's just supposed to make you think something, or feel something."

A pause followed as Sidney took this in.

"What I feel is that I don't get it," she replied.

Sidney wanted to shine a light into the dark space to really see what was back there, but Mom always kept us from doing that. I guess she didn't want to ruin the illusion. Maybe that was part of the piece—not knowing how far back the darkness went, how much depth was really there.

That was where Jamie was headed that day on the eighth-grade field trip, and that's where Alexis gestured me—down the little hallway leading to *Acton*.

I took a deep breath and then followed.

Pausing in the doorway, I could see Jamie's silhouette in the dim light. He was standing in front of the darkened rectangle, but he wasn't reaching in.

"I like this one," I said, voice hushed, even though we were the only people in the room, and there was no need to be quiet. Something about the low light made it feel . . . special, somehow. Sacred, like a church or a monument.

Jamie glanced back as I approached, smiled a little. "Me too."

I stepped up, shoulder to shoulder with him in front of the rectangle, and then gave him a glance and moved closer to the space, reaching out my hand.

"What are you doing?" he said with a hint of panic, grabbing for my wrist.

"It's empty," I replied, and Jamie's expression shifted to one of confusion.

I held out the other hand and plunged it into the darkness.

He let out a shocked laugh. "For real?"

"Yeah." He was still holding my wrist. I swallowed. "Try it. Just reach out your hand."

He stepped closer, moved his other hand up tentatively, fingers extending into the empty space.

"Whoa." I could see the white of his teeth as he grinned through the dimness. "I couldn't tell." He was speaking hushed too. "I thought . . ."

He looked over at me.

This was it. This was the moment. Like standing on a high dive, toes lined up at the end of the board, that moment just before the jump.

As Alexis had instructed, I looked at Jamie's mouth and then his eyes. And then his mouth. And then his eyes. *Linger.* I stuck with eyes for a moment. Watched them crinkle a bit at the edges as he smiled a little.

"What are you doing?"

*Just say whatever will make him kiss you.*

I shook my head.

"I like . . . I like you," I said, and looked at his mouth. His smile grew.

"Really?"

I nodded and watched the smile dim slightly. I flicked my gaze back up to his eyes. "*Really* really?" he asked, quieter.

I didn't reply, just nodded and leaned in toward him.

He leaned in too and softly pressed his lips to mine.

It was gentle, and sweet, and lasted for just an instant, until someone nearby let out a high-pitched squeal. They were quickly cut off by a flurry of *shush*es.

We broke apart, and I could see it happening in real time in Jamie's eyes, I could see happiness deflate into devastation and then quickly shutter off.

His voice stayed the same, just as soft, but everything had changed. "You know," he said, "you probably should've had Alexis and them wait farther away."

I turned and could see the back of Alexis's phone disappearing around the corner.

When I looked back at Jamie, he had stepped away from me. He shook his head, his voice tightening. "That game is mean, Nina. It's really . . ." He swallowed. "It's just mean."

It was. I knew that. And I knew that maybe he liked me, and I knew that it would hurt him if he found out, but I did it anyway—I don't know if it's because I wanted Alexis to like me or because I wanted to fit in so badly or because part of me just wanted to kiss Jamie without having to be the person who chose to do it, without having to be responsible for it. I wanted to know what it was like, if his lips were as soft as they looked. I wanted to see how they felt against mine.

I was selfish and terrible and had never been more aware of it than in that moment, with Jamie blinking at me, hurt writ large across his face as much as he tried to hide it.

"Sorry," I mumbled. I couldn't even manage the *I'm*,

which barely made it an apology. There was no owner-
ship to it without that. There was no admission of fault.
I swallowed hard and tried again. "I . . ."

He didn't say anything, just shook his head, and for
a moment there was nothing but terrible silence. Then
he walked away.

It was never the same between us after that.

**37.**

**IT WASN'T LIKE JAMIE IGNORED** me completely, never spoke to me again, walked in the opposite direction whenever he saw me. If anything, I was the one who avoided him. I didn't know what to say, how to make it better. So it sort of just . . . faded away between us.

Maybe it would've happened anyway because of high school—more people, new friends, new after-school commitments. Meridian North was massive, so I didn't have any classes with him anyway. I didn't see him much once high school began except when we would run into him at the Eastman, in the elevator or at the mailboxes. My mom would ask him about his grandparents, or how school was going, and he'd chat good-naturedly. He'd show up to the bus in the mornings at the last minute, board and sit near the front with a couple of other guys on our route. Walking back from the bus stop in the afternoons—if we both happened to be riding—I'd slow my steps so we wouldn't have to catch the elevator together.

When he showed up at our place on Christmas with Gram and Papa, that was the first time I had really had a conversation with him in ages.

And I liked having conversations with Jamie. There was a time when talking to him was one of my very favorite things to do. Sitting across from each other on the rides to and from school every day, asking *Would you rather only eat breakfast foods forever or have to give them up forever? What if you could transport yourself to anywhere you wanted in the world, but only for five minutes at a time? Would you marry the clown or be the clown—* that one came up a lot. Jamie's eyes shining, smile a little bashful, *You should marry the clown, Nina, it's the perfect solution.*

*Is it?*

*Well, yeah. I already said I'd be the clown.*

I looked down at my phone the afternoon that Jamie had walked out of radio class. I couldn't get his look of disappointment out of my mind. I wished, with a sudden fierceness, not to be the kind of person who let Jamie Russell down. Not again.

I stared at the contact name on the screen for a moment before pressing it.

"Nina?"

"Hi, Dad."

"What's going on? Everything okay?"

"Oh yeah. Uh . . . I wanted to ask you something. About when you come for Sidney's play."

"Sure thing."

"Do you think you could do this thing for my radio class?" I described it to him—the interview, the talk for the class. "Nothing huge or, like, that you'd have to prepare for or anything. Just answering some questions about being in the industry and stuff like that."

"Uh . . ." A pause. "Uh, yeah. I think that should be all right."

"You can make it? For our show on Thursday and for class on Friday?"

"Yeah, I'm gonna take a couple days off work. I'll be there."

"For real?"

"Definitely. Sounds good. Anything for my favorite deejay!"

I hadn't mentioned that I wasn't actually on-air.

"Thanks. That would be really great."

"Everything else going okay? Rose and Sid? Mom's all right?"

"Yeah, everyone's good."

"Good. Good, good. Okay. Love you."

"Love you too."

He hung up.

---

There was a knock on our front door that evening. It wasn't Dan, because he was there, and he was the only person on our "approved visitors" list. Everyone else had to be buzzed up.

I swung open the door, and there was Jamie.

"Hey," he said. "Do you have a second?"

I hesitated. We were just sitting down to dinner. If I invited him in, I knew Mom would ask him to join us, and then I'd have to sit through a bunch of awkward small talk, all the while knowing he came to have a *conversation* with me.

"Nina?" Mom called.

"Be right there," I said, stepping into the hall and shutting the door behind me.

"Sorry, we're just starting dinner—" I began at the same time Jamie said:

"I can come back. I didn't mean to—"

We both broke off.

Jamie flashed an awkward smile that faded quickly. "I just . . . wanted to say I'm sorry for earlier. At school. I shouldn't have just left like that."

"No, Jamie, I—"

"I'm just stressed. That's all. I shouldn't let it affect the show or the group or anything like that, and I shouldn't . . . I mean, that's not an excuse to be a dick."

"You weren't," I said. "You were right. I should've asked him already. I was being stupid." A pause. "But I checked with my dad, and it's going to be fine. He'll definitely do it."

"For real?"

"Yeah. One hundred percent confirmed."

"Awesome." Jamie nodded. "Thanks. For that."

I nodded back.

He shifted from one foot to the other for a moment and then said, "Well, I, uh . . . ."

"Why are you stressed?"

He shook his head. "It's not really about school or anything."

I smiled a little. "Would I only care if it's about school?"

"I don't know," he said, in a way that made me think he really believed that, and it broke my heart a little bit.

"What's going on?"

"Don't you have dinner?"

"It can wait."

I stepped to the right of our door and sat down with my back against the wall. Jamie smiled a little, leaned against the opposite wall, and sank down too.

"I'm just worried 'cause . . ." He shook his head, the corners of his mouth pulled down. He shut his eyes after a moment and rested his head back against the wall.

"My grandpa can't really work anymore," he said eventually. "But my gram is working a ton. She works for this nonprofit, but it's kind of been struggling this year, and she might . . . like, she keeps playing it off, but I think they might have to let her go. And I feel like shit because she was basically retired already from teaching when they—when I came to them, and she had to start working again, and if she loses her job, I don't know . . . With Papa's health stuff, and—" He cut off, shrugged. "It's just a lot."

*I'm sorry* or *I wish I could help* or *Is there anything I can do?* were all things that I could have said. Should have said. But I was me. I was supremely versed in *Not Knowing How to Deal with Things*, the Chief Executive Officer of *Feelings Are Uncomfortable*. So I just made a sound kind of like *hmmmmyah* in the back of my throat and studied the carpet—black, patterned with white diamonds, low pile, a staple of the Eastman for probably the last twenty years at least—and only looked Jamie's way when I was sure he wasn't looking back.

Right now he was staring off in the direction of

apartments 903 and 901, which faced the front of the building. 901 still had their Christmas wreath up, all these weeks later.

"Existential Dead probably has a good song for this kind of thing," I said eventually, because I couldn't stand a silence for too long. I was too much like my dad.

"You think so?"

"For sure." I screwed my face up in thought. "You know, something like . . . *Grandma's working hard for bucks . . . A cruel twist of fate steals well-earned luck . . .* Then, you know, the chorus." I shrugged. "*Eat my face, eat my face . . . eat my face, eat my face, eat my face.*"

Jamie just looked at me for a second and then burst out laughing.

I felt weirdly proud. "It's called 'Lament for the Lost Souls Who Wander and Wait for the Bus That Never Comes.' It's a bonus track from their unreleased 1996 album . . . *Satan's Shoehorn.*"

"Oh, for real?" he said, still laughing. "It's a bonus track?"

"Yeah. It was a live recording from a concert they gave in the basement of a Chili's in Muncie. On the night of a lunar eclipse. They played that song only, and then they torched the Chili's. Like, literally burned it to the ground." I leaned in and dropped my voice conspiratorially. "You know the wildest part is, their original bassist was still inside."

Jamie buried his face in his hands, shoulders shaking, and when he looked at me again, there was a wide grin on his face, moisture in the corners of his eyes.

I dropped my gaze back to the carpet, and I don't know why I said it now, except that there was something in his smile, in making him laugh, that was so deeply gratifying that I felt like I couldn't enjoy it—like I didn't deserve it—until I did this one thing right. The way I should have done it before, originally, or at least a long time before now.

"Hey, Jamie?"

"Mm. Yeah?" He was wiping his eyes on his sleeve.

"Remember in middle school . . ." I swallowed. "You know that dumb thing . . . like, with Alexis . . ."

I dared to glance at him, and he met my eyes, the smile fading, his expression shifting to something neutral.

The carpet was my friend, my constant companion.

"I'm . . . sorry about that," I said. "I'm really sorry."

It was quiet. I couldn't make myself look up at his face.

"Nah, it's . . ." Jamie's tone was even, just a touch hesitant. "I mean, that was just . . . kid stuff. Right?"

"Yeah, but . . . no," I replied, because Sidney was almost the same age now that I was then, and I knew she was perfectly capable of not acting like a complete and utter dick to someone she cared about. "It was . . . a jerk thing to do. And I'm sorry."

"It's fine," Jamie said. "No worries."

There were still worries, though. I wanted to apologize more, to press him further, and I wasn't even sure why. That would just make it even more about me and about making myself feel better. Maybe sometimes you just have to ride out the discomfort of your own guilt. I don't know what more I wanted from him other than *No worries*. To demand the exact words *I forgive you*? That was absolutely unreasonable.

It didn't stop me from wanting more, though, and I didn't know why. I just know I didn't feel . . . absolved, or whatever.

But I just said, "Cool," and then it was quiet between us.

"I should, uh, get going," he said finally, and gestured to the door. "You've got . . . dinner and stuff."

"Oh yeah."

We got to our feet. "But . . . are you scheduled for Saturday?"

I nodded.

"Awesome. See you then, I guess?"

"Yeah. For sure."

He headed away, and I resisted the urge to watch him go. But just barely.

# 38.

**DURING SATURDAY'S WEDDING, THE BEST** man pulled a crumpled sheaf of paper from his suit jacket, tried to smooth it against his leg, and fumbled with the mic before swinging around to the bride with a grin.

"Katie, as Mike's best friend, I have just one thing to say to you."

A dramatic pause before the follow-up:

"You can do better."

The room broke into laughter.

I caught Jamie's eye across the room. He made a face and then smiled.

I smiled back.

---

My phone buzzed with a text that night after I had gotten home, showered, and collapsed into bed.

*There should be a wedding rating system, and the You Can Do Better speech should get minus thirty points*

I grinned. Read it, and read it again before replying.

*Agreed.*

# 39.

**MR. TUCKER CAME OVER DURING** class on Monday as we were gathered in our groups having "programming meetings" (ostensibly—the group next to us was discussing March Madness).

"So," he said, taking a seat at the empty desk next to Jamie. "I wanted to talk with you all about a potential fundraising opportunity related to Nina's dad's visit."

"Okay," Jamie said, with none of the reservation that I suddenly felt.

"I've been thinking about the whole thing—the interview on your show, the visit with our class. You guys are pulling in really decent numbers." His voice dropped down. "The best in the class at the moment, to be honest. So here's what I'm thinking: We could—*potentially*—turn this into a ticketed event."

"What?" I frowned. "No, it's just the interview in-studio, and a talk for people in class, right? Like it's just supposed to be an educational thing."

"Well, I'm thinking we could combine the interview and the talk, have it the evening of your show, and make it open to the public. The members of our class and all the volunteer hosts would get free entry, of course. Absolutely. But I think it could be a really cool fundraising opportunity for the station. You guys are growing a listenership, and I think we could potentially capitalize on that. I also think it's a great chance for members of the community to learn more about what we do here at the station."

This was a good idea in theory, but in practice, in this particular situation, it was not a good idea at all. I looked at the group, not wanting to be the one who had to say it, but to my surprise, Jamie spoke:

"Can a portion of the ticket sales go to charity?"

Mr. Tucker smiled. "That's a great idea, Jamie."

"I know one. That we could pick." He avoided all of our gazes. "I know a charity we want to pick."

"Awesome. We can definitely coordinate that. Let's discuss this more later, okay?"

"Great," Jamie replied, and Mr. Tucker headed off to the next group.

"What the hell?" Joydeep hissed. "What about *the situation*?"

"The *Nina's Dad's not coming* situation, or the *Existential Dead* situation?" Sasha asked.

"Either! Both! This is a multifaceted situation!" Joydeep replied.

"He can come," Jamie said. "Nina checked with him. One hundred percent confirmed, right?"

I had to agree: "Right."

"So we have a guest, just like we promised," Jamie continued.

"Not a guest that anyone would buy a ticket for!" Joydeep said.

"Hey!"

"I'm sorry, I thought we were past stroking your dad's ego."

"I don't want to stroke Nina's dad's anything," Sasha interjected.

"We said that it's not Tyler Bright," Jamie said. "Multiple times. It's not our fault if people ignore us and think what they want anyway, is it?"

No one spoke.

"If we could do this, it would really . . ." Jamie met my eyes, and then quickly looked away. "There's this food bank, on the west side . . . My grandma works there. It would be really cool if . . . I mean, it would help a lot—if—"

"I think it's a great idea," I said.

Sasha looked skeptical. "You do?"

"Sure."

There was gratitude in Jamie's expression when I glanced back at him.

"But what are we gonna do if a horde of angry Tyler fans comes at us when they realize their idol isn't there?" Joydeep asked.

"It probably won't even be a thing," Jamie said. "We haven't even sold any tickets yet. We're overthinking this."

We were under-thinking it. Over the course of the next week, Mr. Tucker set up a webpage for the event, scheduled for the Thursday evening of Dad's visit in April. We linked it on all our social media pages.

### 98.9 THE JAM: SPECIAL DISCUSSION WITH MYSTERY GUEST!

**Sounds of the Nineties** *(Thursdays from 5–7 p.m.) is hosting a special discussion with a mystery guest familiar to the airwaves of Indianapolis. Join us for a live interview with this radio legend at Meridian North High School on April 11!*

We sold thirty-two tickets in one day.

*It's chill*, Jamie said in the group chat. *It's not too many, and it's good money for the charity.*

Joydeep replied: *No offense, Nina, but if people knew it was your dad, would we sell that many right off the bat?*

*Probably*, I said, and then kept typing:

*Yeah*

*I mean*

*Maybe?*

The next day, we only sold only twelve tickets. The day after that, just five.

"See?" Jamie said before class started. "Totally chill. The first wave was probably just . . ."

"What? Bots and stuff?" Joydeep said skeptically.

"The hardcore fans. Of our show."

"Of *Tyler*," Joydeep corrected.

"It'll be fine," I replied.

---

It *was* fine. Until Friday, when Sasha logged on before class started and saw that we had sold fifty-four tickets so far that day.

"What the hell?" Joydeep said, standing to peer over her shoulder at her laptop screen, like visual confirmation was necessary.

"I don't know," Sasha replied. "It just spiked."

"Check the Deadnoughts. See if they're saying anything about us."

Nothing came up besides the usual:

> *Omg @soundsofthe90s please play Velvet Flycatcher #bestalbum #no contest #threedeepcansuckit*

> *TB DOING A LIVE INTERVIEW APPARENTLY????*

> *did u see? classic ExD denial tho lol*

"We'll just have to . . . monitor it," Jamie said. "Over the break. We'll just keep an eye on it."

---

After radio class that day, only one more period stood between us and spring break. There would be no show next week. We had reached 1999 with this week's episode and had resolved to start the theme over again when classes started back up.

"Got any plans for break?" Sasha asked as we filed out of the classroom into the hall.

Jamie shrugged. "Just working."

"Me too," I said.

"Tomorrow?" Jamie asked.

I nodded.

"Cool, same."

"I'm planning on doing nothing, literally nothing, and I'm gonna enjoy the hell out of it," Joydeep said. "How about you, Wonder Woman? Fighting for truth and justice?"

"I'll be around," Sasha said.

"Good. Our planet is safe in your hands," Joydeep replied with a salute, and then headed off down the hall.

"Have a good break," Jamie added, and then he took off as well, leaving Sasha and me standing alone.

"Where are you headed?" Sasha asked.

"World Lit."

"I've got AP English that way," she said, and we started to walk together. "So you and Jamie work at the same place?"

"Uh, yeah. This catering company. It's in our apartment building, so it's pretty convenient. Don't even have to walk outside to get to work."

"Nice. You guys knew each other before, right?"

"Yeah, we kind of grew up together."

She cut a glance over at me. "You know, I actually knew Jamie before the show too."

"Oh. Really?"

She nodded. "Not well or anything. But we both worked on the musical last spring. Did you see it?"

I had seen the last six Meridian North musicals, courtesy of Sidney's obsession. Last spring's show was *Bring It On: The Musical*.

"Yeah." I had no idea Jamie did theater. And I couldn't remember seeing Sasha up there either, but admittedly the musicals were always jam-packed. I think it was a prerequisite of every high school musical that they had to cram as many people onstage as possible. In the production of *Godspell* my sophomore year, Jesus had no less than eighteen disciples. "I didn't know you were into theater."

"Nah, I just wanted an arts extracurricular. In case the sports scholarships didn't pan out, I wanted to be as well-rounded as possible, you know? So I did a crew thing. Specifically, I ran lights. More specifically, I ran the spotlight."

"Oh . . . cool."

"Did you happen to see opening night?" she said ruefully.

I shook my head. We went to the weekend matinee. Dan came too and entered the silent raffle, bidding on and winning about five tons of kettle corn.

*Aren't you supposed to stop us from eating stuff like this?* Sidney had asked.

*I'm a dentist, not a monster*, he'd replied with a grin.

"I was scared of messing up," Sasha said now. "So scared, actually, that my hands were shaking really badly. To the point where I could barely keep the spotlight trained in the right spot, and when I did, you could still see it shaking. Like, *violently* shaking." A pause. "You know Alyssa Charles, the lead girl? She had this huge solo song early on in the first act, and I totally messed it up. She apparently threw a fit backstage afterward. Said the show needed a seizure warning because of me." She shook her head, expression a little bit sheepish. "Jamie was helping run the light board. He was up in the booth too. I remember being like, *What do I do? What should I do?* and he said, so serious: *Pray for an earthquake.*"

I couldn't help but smile, and Sasha smiled back.

"He helped me hold the light so it was steady. He was there whenever I needed him for the rest of the night, and the rest of the weekend too—said he'd be standing by just in case."

It was quiet.

"I know this whole . . . event thing is kind of risky," she continued as we neared the World Lit room. "And

I don't like that. I don't like messing up. But if it can help Jamie with his grandma's charity thing, then that's something, right?"

"Is doing a bad thing for a good reason still bad?"

Sasha shrugged. "Probably depends on the circumstances." A smile. "Here's hoping not?"

# 40.

SASHA AND I ENDED UP hanging out over spring break. One afternoon we met at the mall uptown and walked around, tried on some deep discount clothes that were clearly discounted for a reason, got overpriced frozen yogurt.

Sasha was really easy to talk to, easy to be around. I told her about Rose and Sidney, about Mom and the impending marriage. I heard about her friends on the volleyball team. Her brother Quincy, who was ten. Her potential volleyball scholarships—she had been recruited by a few schools, and had just committed to Notre Dame.

"That's really cool," I said, stabbing a strawberry with my spoon. "Must feel good."

"Mm," she replied.

"What?"

"No, it does. Definitely. But it's also kind of scary?"

"Why?"

She shrugged. "I don't know. Makes it real, I guess. The stakes seem way higher. I love playing, but now it's like, I won't just be playing 'cause I love it, I'll be playing to stay in school. I just hope it doesn't put too much pressure on it." She took a bite of yogurt, then a smile crept across her face. "You know like how it's easy to flirt with someone if you don't actually care, but as soon as you get feelings, suddenly it's the hardest thing in the world?"

"Can't relate," I said. "I never flirt with anyone."

"No, whatever you and Jamie got going on kind of transcends flirting," she replied, giving me a look before going in for another bite of yogurt.

"What? We don't—what?"

"Come on. There's a little something there."

"No."

"A liiiiittle something."

"Sasha."

"Just a teeny, tiny, little itty bitty—"

"We kissed *one time*."

Her eyes grew wide. "I knew it! When? Where? Was it at school? Was it at the studio?"

"Ages ago," I said. "In junior high. It's over and done. He would never—" I shook my head. "It's nothing."

"But—"

"I want to look for some sneakers." I didn't have the budget for sneakers—most of what I was earning at Pipers was going into the Dantist's Camera Repair Fund. But Sasha didn't need to know that. "Should we get moving?"

"Yeah, okay." It looked like there was more she wanted to say, but she didn't press further.

When I got home that evening, I could hear Rose's voice coming from our bedroom and increasing in volume. I could only make out snippets—"didn't want to make it a big thing" and "wasn't *hiding* anything" and "kidding me right now?"

"What's going on?" I said to Sidney, who was curled up on the couch watching TV.

"Rose might lose her scholarship," she said. "She got a thing from school. Mom found out, and they had a fight, and Rose told Dad, and now they're having a fight."

I moved into the hallway. Mom's bedroom door was shut, but the door to our room was slightly ajar. When I pushed it open, I could see Rose standing by the window, her back to me. She didn't turn around, her phone pressed to her ear, her posture tense.

"Yeah, I am," she was saying. "Because I—no, listen—because you think, like, a ten-minute phone call every week gives you the right to suddenly *parent* us. When you've never done the job of actually *being a parent*. You only want to chime in when it's convenient for you. You know, when we were kids, if something was wrong, if we needed help, we'd go to Mom, do you realize that? If we were sick on your weekend, we'd stay with her. Because you didn't want to deal with it, and because we knew deep down that she would take care of us, that you couldn't even—listen to me—you're not even listening to me!"

She lowered the phone abruptly and hung up. When she turned around and saw me, her expression went hard.

"I don't want to hear it," she said.

"Hear what?"

"I don't know. Whatever you're gonna say."

"I'm not saying anything."

"You're literally talking right now."

Arguing with Rose in this moment was absolutely unproductive and I knew it. And yet . . . "So I can't speak out loud? Is it okay if I think really hard?"

"Nina, I swear to god—"

Mom's door opened then, and she stepped into the hall, noticed me there. "Ah, you're home."

"I'm going out," Rose said, and then moved past me.

"Rose," Mom called as Rose stomped through the living room.

"I'm going out," she repeated, and the front door opened and slammed shut.

———————————————

I got a text a little while later from Jamie.

*Hey your sister is down at the playground*

Two more messages popped up as I looked at the screen:

*Should I go talk to her?*

*I'm gonna go talk to her*

I went to get my shoes on.

The playground stood about a block away from the Eastman, tucked back among the houses there. It had a blacktop with benches bordering either side, a basketball hoop, a swing set, a little jungle gym, and one of those metal roundabouts that turn in circles.

Jamie and Rose were sitting on one of the benches near the basketball hoop when I arrived.

"Hey," Jamie said, looking over as I approached. "We're discussing plot holes in *Harry Potter*."

Rose smiled weakly at me. She looked like she'd been crying.

"There are no plot holes," I said, just to be contrary. "That shit is airtight."

"In book four, why didn't they just make a port-key out of something Harry would encounter in a normal day? Why did they have to stage an elaborate festival that Harry had to win his way through just to get to the trophy portkey? Why didn't they turn a pen or something into a portkey and then hand it to him?"

"It's not worth thinking too much into. It'll keep you up at night," I said, and as I settled down on Rose's other side, Jamie stood.

"I should, uh . . . I just wanted to . . . make sure you were . . ." He gestured around. "You know. It's getting dark. Safety in numbers and all that."

"You don't have to leave, James."

"I just thought maybe you'd rather talk about . . . *Harry Potter* plot holes . . . with Nina."

"We'll probably talk about the shambles my life is in instead," Rose said. "And you're welcome to join."

Jamie sank back down, and it was quiet. The sun had dipped low, the sky that kind of watery twilight blue of early spring.

"I don't know what I'm doing," Rose said eventually.

"Trying to justify the Triwizard Tournament in your mind?" I said.

She didn't laugh. Instead she just shook her head, and when she spoke, her voice was hoarse: "It's like I'm at the point where I can't even remember why I liked doing art in the first place. And I can't even tell . . . like maybe I was only good at it before because it didn't matter."

I thought of Sasha, of her words in the food court today. "Like how it's easy to flirt with someone if you don't actually care, but when you're like, legit interested, it's really hard?"

"Can't relate, I'm always good at flirting," Rose replied.

I smiled.

"I think you're an amazing artist," I said after another pause. "But I think . . . if you're not happy at school . . . if you're having a hard time doing what you're doing and you're not enjoying it at all, then . . . why don't you just do something else?"

She shook her head. "I can't."

"Why not?" Jamie asked.

"How can I just give up on my dream like that? What

if it's supposed to be hard? And even if it's not, what kind of message would that send to Sid? How messed up would that be?"

"What does it have to do with Sidney?"

"She wants to do the theater thing so bad. What will it say to her if I just give up?"

"It's not giving up," I said. "It's just . . . admitting that what you thought you wanted isn't actually what you want. What's wrong with that?"

"But I told everyone! I made this whole big thing about *following my dreams* and *living a creative life* and all that, and what am I supposed to do now? Just say I changed my mind?"

"Yeah."

"But—"

"But what? It's not a crime, saying something you thought before isn't what you think now. I actually think it's a pretty decent thing to do, isn't it?"

"I don't want to have to say I was wrong," she said sullenly.

"Well, that sounds like a Rose problem."

She huffed a laugh.

"You could switch majors," I said. "You could go to a different school. You could take a semester off, just work for a bit. There are lots of options."

Rose nodded, and it was quiet again.

"What do you think, James?" she asked eventually.

"I think Nina's right."

"That's an awesome thing that people should say more often," I said.

Rose smiled a little brighter this time. A little more like normal Rose. "Maybe I think you're right too."

I held out my arms. "God, it's like a drug."

# 41.

THAT SATURDAY BROUGHT A WEDDING to the Eastman that was unlike any of the ones I had encountered so far during my time at Pipers. This wedding was themed. And not in the way that they usually are—*vintage* or *romantic* or *rustic*. This wedding was Shakespeare themed.

Sonnets or passages from Shakespeare weren't uncommon for readings during a ceremony, Jamie told me as we filled pitchers with water that evening. But this wedding was next level, totally full-out, Shakespeare to the max.

"There are *lutes*," one of the other waiters told us excitedly. "They've got dudes out there playing *recorders*, wearing *doublets* and shit!"

The bride and groom, the rest of the wedding party, and even the officiant wore elaborate period dress. The musicians indeed played instruments of the era. There were definitely sonnets, and while the best man and maid of honor speeches were original works, according to the enthusiastic discussion among guests they had been composed in iambic pentameter.

"If my best friend told me my speech had to be in iambic pentameter, I'd find a new best friend," Celeste murmured to me at one point, and I snorted.

"Can you imagine?" I said to Jamie as we were getting cake service ready. "Being like, let's get married, but it has to be *Shakespeare style*. Let's spend all this money on a big fancy wedding, except it's . . . I cannot stress this enough . . . *Shakespeare style*."

"You know, it's not even the weirdest theme I've seen."

"What was the weirdest?"

"There's been a bunch. Space cowboy. *Hunger Games*. Zombie apocalypse."

"You're lying."

He grinned. "Maybe. One of them is real, though."

"Which one?"

"I'll never tell."

"Jamie!"

We were bringing back our trays to transfer more plates of cake when Jamie said, "I think it's nice, though."

"What? Shakespeare style? Or the *Hunger Games*—for real, was it *Hunger Games*? I need to know everything."

He began loading my tray with plates. "I just think it's cool that they each found the, like, one other person who thought this was a great idea. They're . . . on the same page. And that's kinda what the whole thing's about, right?"

He glanced up at me, and something about the

211

moment—facing down the full force of Jamie Russell's earnestness—was too much. I was afraid I'd do something stupid, like drop my tray and grab his face and press five or six dozen small kisses there.

Instead I just swallowed and looked away. "What would your wedding theme be?" I asked eventually, watching Jamie rearrange a few plates on his own tray to fit a couple more.

Jamie thought for a moment. "Big top circus."

"Yeah?"

"Oh yeah," he said, meeting my eyes once more with a small smile. "Peanuts, tiny car, red-and-white-striped tent. The whole nine yards." Then he shouldered his tray and headed back toward the ballroom.

# 42.

**TO OUR DISMAY, TICKET SALES** for our event continued steadily over the course of spring break.

I had mentioned the event at one point over break and Mom had looked surprised—"Your dad is doing a school thing? And they're actually selling tickets?"

"Yeah, I mean . . . a few."

"We can get in for free though, right?" Sidney had asked.

"It wouldn't hurt to buy them," Rose had replied. "Support the station and all that."

"No, we've got *two* people on the inside of this. We should get comps," Sidney insisted, and I couldn't help but smile.

"I'll see what I can do."

When Sasha sent an updated total to the group chat on Monday morning, I had to double-check to make sure I hadn't read it incorrectly. It didn't seem possible.

That first afternoon back, Mr. Tucker approached us before the start of class as people were still trickling in.

"I'm blown away," he said. "Absolutely floored. I never thought . . ." He shook his head. "We've sold almost three hundred tickets. This is going to be amazing. And the thing is, because of the number of advanced sales, we obviously can't have the event in any of the classrooms. Even the black box theater would be too small. But luckily . . ." He paused like he was about to drop something truly spectacular. "I managed to get permission for us to use the auditorium."

I shook my head. "What about the middle school show? They open the next day. Don't they need it for . . . dress rehearsal or whatever?"

"I was told they'd wrap up that afternoon with plenty of time for us to get in there. They'll have their backdrops up, but that won't really make much of a difference, right?"

"Right," Jamie replied.

"I'm looking forward to this," Mr. Tucker said with a smile. "It's going to be great."

That was definitely debatable.

---

We had just risen from dinner a couple of nights later when Sidney's phone rang. She looked over at Mom:

"Technically, the forks are down."

Mom waved a hand, consenting. "Go for it, you quibbler."

Sidney grabbed her phone and disappeared into our room.

She came back a few moments later, her face stormy, and handed the phone to Mom.

"Hello?"

"What is it?" Rose said as Mom began on a series of *Hm. Mm-hm. Yeah.* Sidney didn't answer, just threw herself down on the couch.

"What is it?" Rose repeated.

"Dad's not coming," Sidney said.

I blinked. "What?"

"He said he can't make it. Something came up."

My stomach seized.

---

I took the elevator downstairs to make the call. The chances of being overheard in the hallway felt too high.

I stood in the doorway of the Papa Bear ballroom. The overhead lights were half on, the chandeliers off. A cluster of round tables and bamboo chairs were out, but they weren't set yet, instead standing bare in preparation for whatever decorations the weekend's weddings would bring.

Dad picked up on the fourth ring.

"Hey, Nina, what's going on?"

"You're not coming for Sidney's show?" I said without preamble.

He let out a sigh. There was a long pause. "I really hate to miss it, but something's come up at work and I—"

"You said, though." There was a plaintive edge to my voice that I tried desperately to quash. "You said you'd come and that you could do the thing for my radio class."

"That's just it," he said. "I can't get out of work on Thursday, so I'd miss your show for sure. Even if I made it in time for Sid's play on Friday, I couldn't choose between the two of you like that. I can't. It's not fair to either of you. So I'm just gonna have to sit this round out."

Silence.

"So you're not coming at all. Even though you could make it for Sidney. If you wanted."

"I couldn't do that to you, kid."

There was a lump in my throat. "Forget about my radio thing. Just come for her show. It's important to her."

Silence. And then:

"I'm sorry, Nina. You know I am. I'm really—"

I didn't hear the rest. I had already hung up.

# 43.

ROSE CAME DOWNSTAIRS EVENTUALLY. I was sitting on one of the bamboo chairs in the ballroom, mindlessly scrolling on my phone.

I passed a picture of a fancy dessert from Alexis's account. Joydeep and two other guys posing in front of a car. Three celebrity *#sponsored* posts. I didn't absorb any of it.

Rose leaned against the doorway. She was wearing workout clothes. "Wanna go to the gym?"

"No."

A pause. "Couldn't get Dad to change his mind?"

"That would be a no as well."

I paused on a photo of a beach with a heart drawn into the sand.

"That sucks," Rose said eventually.

That was an understatement. "I don't know how he can do it. Just bail like that."

"Seriously? It's kind of his whole deal."

"That's not true." I shook my head. "I know that you and him fight about stuff, but . . ."

"But what? Seriously, Nina. Where is he right now?"

He hadn't mentioned on the phone, though I hadn't given him much of an opportunity. "I don't know. The grocery store?"

"He's on the other side of the country." It was quiet for a moment. When Rose spoke again, her tone was measured in that way that reminded me of Mom. "You know, there's this thing we learned about in psych class called a parasocial relationship. It's when there's a false sense of connection between you and a famous person. Listening to Dad's show every day makes you think that you know him. But you don't. Not really."

Like the Deadnoughts thinking they know Tyler or how he would act: *He's faking us out. He'll definitely show at the interview! A classic TB denial!*

I shut off my phone screen, looked up at Rose. "When did you take a psych class?"

"Last semester. It was a gen ed thing."

"How'd you do?"

She smiled a little. "Pretty well. I liked it."

"You know, art therapy is a thing."

"Are you saying I need some?"

"No, I'm saying you could, like, give it—be an art therapist."

She just looked at me for a moment and then said, "Let's stick to one life crisis at a time."

"This isn't a life crisis. It's just . . ." I shrugged. "It is what it is."

She nodded.

"You'll figure it out," she said. "It'll all be okay."

I didn't believe her for a minute.

# 44.

WHEN I WENT BACK UPSTAIRS that evening, Sidney was in our room, going through some dance moves in front of the mirrored doors on our closet. I watched as she swung her arms above her head, jumped forward, pivoted, kicked one leg out . . .

"Yes?" she said eventually.

"What number is this?"

"It's right before the act break."

"I'm not seeing a lot of jazz hands." I leaned against the doorframe. "I hope this show's not light on jazz hands."

"There *might* be some jazz hands."

"I won't sleep well without absolute confirmation."

It was quiet. She spun in one last circle and then struck a pose, arms in the air, one hip cocked. Shooting me a look, she jazzed her hands. "You're welcome."

I smiled and she dropped the pose, went and flopped down on her bed and picked up her phone.

"Sorry about Dad," I said.

She shrugged. "He's missing your thing too, right?"

"Yeah, well . . . That's not important."

"It's important to you."

"Nah."

Sidney looked up at me for a moment. "You don't have to do that."

"Do what?"

Her gaze dropped back down to her phone. "You know what."

It was quiet. "Yeah, okay," I said, and then I held my arms up and did jazz hands. "What do you think?"

"Mediocre at best."

"Hey!"

"Okay, let's say *room for improvement*."

"I'll take it."

# 45.

**I WAS SITTING AT LUNCH** the next day when my phone buzzed. Twenty-two tickets so far today and counting. The group chat had been going off periodically—updates on the ticket sales from Sasha, exclamations of concern from Joydeep. Jamie was trying to downplay everything. I didn't respond to any of it. I didn't know what to say.

I assumed it was another text from one of them, but when I checked, it was from Alexis. *Question*, was all it said. I would have to wait a moment for the follow-up—a typical Alexis texting convention. She liked building suspense, I think.

As I watched the text bubble, I thought of the eighth-grade field trip—the ill-fated visit to the IMA. Alexis had slid into the seat next to me on the bus ride back to school, after the kiss, the fallout.

"So?" she had asked, leaning into me. "Did it work? Are you guys together now?"

"Are you serious?"

She blinked at me. "We saw you kiss."

*But not the part afterward.* I just shook my head and stared out the window. "That was stupid. It was a stupid idea. I never should've . . ." The passing streets grew blurry. I blinked against it.

Alexis was quiet for a moment, and then said, "I only picked him because you like him, and he likes you. It's super obvious."

"He's mad it was for the game," I said, voice thick, but that wasn't even accurate by half. Mad wasn't right. Hurt. He was hurt. Because of me. I did that.

Alexis looked troubled for a moment, but it quickly cleared. "He'll get over it. It's nothing."

"It's not *nothing.*"

She huffed a breath, frowned. "I'll fix it," she said finally. "I'll talk to him."

"Don't," I replied. It would only make it worse.

"I didn't mean to—" I had never heard Alexis sound uncertain before. "I thought I was helping."

I shook my head. I couldn't blame her. It was her dumb game, sure, but I was the one who agreed to play it. "Just leave it alone. Forget it."

She left it alone. But a couple weeks later on the schoolyard after lunch, when one of the girls suggested a round of Kiss Cam, Alexis shot me a look and then said, "I'm over that game. Let's do something else."

Our friendship mellowed after that. I think high school was responsible for that a little bit—scattering our friend group across a giant freshman class, lessening Alexis's pull. She sought me out more than I sought her out. Never in a needy way—it wasn't in her nature—but the dynamic had definitely changed. That kind of queen bee hero worship thing was gone. Somehow the Kiss Cam incident leveled things out between us.

Right now, I watched as Alexis's follow-up message popped up my phone:

*So is it true some group from your radio class is having Lucas on?*

I frowned. *What?*

*Everyone's been talking about it*, she replied. *Is it true?*

*Who's Lucas?*

*From TION*, she replied. *The blond one. Not as hot as Kenji but more accessible than Tristan?*

More messages appeared quickly.

*He's the one you want to drink hot cocoa in front of a fire with*

*In some mountain cabin somewhere*

*Wearing matching sweaters*

*While he bones you*

*ALEXIS*, I typed. *Who is having them on their show?*

*That's what I'm asking you. It's this huge thing apparently*

Dread was growing in the pit of my stomach. *Who did you hear this from?*

*Some girl on the dance team.*

Another message followed, the nail in the coffin:

*Anyway they've been selling tickets for it*

And another:

*Should I buy one?*

I left before finishing my lunch, making up some

excuse to the other people at my table and pitching my half-eaten sandwich on my way out of the cafeteria.

*Emergency meeting at the gallery*, I texted while pushing through the doors.

*Right now!*

*RED ALERT*

I almost ran straight into Jamie in the hallway. My phone slipped from my hands, but he managed to grab it.

"Hey," he said. "What's up?" A frown. "You okay?"

"We have a problem."

# 46.

**WE ALL HUDDLED AROUND SASHA'S** laptop screen and peered at an image of five faces—one brooding, one smoldering, one smiling shyly, one grinning, and one looking pensive.

"Which one is he?" Jamie asked.

Sasha pointed to the one who was grinning. "He's the hot one."

Joydeep looked offended. "Are we looking at the same picture?" He jabbed at the smoldering face. "That guy's the hot one."

Sasha screwed up her face. "Kai?"

"Yeah."

"I didn't know you were a fan," I said.

"I'm not," Joydeep replied. "I just have eyes."

"How could this have happened?" Jamie asked.

"I don't know. But it's a thing, apparently. People think he's the mystery guest."

"How do you know?"

"Alexis told me, Apparently some girl on the dance team told her."

Joydeep gasped.

"What? What is it?"

His eyes were wide. "Sabotage!"

# 47.

**WE ALL WAITED IN THE** hall before radio class on Friday, and eventually Sammy showed up, walking hand in hand with Colby. Colby slapped palms with Joydeep and they exchanged "Bro!"s.

"Hey, could we talk to you real quick?" Jamie asked Sammy.

She looked a little annoyed. "It's almost time for class."

"We just need a minute," Jamie said.

Sammy squeezed Colby's hand and then let it go. "Be right in, babe."

Colby gave us all an odd look but headed in.

Sammy looked at us expectantly. "What do you guys want?"

"Saboteur!" Joydeep cried.

"We heard you've been spreading rumors about our show," Sasha said, more calmly. "About our mystery guest."

Sammy just blinked.

Sasha had never seemed taller than in this moment. "Why would you do that?"

There was no doubt she'd been made, and Sammy knew it, so she huffed a breath, folded her arms, rolled her eyes. "Um, let me see. 'Dear *Cat Chat,* I think I'm a tree. I jizz sap everywhere. Blah blah blah.'"

"Uh, the letter writer didn't think they were a tree. Their *boyfriend* thought they were a tree," Joydeep said.

"Either way, it was *completely despicable* of you to *tamper* with our show like that—"

"Hey, check your ratings, sister, I fucking *made* your show—"

"How did you even find out what Joydeep did?" I interrupted.

"Funny story," Sammy said. "Our producer Lily was driving home from track practice one night and heard the craziest thing on the radio. Four idiots who didn't realize that they hadn't pressed the right button, sitting around talking about how *super funny* their prank was."

"Okay, that was one idiot who hadn't pressed the right button, and a separate idiot who did the pranking, thank you very much," I replied. "Leave the others out of it."

Sammy made a face. "Either way, it was messed up, so obviously I had to do something. And honestly, you guys made it easy when you were basically giving out Lucas facts about your stupid secret guest anyway. No one really believed me at first, but then you started selling tickets and that totally clinched it, so thanks for that."

"What are you talking about?" I said. "Those facts are about my dad."

Sammy let out of breath of laughter. "Are you serious?" Her eyes widened with realization, and her grin grew. "Are you for real? Is your dad Lucas from TION?"

"Uh, not to my knowledge."

She looked between us. "You really didn't know?"

"Know what?"

She shook her head, still grinning. "Good luck, is all I can say."

# 48.

**"WHAT THE FUCK WAS SAMMY** even talking about?"
Joydeep said. We met back in the gallery after school
for another emergency meeting—though admittedly
*emergency* had lost some of its urgency since all of our
meetings these days seemed to be emergency meetings. Mr. Tucker had sent out an excited email that
morning:

> *Ticket sales have reached four hundred!*
> *This is so amazing! Congrats Sounds of*
> *the Nineties team, cannot WAIT for the*
> *big event!*

"Apparently, there have been some other . . . coinci-
dences," Sasha said, looking my way. "In the facts we
compiled about your dad."

"What? How? Genuinely, tell me how my dad could
*also* be mistaken for Lucas from This Is Our Now?"

"I did some looking during class," Sasha said carefully. "And apparently, a lot of stuff just . . . happens to

be similar. He's actually lived in Indiana. He's been heard on the radio for years. His favorite TION member is Josh—there's this whole thing with him and Josh, this bromance. The color yellow—"

"How could yellow *possibly* factor in this time?" I asked.

"Apparently he sings a line in one of their most popular songs: *My heart burns yellow sun / Your soul answers midnight blue.*"

"Bleh." Joydeep looked disgusted.

"I don't hate it," Jamie said. "Lyrically."

"Anyway," Sasha continued. "It's a thing, apparently. They have like, yellow sun shirts and stuff. I guess people thought we were referring to that."

"TGI Fridays, though?" Joydeep burst out, incredulous.

"He, like, famously loves their loaded potato skins. He's tweeted about it."

"No," I said. "No no no. It's enough we've got the Deadnoughts. We're not dragging the TION fandom into this."

"We didn't do anything," Jamie said. "People interpreted something wrong. That's not our fault."

"Yeah, but once it's out there, it's out there," Sasha said. "Even if it's not true, just the *idea* that it could be is enough for people."

Joydeep nodded. "I say we just announce your dad once and for all. If people want their money back, that's their own fucking deal."

Sasha nodded, then glanced my way. "At least we

have some kind of guest, even if it's not the one every-one's expecting."

I swallowed. Anxiety roiled in the pit of my stomach. I didn't want to have to rip this Band-Aid off.

But there was no avoiding it. Or at least I knew that avoiding it any longer would only make it exponentially worse.

"We actually . . . don't."

They all looked my way. "Sorry, what?" Joydeep said after a moment, voice ominously calm.

Mine was small in response: "We actually . . . don't have a guest. He can't . . ." I shook my head. "He's not coming."

The silence that followed seemed interminable, though in reality it was probably only a moment or two before Joydeep stood and walked over to one of the pottery stands.

"Let me get this straight," he said, turning back to face us. "The event is one week away. We don't have Tyler Bright. We don't have Lucas from TION. And now we don't even have the *actual person* that we were *actually supposed to have in the first place*, your own dad, we don't even have *your own dad*. That's what you're telling me. We have nothing."

"Except ticket money from four hundred people," Sasha said hollowly.

"And each other," I added, because I'm an idiot.

"Oh, great," Joydeep said. "Great. This is great. Really great."

"You have to stop saying great," Jamie replied.

"*Fantastic!*" Joydeep exploded. "Is that better? Nina,

how did this even happen? You said he was *for real* confirmed this time. You said *one hundred percent*! How could this have happened?"

I looked at them for a moment. Three expectant faces.

"I lied," I said.

# 49.

**"WHAT THE FUCK?" JOYDEEP SAID,** quietly and with great sincerity.

I shrugged. The looks on their faces were too much to handle, so I fixed my eyes on the series of fake magazine covers lining the back wall. The one in the center was a *Rolling Stone* cover mock-up featuring a girl wearing a pink leotard, posing provocatively.

"I . . . I'm sorry," I said.

And then there was nothing to do but bail.

Jamie followed me out and caught up with me, longer legs carrying him faster so he could circle around and cut me off at the end of the hall.

"Why would you do that?" he said. "Why would you lie?"

What it all boiled down to was this:

I couldn't admit the truth. That my dad didn't want to be there for either me or Sidney. Because that's what it was, wasn't it? He was just waiting for an opening. For a reason to not have to come, and it took care of itself. He couldn't pick between us. That made it about us, not him.

So I made it about me, not him, because that was just easier, wasn't it, than saying the reality of it out loud.

"Because I suck, Jamie," I said. "You're just too nice to admit that. Or to realize it in the first place, maybe, I don't know. I suck, and I fucked this up for all of us, and that's just how it is. Sorry. I'm sorry." I met his eyes now. "I'm sorry."

He shook his head. "You lied about lying."

I let out a pathetic breath of laughter, trying to sound cavalier. "What?"

He was completely serious. "He did confirm. You did confirm it. I know you did. So what happened? Why can't he come?" He looked concerned. "Is everything okay?"

"Everything's fine." I swallowed. "Everything's exactly the way it always is." I wanted to cry for some reason. Instead I just looked away, squeezed the strap of my backpack, and nodded.

Then I walked away.

# 50.

**THE KISS BETWEEN JAMIE AND** me wasn't the actual
end of the Kingdom revival. Remarkably, Iliana, Aurelie,
Hapless, and Quad met once more after that.

It was a week or so after the eighth-grade museum
trip, after I messed things up with Jamie. I was working
on homework in our room when Sidney burst in wearing her Quad outfit.

I looked up from a row of geometry problems. "What
are you doing?"

"What are *you* doing?" she replied. "Jamie's coming.
We're playing."

"What?"

"I saw him in the lobby with Mom on Tuesday and
he said he'd come. He was busy yesterday, but he's free
today and he's coming over"—there was a knock at the
door—"now!"

I had no choice but to join in. I couldn't tell Sidney
and Rose what had happened between us. But Jamie
must have not hated me entirely if he still agreed to
play?

When I met them in the living room—Rose was buckling Iliana's belt—he didn't meet my eyes. He looked right past me as Sidney explained what we were going to do.

The last time we had met for Kingdom, we were outside, wandering through the Wilds looking for a scroll that would lead us to a sacred pool where Hapless's curse could be broken. We had secured the scroll (it was a rolled-up menu for a Chinese restaurant), and today Sidney commanded we follow it to the sacred pool (the indoor pool, which we had formerly dubbed a swamp, and which was located downstairs by the back entrance to the building).

It was quiet as we got in the elevator. I think Rose could sense it, that something intrinsic had changed—I hadn't told her what happened at the museum, but she was Rose, she could intuit anything—and maybe Sidney could too, because she glanced back at me.

"Hapless doesn't remember you anymore because you weren't mean to him," Sidney said. "Remember how you didn't want to be mean to him?"

My stomach twisted.

"She's our friend. She's okay," she told Jamie, who nodded, not looking my way. "We trust her, so you can trust her too."

"Got it," he replied.

The hall outside the service elevator was empty, and we made our way past the back door, past the vending machines, peered through the window in the hall that looked down onto the pool area. It was empty too.

"What do we do?" Jamie said when we were all assembled inside. The pool room was always warm, the air thick with humidity.

"According to lore—"

I snorted. "What lore?"

Sidney glared at me. "According to *lore* of *old*, the sacred pool will wash away your curse."

"Just like that?" Jamie said.

"No," Sidney said. "It demands a sacrifice first."

"We're not throwing stuff into the pool," Rose said.

Sidney glared at her too. "We have to do a ritual, then."

So we did a complicated ritual, which involved my scrying stones, a small desiccated piece of wood that Sidney had picked up from who knows where, and a sprinkling of water from the hot tub (aka the anointed spring).

"Now what?" Jamie asked when we were done.

"Now you have to let the sacred magic of the pool consume you," Sidney replied.

Jamie considered this for a moment, and then took one step backward, and then another, until he was at the edge of the pool.

"Jamie—" I began, but all at once, Prince Hapless tipped over and broke the water with a large splash, disappearing into the depths, leaving only ripples behind.

Sidney let out a choked laugh, and next to me, Rose tensed.

We could all see Jamie at the bottom—the pool wasn't that deep—but he wasn't coming up.

"Jamie," Rose called.

"Hapless!" Sidney tried.

But he stayed down there, a dark shape against the pale blue of the pool floor.

Maybe Iliana the bounty hunter would have looked skyward and let out a lengthy curse to the gods before diving gracefully to Hapless's rescue. But Rose just let out a sound like *sflkjfsfjk* and then jumped into the pool.

She disappeared under and broke the surface again with Jamie in tow. They both thrashed around a bit and then made their way over to the side of the pool.

"What were you doing?" Rose said, climbing to her feet. Her clothes hung wet, water streaming in rivulets off of her. Jamie pulled himself out of the pool but stayed sitting in a puddle on the concrete. "Why didn't you come up?"

"I was letting the water consume me," he said simply. "Am I cured?"

Sidney considered him for a moment. "No. And you're unconscious."

Instantly Jamie fell back on the ground, a marionette with its strings cut.

I spoke before I could even think: "Sidney, no. He has to be cured. This can't go on forever."

"I'm in charge and—"

"You're not. We're all playing, not just you. I say he's fine."

Sidney turned to Rose, her expression clouding over.

Rose sighed too. "I mean, Nina's kind of right. We can't play forever."

"But—" Sidney broke in.

"*But*," Rose continued, "Sidney should get . . . the ending she wants." She looked at Sidney. "So what happens now?"

Sidney was quiet for a moment, considering, and then she raised her chin defiantly. "Now Prince Hapless dies."

"He can't *die*," I said.

"Sure he can. He's not immortal. He's not magic. He doesn't have any charms or shields or anything." A shrug. "It's realistic."

"Nothing about Kingdom is realistic," I replied. "Rose's hairbrush is a dart gun! You're a *literal* troll!"

"I get to pick the ending and I say we did everything we could and it didn't work." She shook her head. "Sometimes things just don't work."

I thought of my mom's words to Sidney—to all of us—during a discussion once about the divorce. We didn't talk about it often, but Sidney was just a toddler when it happened, so she would have questions every now and then. Once she asked, *Who made you get divorced?*

*No one made us.*

*But whose fault was it?*

A complicated series of emotions had passed over my mom's face, and then she replied: *It doesn't have to be someone's fault. Sometimes you can do everything right and it just isn't meant to be.*

I looked at Jamie's prone form on the ground and then back up at Sidney. "No."

"What do you mean, no?"

I swallowed. "What about true love's kiss?"

Sidney shook her head. "That's fake."

"At least let me try." I blinked at her, my heart pounding in my chest. "It always worked before."

"Hapless already forgot you."

"This could help him remember."

I glanced down at Jamie, but he was still lying motionless, eyes shut. He had always been the best pretender when we played Kingdom—I knew he wouldn't break. At least, I desperately hoped that this time he wouldn't.

He stayed completely still as I knelt down on the ground next to him. His hair was plastered down against his head, little drops of water beaded up on his face. Before I could do anything, Sidney burst out: "Wait!"

I froze.

"Hapless only wakes up if he *really* loves you. That's the only way. He can stay alive as long as his love for Aurelie is real. But if not . . ." She shook her head. "He's a goner."

I swallowed, then leaned in, rested my fingers over Jamie's lips, and pressed a kiss to my knuckles. A beat longer than I would normally, and unnecessarily gently, considering Jamie couldn't even feel it. But I hoped, stupidly, that he got the message.

I pulled back, and Jamie blinked up at me.

"Noooo," Sidney wailed. "Come on, it should at least be more dramatic than that!"

Jamie's eyes were everything.

"At least cough or, like, gasp for air or something," Sidney continued.

Jamie just looked at me for one moment more, and then moved to sit up. I sat back on my heels.

"I think we should probably call it here," he said, getting to his feet. "It's been . . . a good game, right?"

"That's it?" Sidney said. "That's all? You're not even gonna thank us for saving your life? Restoring your memories? Are they even restored?"

Jamie thought for a moment, and then nodded. "I remember everything."

"You don't sound happy enough to be a person who just got the memory of mac and cheese back," Sidney said.

That teased a smile from Jamie. "You're right." He dropped down to one knee in front of Sidney, bowed his head.

"Thank you, travelers, for your assistance. I will forever be grateful. I hope your next adventure brings you riches and happiness and . . . good things." His eyes flicked up toward me, and then away. "All good things."

Then he stood, and with an awkward nod at Sidney and Rose, headed out, boots squishing with each step.

By the time we got into the hall, there was a trail of wet footprints leading to the elevator, and he was already gone.

# 51.

**THERE WAS A WEDDING ON** Saturday night. The ceremony was in the atrium, the reception in the Papa Bear ballroom. I worked my way through the meal mechanically, bringing salads and filling cups and clearing dishes. I was topping off water glasses when the speeches started. One of the women at the head table, clad in a royal blue dress, stood and turned to the two brides in the center.

"Andrea," she said, and one of the brides brought a hand up to her face. "Oh my god, don't cry yet, I haven't even started."

Gentle laughter rippled through the crowd.

"Okay. Keep it together or I won't be able to—okay. Andrea, you've always been my best friend. You've been like a sister to me—stop it, I mean it! Don't cry, oh my god." She dabbed her eyes with a napkin before continuing: "You've always looked out for other people, you've always put others before yourself. You're the most selfless person I've ever met. There's no one I'd trust more in this world than you, and honestly, truly, there's no one I'd want you to trust your heart to more than Yvonne. I know she'll take care of you, the same way you've always taken care of so many of us here."

It was sweet, too sweet for me to bear, somehow. Too much. The air in the room felt too close. I moved to the side, set my water jug down on one of the tray stands, and then ducked into the lobby, out the door, down the small flight of steps, and out into the night.

I leaned up against the brick of the building. The windows of the ballroom faced onto the parking lot, and although the shades were drawn during events, I could hear the murmur of voices inside.

I didn't have my jacket, so I just stuck my hands in the pocket of my apron, let out a breath and watched it billow up in front of me. It was a cold April so far—nothing had bloomed yet.

I looked out over the parking lot, the bare branches of the trees swaying a little in the wind. *The sacred glen*, I thought absently.

Where was Aurelie now? *Baking or hustling people at magic pool.* Maybe she had her shit together in some capacity. Maybe her magic powers had helped her somehow in that way.

And what of Prince Hapless? He was dead now, apparently, according to Jamie. I thought about Hapless wandering through the glen. Maybe a warlock enchanted him, or he was struck by a poisonous dart. I thought about him alone, crying out for Aurelie and Iliana and Quad and no one coming. And Sidney's words: *He can stay alive as long as his love for Aurelie is real. But if not, he's a goner.*

It made me want to cry. How stupid was that. Imagining something too hard and upsetting yourself for no reason.

The door opened, and a pair of black-clad legs descended the stairs.

"Hey." Jamie sidled up to me. "Celeste was looking for you." A pause. "What are you doing out here?"

It had been silent in the *Sounds of the Nineties* chat since the revelation yesterday. I didn't know what to say to everyone, how I could possibly make it right.

I swallowed, looked away. "Just, uh . . ." I didn't know how to explain it. "That speech was really nice."

"It was." Jamie's voice was soft. "Sometimes they get me too."

I looked over at him. His tie was off-center. My fingers itched to straighten it.

His brow furrowed a little. "You okay?"

"Yeah." Then I shook my head. "No. Probably not."

And suddenly wanting to cry wasn't just an impulse, but an actual thing that was happening.

"Hey," he said. I turned my face away, looking toward the back gate. "Hey, what is it? What's wrong?"

I just shrugged, and when I could speak, the only thing I could think to say was, "That M&M cake was really nice."

"Nina—"

"Remember, for my birthday? I never told you. I was so . . . That was so nice of you, you didn't have to do that, it was—you're too good. I don't know how to be good like that. I don't know how to not be a human garbage can, Jamie."

"You're not a garbage can. Jesus." He now looked both concerned and bewildered.

"How do you know that?"

"Well, for one thing, no one would throw that many M&M's away."

I let out a puff of air, not quite a laugh. When I looked back at Jamie, his expression was too open, too honest.

"I let everyone down," I said, and hated how pitiful my voice sounded, how small. "Everyone hates me."

"They don't."

"You don't hate me?"

"I don't."

"But you should. After everything . . ."

He shook his head. "I don't."

I nodded. Swallowed, wiped hastily at my eyes.

"Are you free tomorrow?" Jamie asked after a moment.

There was no wedding tomorrow. We had dinner plans with the Dantist, but I could cry off.

"Yeah."

"We could meet up," he said. "Try to figure the whole thing out. We have till Friday, right? We can fix it, I promise. No one hates you. We'll fix it. Okay?"

I nodded. "Okay."

# 52.

**WE DECIDED TO GO TO** a sushi place on Sunday, near the IUPUI campus downtown.

It was not a date. It was a brainstorming session. But I still put on a nice shirt and my cleanest sneakers, and I even tried to do a hair tutorial from YouTube. Rose walked in when I was sitting on the floor in front of the mirror on our closet, trying to replicate the French braid twist by Beautyglitterqueen99.

"What are you doing?"

"Practicing for prom," I said, and Rose must've been truly distracted, because she didn't question it, despite me having never once shown interest in having decent hair for prom—or honestly, prom in general.

Rose was working that evening. Mom and Sidney were going to Dan's. I insisted that I couldn't join since I had plans, and headed down to the lobby at ten till four to wait for Jamie. I figured we'd take the bus together, or maybe he would borrow Gram's car.

It wasn't a date. It was a brainstorming session.

I tapped my foot against the tile floor absently while

I waited. The desk attendant glanced my way, but then went back to staring at his cell phone. The desk phone rang eventually, and I could hear him: "This is Joe at the Eastman, how may I help you?"

I waited. I listened to Joe's side of the calls that came in. I checked my phone—it was possible I got the time wrong. Maybe we said five? But I remembered it clearly, after work last night: Jamie shifting back and forth in the elevator, *Is four okay? Gram doesn't really like me staying out late on Sundays.*

I went on the Instagram page for *Conrad and Co.* while I was waiting and scrolled through pictures of the team: a bearded man (Will) at the soundboard, a woman with bleached blond hair pulled back in a ponytail (Tina) holding two giant coffee mugs. My dad, wearing sunglasses inside, throwing up a peace sign at the camera.

I switched to playing a mindless game on my phone when the *Conrad and Co.* pictures began to stoke an unpleasant feeling in my chest.

I texted Jamie, *hey it was 4 right?* at ten past. I was suddenly way too conscious of my Beautyglitterqueen99 hairstyle.

At twenty past, a thought struck me: Maybe we were supposed to meet at the restaurant? I just assumed we'd meet here—we both lived here. What was the point in going separately? But maybe he was coming from somewhere else. Maybe he was already there.

I sent another text: *Are we meeting there?*

What if he didn't have his phone?

I hated talking on the phone, but I gave him a call anyway. It went straight to voicemail—maybe it had run out of battery or maybe he forgot to turn it on (as if I ever turned mine off).

Finally, at four thirty, I went upstairs to his apartment and knocked lightly on the door. No one answered.

That sealed it for me. Jamie had already left. He probably thought we were meeting there. He was probably there already. Or maybe not, but the idea of Jamie sitting at a booth alone waiting for me, wondering where I was, propelled me back downstairs and outside.

I walked to the bus stop. It was a little chilly, the sky overcast. I hadn't worn a jacket, just a sweatshirt, and I pulled my hands in the sleeves.

I took the bus downtown, and by the time I approached the strip mall where Sushi Boss was located, heavy clouds had gathered.

I pulled open the door, stepped inside. A quick scan of the place revealed that Jamie wasn't there.

If he was, he had left. Or maybe he hadn't come in the first place.

I had come all the way down there, though. I ordered a roll, even though I didn't want it.

I sat by the window and scrolled on my phone, refreshing the same three apps over and over despite knowing that I should stop, that we were getting short on data this month, then switching over to this dumb woodblock version of Tetris. I kept getting the urge to check my phone for messages, which made absolutely no sense, because I was literally looking right at it. No texts came through.

I poked at my food, stomach uneasy, ate a little despite my better judgment, and asked for a box.

It was raining when I left. I pulled up my hood and headed back to the bus stop clutching my leftovers, but it was Sunday evening, and the next one wasn't for almost half an hour.

It was stupid to come here.

I thought about calling Mom, but I had made a big deal about missing dinner because I had plans, and anyway, she was all the way uptown at Dan's and it would take just as long to get down here. I was embarrassed, and annoyed, and sad, and I knew deep down that I deserved something like this, for sure, at minimum, but I thought that Jamie was being genuine the night before. Jamie was always genuine—it was like the number one Jamie quality, it was among the things I liked best. He wouldn't stand me up.

Except he did. And I was too obtuse to even accept that it was happening. I went forward with the not-date brainstorming session all on my own, despite all evidence that I was being stood up.

By the time I reached the Eastman, I was drenched in rain. No one was back yet, thankfully, to see my pathetic return. I was fumbling with the key to our apartment when my phone buzzed.

It was Jamie.

*Papa's in the hospital*

I blinked.

Before I could reply, four messages came back quickly:

*He had a mini stroke today*

*He's doing a lot better now*

*But he has to stay there for a couple days*

*Gram's still there but she just sent me home*

The next message came through as I was on my way back to the elevator:

*I should've texted you sooner, I totally forgot*

*Don't worry about that*, I sent as I pressed the 7 button on the door panel.

Jamie swung open the door to their apartment just after I knocked. He still had his coat on.

"Are you okay?" I asked.

He nodded. Then his lips twitched in that way that people's lips do when they're trying not to cry. Or at least, in that way that Jamie's lips twitch when he's trying not to cry. I had seen it before—it was the same look he had when we were little kids and he accidentally let go of his balloon at the zoo, all of us with our faces turned upward, watching the red balloon float off into the sky—

"Come upstairs," I said. "Rose will be home soon. She can take care of us."

He blinked at me. "Why are you all wet?"

"I forgot my umbrella."

The balloon look flickered again. "Did you go to Sushi Boss?"

I just held out a hand. "Come upstairs."

# 53.

ROSE WASN'T HOME YET WHEN we got up there. Our room was a disaster area, but at least my side was manageable, so Jamie sat on the bed. I pulled out some sweats from the laundry.

"Be right back."

I changed in the bathroom, and when I came back in, Jamie was still sitting on the edge of my bed, coat on, looking lost in thought.

"Take off your jacket, stay a while," I said, and stretched out on Sidney's bed.

"Cold," he replied.

"Get under the covers, then."

He looked at me for a moment, then shrugged out of his coat, toed off his shoes, stretched out on my bed, and pulled up the sheets.

Our beds were close—there was a narrow nightstand in between, where Sidney would stack books and leave her glasses. I'd keep my phone there.

When we first moved to the Eastman, Sidney was only three. She'd get scared at night by the traffic sounds and the elevator, so she'd sleep in my mom's room a lot of the time. Eventually she started staying in her own bed, but she would still get scared every now and then, in the dark of the room at night. She would want Rose to sing to her so she would know Rose was there. She would want to hold my hand across the space between our beds. I remember forcing myself to stay awake until she fell asleep, until I felt her little hand slacken in mine.

I thought about reaching across the space for Jamie's hand, but I didn't. Instead I just looked over at him, his head resting on my pillow. His eyes were shut.

I wanted to know what happened, how it happened, where they were, if Papa was going to be okay, but I didn't want to make him recount anything he didn't want to in this moment. I had never seen him look more tired.

He opened his eyes while I was looking at him, blinked at me.

"I should've texted you earlier," he said, voice croaky.

"Jamie, you had actual real-life important stuff going on. It's seriously no big deal."

He nodded, then shivered.

I stood, and moved over to my bed. I was going to pull up one of the blankets that had fallen on the floor and lay it over him. That was my intention. It was definitely my original plan. But I didn't reach for the blanket. I just stood there, at the edge of the bed, until Jamie scooted over a bit and held open the covers.

I got in.

# 54.

**I TOLD MYSELF THAT CUDDLING** Jamie was a necessary accommodation to fit two people into a twin bed. Space conservation is what it was. It was efficient. If I was going to lie here next to him, actively cuddling him was just common sense.

And anyway, maybe it was making him feel better? Was that thinking too much of myself, of my, like, comforting abilities?

He was bigger than me, but he hunched down, pressing his face into my neck. I ran my fingers through his hair absently. It was really soft, way softer than anyone's hair had a right to be.

"Feels nice," he murmured after a while.

"Mm," I replied, because it did; everything in this moment felt a lot nicer than it should have, given the circumstances. Maybe that whole pause-the-battle-scene-or-apocalypse trope where the protagonists drop everything to make out wasn't entirely inaccurate.

This wasn't a battle scene though. Jamie was upset, he was stressed, and I shouldn't have liked the feeling of his arms wrapped around my waist so much, his breath on my skin, but I did.

He adjusted slightly after a bit, and I could feel his lips brush up against my neck, almost a kiss.

I tightened my grip in his hair unconsciously.

"Sorry," he whispered, pulling back a little.

There was a hush to it, to everything. Like when we stood in front of *Acton*, the dark and unknowable and irrepressible space just beyond us.

*Try it. Just reach out your hand.*

I lifted my other hand to his face, traced the line of his jaw with my fingertips, feather light. His eyes flickered shut. And then he dipped his head again, pressing his mouth to my collarbone purposefully this time, lips parting with each kiss he placed there.

My skin felt too tight, like it might burst, but in the best possible way. When he shifted to kiss my neck, I thought I might combust. Just spontaneously erupt in flames. Could he feel that? Could he tell? Was he feeling it too? He moved up and we were face-to-face now, close, closer than we'd been in so long, my eyes almost blurry with it, and this was it—lips almost brushing—almost—

Then the front door opened.

Jamie startled, sat up quickly, and shifted off the bed just as Rose appeared in the doorway to our room. I was still lying in the exact same spot, now suddenly bereft as Jamie moved toward the dresser, his back turned to the door.

Rose looked between us. "Hey."

"Hi," I said. Jamie didn't turn around.

"I, uh." Rose contemplated us for just a moment. "Forgot something. In the car. I will be back in . . . ten minutes." Her eyes flicked to me. "Fifteen? Fifteen minutes."

"Okay."

She disappeared, and the front door opened and closed again, and Jamie and I were alone. Again.

I didn't know what I wanted. Except that's a lie—I did. I wanted Jamie to cross back over, get in bed, kiss me everywhere and anywhere he wanted, and give me the liberty to do the same. But I didn't know how to express that. And I knew realistically we couldn't accomplish that in the ten to fifteen minutes before Rose returned, but I wanted it anyway. Wanted him.

He just stood there, scratched the back of his neck, rubbed at one eye.

I felt suddenly stupid, still being in bed. Still being a part of something that didn't get far enough to actually *be* anything, but was definitely still . . . something. I stood too, leaving the warmth of the covers behind.

He looked back my way. Not at me specifically, but in my general direction.

And then, finally, he crossed back over. He was coming closer, and closer, he reached out—

And grabbed something on the shelf behind my head.

We both stared down at it: the jar packed with little tinfoil squares.

When his eyes flicked back up to me, there was an

odd expression on his face. "You still save the wrappers?"

There it was, all at once. Eight-year-old Jamie, lamenting that Grammy wouldn't let him have gum. He didn't care about the candy; he just wanted the wrappers to "build something."

*Something like what?* Rose had asked skeptically.

*Like a space suit,* he had replied with a grin. *One of those shiny metal ones.*

We were allowed to have gum (or at least, my dad let us have gum when we were with him), so I always asked for the kind with foil wrappers, so I could save them and give them to Jamie.

I kept doing it, even as we got older, even into junior high, despite the fact that the space suit never materialized. I remember presenting him with a bunch of them on the playground in fifth grade. And in sixth grade, dropping a handful of folded rectangles onto his desk in social studies, him grinning up at me. *Still working on it*, he said.

Seventh grade. *It's gonna be Mars-ready.*

Eighth grade. *Almost there.*

And then I stopped. It stopped, we stopped, but I didn't stop saving them. I just stopped giving them. And if that wasn't me in a nutshell.

I told myself it was out of habit. It was a habit that had become mine. It was my thing now. But seeing the jar in Jamie's hand, all those neatly folded rectangles packed in on each other, shiny and incriminating, I knew that I was really only fooling myself into thinking that they were anything other than a way I could tell Jamie I loved him without saying it out loud. And I never stopped collecting them because I never stopped loving him, and the idea of me convincing myself I had would be laughable if it weren't so pathetically sad.

*You still save the wrappers?* hung between us, a question I was meant to answer.

The word caught in my throat a bit, but escaped nonetheless: "Yeah."

Jamie held my gaze. "Why?"

I shrugged, trying to look nonchalant, or something other than absolutely read to hell.

"Just . . . got in the habit."

He looked at me another moment more.

Then he reached past me to the shelf. Stuck the jar of wrappers back up there.

"You can have them," I said, my voice hoarse.

He just smiled a little. "Nah. I couldn't take your collection."

*It's your collection*, I wanted to say, but I didn't.

# 55.

JAMIE LEFT BEFORE ROSE CAME back. He said he
wanted to call Gram and see if she needed anything.

"Let me know if we can help at all," I said, standing
in the doorway. Jamie paused in the hallway. He had his
coat back on. I wondered if he was planning on going
back to the hospital, despite Gram sending him home.

"Thanks." He nodded. "Thank you." And then he was
gone.

Rose came in a few minutes later. I was on the couch,
some cooking show playing on the TV.

*Your mystery ingredients? Scallops! And . . . Honey!*
*Dew! Melon! Chefs, you have FIFTEEN MINUTES!*

Rose took off her jacket, stuck it in the coat closet,
kicked off her shoes. Sat down on the chair across from
the couch and regarded the TV.

"Ugh, scallop gazpacho? That sounds gross."

It was quiet for a few minutes.

*The flavor palate is . . . unconventional.*

*Thank you, chef.*

*I'm not saying it's a good thing.*

"Jamie's grandpa had a stroke," I said eventually.

Rose looked over at me sharply. "Is he okay?"

"I think so. Jamie said he was doing all right, but he has to stay in the hospital for a couple days. It was a . . . mini one, apparently." A pause. "I didn't know they, like, came in sizes. It's like they shrunk a regular stroke in the wash."

"Jesus, Nina, is there ever one second where you're not working on your stand-up act?" Rose looked exasperated.

"I'm not trying to be funny, I'm just—" I shook my head.

"What's going on with you guys?" she said.

"Nothing. I was keeping him company. We were waiting for you, actually."

"That's funny, 'cause he seems to have cleared out now that I'm here."

*Chefs, the entrée challenge today involves everyone's favorite cruciferous vegetable . . . BOK CHOOOOOY!*

"What do you want me to say?"

"I don't know. Just . . . be honest with me."

"About what?"

"I don't know," she said again. "How about, were you having sex with Jamie just now?"

"Agh! No! Geez! I don't want to talk about this with you."

"If you can't talk about sex with me, who can you talk about it with?"

"No one. Ever."

"Wow, not one single person? Not even whoever you're having sex with?"

"No, we'll communicate solely through pictogram."

Rose rolled her eyes but didn't respond. The chefs were bringing up their bok choy entrées for judging when she spoke again.

"Just saying, there were . . . pictogram vibes in the room when I walked in."

*I've never had a vegetable with such a . . . meaty mouth-feel before.*

"Just . . . be responsible, is all I'm getting at," she said.

"There's literally nothing to be responsible about."

"The Conrad family motto," she muttered. I didn't reply.

# 56.

JAMIE MISSED CLASS ON MONDAY. I had texted him that morning: *Everything okay?*

He sent back a thumbs-up emoji a few hours later, but that was it.

I couldn't stop thinking about him. Wondering how Papa was doing. Replaying everything about last night over and over again in my mind, to the point where when Joydeep asked, "Where's Jamie?" as he slid into his seat before radio class started, it was almost a shock to hear his name out loud—like I had somehow summoned it—and a relief to be able to talk about him.

I told them what had happened with Papa.

"Shit," Joydeep said. "Is there . . . like can we do anything? To help? Should I text him? I'm gonna text him."

I looked over at Sasha as Joydeep pulled out his phone. I knew it was astronomically unimportant compared to what was going on with Jamie, but I couldn't help but bring it up. "Look, about the whole thing with my dad . . . I'm really sorry."

"Don't worry about that right now," Sasha replied.

"But—"

"It'll keep," she said with a small smile.

Jamie was back in class on Wednesday and was the first one in the student gallery when I arrived for a *Sounds of the Nineties* meeting that afternoon.

"How's Papa doing?"

"Okay. He's back home now, which is good."

"Good. That's good. Just . . . let me know if you need anything."

"Yeah, thanks." When he spoke next, he was trying very hard to sound casual, which I knew as someone who often tried very hard to sound casual. "Hey, so. About the other day." A pause. "Sorry if I . . . made it weird. I shouldn't have . . ." He trailed off, shook his head.

"Nah, it's . . ." I couldn't say it was nothing because it wasn't nothing to me. Just the idea of kissing Jamie felt sufficient to light me on fire.

But Jamie didn't want that—he was saying so now. He thought it was a mistake.

I swallowed, and tried to convey the vibe of someone whose heart was not plummeting to the floor. "Don't worry about it," I said, like my heart was exactly where it should have been, like this didn't hurt at all.

But I couldn't leave it at that. I didn't want it to be like it was before. I didn't want to drift apart again, not if I could help it. "We're . . . friends, right?"

A complicated series of emotions broadcast across the Jamietron, and then he nodded, a brief jerk of the head.

"Good," I said, and I couldn't stop it from tumbling out, something about Jamie sitting there and the quiet of the student gallery and the memory of the warmth coursing through me that night in my room, in my bed—"I'll always be your friend. I'll always . . . want to be your friend." I swallowed. "Just . . . so you know."

"Yeah," Jamie said. There was something indecipherable happening behind his eyes. "Okay."

It wasn't *I'll always be your friend too*. But it was something. I could work with that.

---

Joydeep and Sasha arrived, and we sat around the gallery—Joydeep stood, periodically pacing between the sculpture stands—and brainstormed.

"I think there's only one real solution," Sasha said eventually.

"Yes," Joydeep said. "Save us, Wonder Woman."

"We've gotta lean into it."

"What do you mean?"

"We can't fake Lucas. The fans will know him from a mile away, there's no getting around that. But we could potentially satisfy part of the audience—the Existential Dead part."

"And how do we do that?"

"Basically," she said, "we need a fake Tyler Bright."

"Sorry, what?" I blinked.

"What else can we do? The guy is a hermit anyway. No one's positively identified him in public since 2001.

He could look totally different now. We just need a guy that's kind of the same age. We can, like, get him a jacket or something."

"What kind of jacket?" Jamie asked.

"A jacket that Tyler Bright would wear, I don't know! Some kind of jacket!"

"For real?"

"He's not going to sing or anything. He just comes out, we do a brief interview, wave wave wave to the crowd, we're done." Sasha looked at each of us in turn. "Come on, who here knows a middle-aged white guy?"

No one replied.

"I can't believe we're actually considering this," Joydeep said.

"She's right, though," Jamie said. "We've got to do something."

"Okay, so think," Sasha said. "Who do we know who's an adult that we can trust?"

I took a deep breath.

I got us into this. I could—potentially—get us out of it.

With some help.

# 57.

DAN AGREED TO MEET AT Lincoln Square the following evening. He thought he was meeting me to talk about college stuff, but he was unknowingly meeting the entire *Sounds of the Nineties* team.

"Hello there," he said, when he reached our booth. We had one of the circular ones in the corner. I was on the end, next to Joydeep. We all shifted over to make room for Dan to slide in.

"These are my friends, Sasha and Joydeep," I said. "And you've met Jamie, from downstairs. We all have radio class together."

"It's nice to meet you, Sasha and Joydeep," Dan said, nodding at each of them. "I'm Dan. It's good to see you again, Jamie."

A waitress swooped in and took our order. Dan ordered a black coffee. The rest of us ordered pancakes.

"So . . . I'm guessing this isn't a chat about college," Dan said, when the waitress had retreated.

"Not exactly," I replied.

"Though our collective futures may depend on it,"

Joydeep chimed in. "'Cause if this thing goes sideways, we may be in some real deep—"

"We were hoping to talk to you about something for class," I interrupted. "We actually kind of . . . need your help . . ."

---

We told Dan the whole story. Our first disastrous shows, the promise to Mr. Tucker, the misunderstandings about the mystery guest. My dad backing out—that was a reveal for the others as well. I tried to downplay it, examining my plate of pancakes as I spoke. "He really was supposed to come, for Sidney's play. And he said he would do this, but . . . something came up at work." I couldn't help but add, "He would've made it if he could," and I didn't even know why.

Dan just listened to it all, nodding at moments, taking occasional sips from his coffee.

Then we got to the heart of the matter—would he help us?

He let out a surprised laugh.

"You want me to pretend to be—"

"Tyler Bright, from Existential Dead," I said.

"You sure have come up with something interesting here." He shook his head. "Tyler Bright." Amusement played across his face. "I haven't heard that name in a long time."

Jamie looked up from his food. "You've heard of him before?"

Dan nodded. "I have, in fact. I may be more familiar than most."

Joydeep's eyes widened. "Are you him?"

"What the hell are the chances of that happening?" Sasha said scornfully.

"Higher than you'd think," Dan said with a smile. "But no, I'm not. I did know him, though. Briefly."

"*What?*" I said, at the same time Joydeep said, "Seriously?"

Dan sat back in the booth, folded up his napkin, and pulled his coffee closer, though he didn't take a drink. "Technically, I knew a guy named John Preciado," he said. He paused like we knew who that was.

"He lived down the street from me growing up," he continued, when no one jumped in. "Our mothers were friends, and we were friends too, even though he was a couple years younger than me. We liked to talk about music.

"I went into the army to pay for college, and after college, after serving for a few years, going overseas and all that, well . . . when I came back from the Gulf, I didn't know what I wanted to do with my life, but I knew it wasn't the military anymore. This was a few years before I went back to school, got my dental degree . . . I don't know if I ever told you that, Nina, but I didn't start on that path until I was in my thirties."

I shook my head. I didn't know that.

"Well, I went looking for work, and I cycled through a bunch of jobs . . . telemarketing, construction, bartending . . . I'd try something for a few months, get fed up with it, try something else. I guess John heard, probably through his mother, when I was between jobs. He offered me a gig traveling around with his band—he was the bass player, had met up with these guys a few years ago. It was roadie work, sort of—loading equipment, tuning guitars, that kind of stuff. I drove their van. Just for one summer. As you probably guessed, that band was . . .”

“The Eagles,” Joydeep said sagely.

I elbowed him, and he grinned.

Dan grinned too. “Well, it was Existential Dead, of course. The unlikeliest little grunge band from Indiana. It was . . .” He trailed off, looking fond. “It was something else, I’ll tell you that.”

“Do you still know them?” Jamie asked, interrupting Dan’s reverie. “Is there any way you could get in contact with them? With John?”

“I’m afraid not,” Dan said. “I fell out of touch with all of them after that summer. I suppose it was one of those . . . moment in time sort of things.”

“But you’ve been around them. Around Tyler,” Joydeep said. “You know what he’s like. So . . . can you help us?”

“By impersonating him? For a ticketed event?” Dan looked . . . mildly concerned. “That has to be some kind of fraud, right?”

“I just don’t know what else we’re gonna do,” I said.

“Well. It must be a desperate situation if this was the best course of action.” Dan took a breath and let it out. Then he rapped his fist against the table. “Here’s what we’ll do. The show must go on. So I’ll be your guest.”

"For real?"

"As *myself*," he said. "As someone with inside knowl-edge about the band that everyone there—or a portion of everyone there, I suppose, with the whole . . . boy band situation—but anyway, at least some of the peo-ple will come away hearing about something they seem to be interested in, and you'll have a guest, as promised. I'll look back through my basement . . . I've probably got some old pictures from that time. I think I . . ." He nodded. "I can definitely find something or other of interest. How's that sound?"

More reasonable than a fake-out Tyler, surely. But also, wildly insufficient for what we were up against? But *also* also: appreciably better than what we had before, which was no guest, nothing even tangential to a guest or to Existential Dead, for that matter.

"That sounds . . . good," Joydeep said, and Sasha nodded.

"That would be great. Thank you."

"Thank *you*, for calling me." Dan smiled a little and flicked his gaze toward me. "I'm happy to help."

# 58.

**THURSDAY WAS THE DAY. THE** interview had finally arrived. Tonight, the mystery guest would be revealed.

I didn't know about the others, but I couldn't eat lunch. Couldn't focus in class. My mind was perpetually fast-forwarding to seven o'clock that evening, when the auditorium would be buzzing, awaiting the reveal of our mystery guest.

Unknowingly awaiting the moment when Dan—nice, kind, khakied Dan—would step out onto the stage.

What would happen? Would they boo him off? Would the TION fans and the Existential Dead fans riot? Would the four or five innocent people in the audience who maybe just wanted to hear an interesting talk be caught in the crossfire?

I couldn't concentrate. I skipped last period and went to the student gallery.

To my surprise, Joydeep was there. He had a textbook and a notebook open on the table, but he was staring at his phone.

"Hey."

He looked up, his expression brightening when he saw it was me.

"Free period?" he said.

I shook my head as I took a seat across from him. "Skipping."

"Rebel."

"I mean, there's not much more that can compare to whatever's gonna go down tonight."

Joydeep looked at me placidly. "I think it's all going to go really well."

"For real?"

"No, it's gonna be a bloodbath. But you know? Maybe we'll still get some money out of it. For Jamie's grandma's thing."

I thought of Joydeep in that very first radio class, gesturing back toward Jamie. *He's with us too.*

"Why didn't you go with Colby and them?" I asked. "Like when we first made groups in class."

"Because." He frowned and mumbled something that sounded like "peaks me."

"Sorry?"

"He picked Sammy," he said more clearly. "Over me. Hana and Lily, those are her friends, and he chose their group over mine."

"Is that why you fucked with their show?"

"No, I fucked with their show because it's funny and I'm good at it. But in general I feel like people shouldn't abandon their friends."

"But if you had been in his group, Sammy would have had to abandon one of her friends."

"No she wouldn't. There's no reason Colby and Sammy *had* to be together in a group. You or Sasha could've gone with her people and Colby could've been with us."

"Great to hear how fast you'd trade one of us out."

"Hey, it was early days! I didn't know—" A shrug. "I didn't know how this was gonna turn out."

"We still don't know how it's gonna turn out."

"But we know about us, though. That we're . . ." He waved a hand between us.

I smiled and raised my eyebrows up and down suggestively. "Soul mates?"

He sputtered a laugh. "You wish." He made a funny face, like he was embarrassed to be sharing feelings. "I don't know. We're kinda . . . bros now."

"Do we have to be bros?"

"Well, not if you don't want to. I just thought—"

"I mean, can't we be friends instead?"

He bobbed his head. "I could be okay with that." It was quiet, and when he spoke again, his voice was oddly careful. "So. What does one friend do when another friend is obviously super in love with their mutual friend?"

I blinked at him. "I'm not—me and Jamie aren't—" I shook my head. "I'm not."

A huge grin split Joydeep's face. "I didn't even say Jamie. I didn't even say you. You just assumed, because you *are*! You are!"

"*You* are!" I said. "Your face is!"

"Hey!"

"Sorry." I put my head in my hands. "Vikrant'll get you first."

He huffed a laugh.

"I knew it. I totally knew it. Sasha and I have a bet going."

"What's the bet?"

"I'm not telling you. I don't want to compromise the conditions of it. But rest assured, I'm going to win."

"Whatever you're doing here is probably tampering, though."

"It's not *tampering* to tell you I think you should tell Jamie how you feel."

"That sounds like tampering."

"That's not the bet! That's just being a good bro."

"Okay, *bro*," I replied, but I couldn't help but smile.

# 59.

**A STEADY FLOW OF PEOPLE** streamed into the auditorium that evening. I tried not to look out into the house as we all stood backstage—me, Jamie, Sasha, Joydeep, and Dan. Mom and Sidney and Rose were out there somewhere in the audience. Their support was not optional.

*You really don't have to come*, I had told them.

*We'll be there whether you like it or not*, Mom replied with a smile. *For both of you.*

We all had our roles for the evening—Joydeep and Sasha would be doing the interview. I was going to record, so we could broadcast it on our show. Jamie was in charge of getting the equipment ready, the mics and the recording set up.

We were in this together.

We had readied the stage—three folding chairs sat in front of what must have been the opening backdrop for the middle school play, showing a row of buildings painted pretty realistically in shades of gray and brown. A projector screen had been brought down in front, partially obscuring it. Dan had given us a PowerPoint full of pictures he found from his summer with Existential Dead, and we gave it to Mr. Tucker to give to AV, so they could project it during the interview.

Dan was wearing a button-down shirt and slacks. No jacket, because *I thought I'd keep it a little more rock and roll*, he had said with a grin. I had tried to grin back.

The buzz in the auditorium was getting louder. I checked the time—ten till seven.

"Ah," Dan said suddenly. "I've gotta go grab one more thing from the car. I'll be right back."

He headed through the black door in the back marked EXIT, and as he passed through, someone appeared on the other side.

"Thank you very much," Dan said to the guy holding the door.

"Oh, hey," the guy said as Dan passed through. "Are you, uh, in charge of this thing?"

"Folks in charge are right through there," Dan said.

"Thanks, man."

Dan disappeared, and then the person—two people, actually—entered the backstage area.

"Hi," the first guy said. He was probably in his late twenties, with close-cropped hair and black sunglasses hooked into the collar of his shirt. "I'm Chris Brewer, I'm looking for—"

"Holy shit," the guy next to him said. "That was Mr. Paint."

"What?"

"That dude, that was Mr. Paint! The YouTube guy! Didn't you—"

If he continued to speak, I didn't register it. Everything went to white noise, because standing next to the apparent Chris Brewer—standing there in front of us—simultaneously existing with us—was Lucas.

As in *the* Lucas. Lucas from TION.

He was a miracle. He was a figment of our collective imagination that we conjured into existence out of sheer need.

I was instantly struck by how young he looked. I knew from Sasha that he was only a little bit older than Rose. But it wasn't just that—it was how *normal* he looked. He was wearing normal jeans and sneakers and a T-shirt, he had on a normal baseball cap. Nothing about him screamed multimillionaire. Nothing said FAMOUS PERSON PRESENT. When he smiled, his teeth were very shiny and almost unnaturally straight, but other than that, he looked like any number of guys from Rose's class, golden seniors now graduated, coming back to watch a football game in a brand-new college sweatshirt.

Chris's voice filtered back through.

"—looking for a place to watch that's a bit discreet, maybe here backstage, or if you have a light booth that's easily accessible—"

Lucas ignored Chris, just as we were all ignoring Chris. "Is Mr. Paint the mystery guest?" he asked.

We all just stared, openly stared, at the TION member voted "Most Likely to Treat You Right (And We Mean Allllll the Ways)" by TeenStar.com.

My mouth had completely dried out. It was barely a word when I got it out: "You're . . ."

"Lucas," he said. "Lucas Kirk. This is my friend Chris."

"Future manager," Chris clarified with a grin.

"What are you doing here?" Sasha said. I had never heard her voice so high.

It was Joydeep who got it together first. It was like a flip switched inside him. An easy smile broke out on his face, and he crossed over to Lucas and Chris with a hand extended. "Hey, I'm Joydeep. We're the *Sounds of the Nineties* team, we're the ones putting on this event tonight."

"It's great," Lucas said, shaking his hand enthusiastically. "We never had anything like this at my school. But my school wasn't anything like . . . I mean, this place is huge. You really have your own radio station?"

"What are you doing here?" Sasha asked again, more urgently, her voice impossibly higher.

Lucas glanced at Chris, looking embarrassed. "I came to see Tyler Bright."

"Seriously?" Joydeep said.

Chris shook his head, exasperated. "I told him it was a long shot. Basically a no-go. Yet he of all people is willing to believe online chatter from some fan accounts."

"I know it's just a rumor. But I was in Westfield visiting some family, and I knew if there was even a chance it's true, I couldn't pass up that kind of opportunity," Lucas said.

"You're a Deadnought?" Jamie asked.

"I'm, like, *the* Deadnought," he replied with a grin. "*Velvet Flycatcher* changed my life. Tyler Bright is a legend." He gave a quick look around. "We were hoping we could watch from backstage?"

The door swung open again, and Mr. Tucker came in.

"Hey, team? Crowd is pretty much seated, we should probably—" He paused when he caught sight of Lucas.

Mr. Tucker's eyes widened. "Hey, you're—I know you. My little girl loves you. You're Blondie!"

"Uh . . ." Lucas looked a little bewildered.

"No, I know that's not right. But my wife, she's got names for all of you!"

"I'm very interested in these names," Lucas said.

"Well, lemme think, there's Blondie, Sparkle Prince . . . Sexy Vampire . . . Champ, and, uh . . ." He snapped his fingers. "The Smolder."

"Oh my god, that's amazing," Lucas said. "Is it weird that I know exactly who's who?"

Mr. Tucker grinned and then looked over at us. "*This* is your mystery guest? I thought—"

"Yes," Joydeep said. "This was our plan all along. We definitely did that. One hundred percent intentionally."

# 60.

WE HAD TO BREAK IT to Lucas that Existential Dead wasn't coming, but he took it well, on account of the baffling fact that he was also a fan of Mr. Paint. And he agreed—lo and behold—to go on, just as long as he was interviewed alongside Dan, so he could ask him questions too.

"I want to know everything about Mr. Paint," he said. "How did he get started? How does he pick the themes? Does he have sponsors?"

Dan returned as Lucas was chatting with us. He sidled up next to me with a dingy looking brown guitar case in one hand.

"Forgot my tour souvenir," he said with a smile, and then noticed Chris and Lucas. "Hello again."

"Hi." Lucas extended a hand and introduced himself once more. It was a disarming habit for a famous person to have. "I can't believe I'm meeting Mr. Paint. And that you toured with Existential Dead! That's wild!"

"I did. Just briefly."

Mr. Tucker, who had ducked out, returned now. "I think everything's set to go out there. You guys ready?"

"I want to hear all about it," Lucas told Dan, and then to Mr. Tucker: "Let's do it."

"Okay. We need our intros first," Mr. Tucker said. "You all good to go?"

Joydeep turned to Sasha. "Ready?"

Sasha looked past him, to the sliver of audience we could see from the wings, and then took a few steps away from the group and gestured me over.

"What's up?"

"I can't go out there," she said in a low voice.

"What? Why not?"

"I just. I can't. I'll ruin it."

"Are you serious? You're great at this."

"I'm great at this when it's the four of us alone in a room and I'm not looking at the faces of the people I'm talking to. But this? It's too much. It's the spotlight thing all over again. I'll mess it up."

"Sasha—"

Joydeep and Jamie joined us now. Joydeep had his list of questions in one hand, a mic in the other. Jamie had a second mic, and he held it out to Sasha, who regarded it like he was offering her a king cobra.

"What's going on?" Joydeep said.

"I can't go out there," Sasha replied. "I'm sorry. You have to do it."

Joydeep looked confused. "But you're my co-host."

"I can't." A pause. "You can do this, though. You don't need me."

"False," he said.

"How are we doing, guys?" Mr. Tucker called.

"Almost ready!" I called back.

"Someone's gotta go out there," Jamie said.

"You've got this, Joydeep," Sasha said.

Joydeep took a breath to steel himself, and then nodded. "Okay. Yeah, okay." And with that, he headed out to do the introductions.

"My name is Joydeep Mitra from *Sounds of the Nineties*. I want to start by saying thanks to everyone for coming out. I'm excited to announce we have *two* very special guests here with us tonight." There was a murmur through the auditorium, several excited squeals, a whoop from the back. "First up, is a local guy—a hometown hero, you might say—who is intimately acquainted with the insides of your mouths, owing to his job as a dentist." A ripple of confusion went through the crowd. "*But*, he also has some inside knowledge of a little band called . . . Existential Dead."

A cheer broke out from a portion of the audience, the kind that cheers for their favorite band name no matter the context.

"Please welcome Dan Hubler!"

The applause that followed was more . . . a smattering of perplexed clapping. Dan walked out onstage holding the guitar case. He nodded to Joydeep and then turned to acknowledge the crowd. Joydeep went on: "Dr. Hubler is going to tell us all about the time he spent touring with Existential Dead."

Murmurs ran through the crowd again.

"Our second guest is from a band that you may be familiar with. They're on the radio, much like myself." Joydeep grinned in our direction, and then turned to the crowd. "Please welcome, from This Is Our Now, Lucas Kirk!"

There was a loud exclamation, one of mingled confusion and hope, but as soon as Lucas stepped onstage, earsplitting shrieks rent the auditorium.

I'd never heard anything like it. It was hard to tell if it was because the audience skewed that much more toward TION fans than Deadnoughts, or because their collective lung capacity was just that much more powerful.

Lucas crossed the stage to Joydeep, waved to the crowd, and then shook his hand and clapped him on the back like they were old friends. Then he, Joydeep, and Dan took a seat.

Dan set the guitar case down at his feet. The screaming had not paused for one moment.

Lucas just looked good-naturedly at the crowd and did that kind of *calm down* motion, which cut the noise by half or so. Then he raised his mic to his lips.

"Hi," he said. The shrieks started again. "All right, all right." He looked pleased. "Thank you. Thanks for that. And thanks for having me here."

"We're happy to, uh. Happy you're here." Joydeep blinked, looking down at his sheaf of questions. "We are happy . . . to see you both . . ."

My stomach seized. Joydeep had nailed the intro, but he and Sasha had prepared all their talking points for Dan.

"We, uh . . ." Joydeep shuffled through the papers again. He glanced toward the wings, toward Sasha and Jamie and me. "We are very excited . . ." His voice was transforming into that of the Radio Joydeep of old.

"Oh, god," Sasha said quietly from next to me. "Okay."

"What should we do?" Jamie whispered.

I imagined that facing Sasha across the net during a volleyball match, you'd see an expression similar to the one she wore now. Determined, decisive, something equal parts intimidating and thrilling. Like she was about to *do that.*

"Give me a mic," she replied.

"Yes, ma'am." Jamie handed the mic over to her.

She took a deep breath. And then she headed out onstage.

Relief played across Joydeep's face at Sasha's approach, and the smile he gave her was radiant. "Friends, audience members, guests, this is my *Sounds of the Nineties* co-host, Sasha Reynolds."

Sasha paused next to the group. There was no fourth chair, since we weren't anticipating an extra guest. Dan stood, gesturing to his, but Jamie ran out just then with an additional chair and set it next to Lucas's.

Sasha sat down stiffly. "Hi." The mic was too close to her lips, and feedback went off. She winced. "Sorry." At a more normal volume: "Hi. Sorry I'm late. I was, uh. Parking my car."

"Well, I speak for the whole *Sounds of the Nineties* team when I say . . . I'm really glad you found a parking space," Joydeep said, and Sasha smiled.

"So." Sasha looked to Dan and Lucas. "Let's get into it."

And with that, the interview began.

---

Sasha and Joydeep asked Lucas about his experiences going from being a normal high schooler, to auditioning on *Pop Talent*, to joining TION. Dan even chimed in with some questions of his own, about the music industry, and finding fame at such a young age. Lucas answered everything thoughtfully. He was funny and charming and self-deprecating. I would later find that my mom had texted me during the show: *He seems like a very good boy!!! Manners for days!!!* Alexis, on the other hand, simply texted me a long string of expletives, key smashes, and exclamation points.

"But what I really want to hear about is you, man," Lucas said eventually, turning to Dan after telling Joydeep and Sasha about his favorite cities to tour in. "How did you get involved with Existential Dead?"

"Existential Dead," Joydeep jumped in, turning to the audience, "if you're not familiar, is a nineties grunge band that started in Indiana."

"They're *vastly* underappreciated," Lucas added.

Dan explained the story of John, his job search, the offer to tour for the summer. Images flashed by on the screen behind them as he spoke. Jamie and I could see them at a steep angle from where we stood—a beat-up van parked at the side of the road, four guys with long hair and sunglasses standing in front of a gas station, posing with their arms folded. A drum set with a plush bear sitting on the bass drum.

"They were never particularly famous," Dan said. "But the people who loved them, *really* loved them. And that music, when you heard it, standing in that room . . . well, it could move you, couldn't it."

He smiled a little. "I remember one night, Tyler was, uh . . . he had, you know, indulged in . . . ." He glanced around the auditorium. "Recreational substances. Anyway, he couldn't play. Said his hands were too numb, but he insisted the show would go on. I knew some guitar myself, had picked it up in high school, and had been playing around since we'd been on the road, practicing with their songs. So they brought me up onstage with them that night, and I played a gig. I played for Tyler. It was at this dingy little club in North Carolina. I'll never forget it."

He leaned down to the case by his chair, rested it on its side, and popped it open.

"Tyler ended up giving me that guitar, and I've still got it today, got it right here."

He pulled an electric guitar out, white with a silver inlay.

Lucas leaned forward. "Holy shit." His mic didn't pick it up, but we could hear it from where we stood. He seemed to remember where he was after a moment, and brought his mic up to his face. "That's his guitar." He looked up at Dan in awe. "That's *his* guitar. That's the Eat Your Greens sticker. And the lightning bolt scratch,

286

and Mitch Presley's initials. This is Tyler Bright's guitar from the *Velvet Flycatcher* album art!"

A ripple went through the Deadnoughts in the audience.

"It is," Dan said. "And I'm very lucky to have it."

"Could I . . . Could I play it?" Lucas asked.

"It may not be in the best shape . . . I restring it every now and then, but it's been a while . . ."

"Please," Lucas said.

There was a flurry of activity to find an amp for it—Mr. Tucker eventually located one in the band room—and in the meantime, Joydeep and Sasha asked Lucas about his experience with musical instruments.

"I'm not the best," Lucas said. "In the band, we don't really . . . We travel with musicians, you know, with our band, so there's not really a focus on us playing or anything. But I've been learning guitar for the last couple of years."

Mr. Tucker had emerged triumphant with the amp by that point, and they set it up onstage and hooked up the guitar.

"Give it a whirl," Dan said, passing the guitar to Lucas.

Lucas stood, looping the strap over his head, and began plucking out a melody, slow but competent. Shrieks of recognition, or maybe just general shrieks of joy, rang through the crowd.

He fiddled around with it for a little while longer, and then handed it back to Dan amid cheers.

"Will you?" Lucas said. "Please?"

Dan looked ambivalent for a moment, but then conceded. He sat—didn't even stand like Lucas had—and with the guitar on his knee, he began to play.

He began, more specifically, to shred that guitar like Tyler Bright himself. Like every heavy, intricate riff we had ever heard preceding an absolutely unintelligible Existential Dead chorus.

The surprise on Sasha's and Joydeep's faces was probably mirrored on my own.

"Holy shit," Jamie said next to me, an echo of Lucas.

When Dan finished, the crowd let out an enormous burst of applause. He smiled and then unplugged the guitar and set it back in the case.

"Thank you," he said, like it was nothing. A dip of his head, a smile, another "Thanks very much," like it was nothing at all.

# 61.

**I STOPPED RECORDING WHEN LUCAS** and Dan left the stage. The sounds of Sasha and Joydeep wrapping up the show were absolutely lost in the noise from the crowd. The two of them joined us in the wings, and the crowd was still cheering when Lucas turned to Dan.

"Can I see it again?" he asked, nodding to the guitar case.

Dan set the case down and pulled out the guitar. Up close, we could see the details Lucas had described—a peeling sticker, a lightning bolt scratch, some initials. The guitar looked beat-up, well-worn.

Lucas held it reverently, and then looked up at Dan. "Twenty thousand."

"I'm sorry?"

"I want to buy it."

"Oh, wow," Dan said. "I think—"

"Twenty-five," Lucas said.

"You'd really pay that much, just for an old guitar?"

"This band means so much to me, you have no idea,"

Lucas said. "And anyway, I've spent way more for way less before. You could set your price and I'd pay it."

Dan smiled. "That's not exactly how you go about bargaining, son."

Lucas flushed. "Would you be interested in selling it, though? Could you part with it?"

Dan considered him for a moment. "Well . . ." He glanced at me. "Give us a second," he said to Lucas, and moved to the side, away from the group. I followed.

"What do you think?" he asked, conspiratorially.

I blinked. "I mean . . . it's yours. If it's important to you, you should keep it."

Dan shrugged. "It was a different part of my life. I'm happy to let it find new life with someone else." His eyes narrowed, crinkling at the edges, looking keenly at me. "Unless of course it means something to you. Then I'm happy to pass it on to you."

I shook my head. Existential Dead was meaningful to me in a completely different way than it was to Lucas, and a physical representation of it mattered less, I think.

"I'm okay. But thank you."

Dan nodded. "It's decided, then." He moved back to Lucas. "What do you say—I'll give it to you for five, with ten grand each donated to the school and the charity being supported here tonight."

"It's a deal." Lucas clasped Dan's hand and grinned, bright and devastating.

Mr. Tucker ducked in.

"Hey, I think maybe we need to go back out and, uh,

reaffirm the end of the event," he said. "I'm not sure people are accepting that it's over."

"You know"—Lucas turned to us with a wry smile—"TION always does an encore."

The crowd roared when Lucas stepped back out with Tyler Bright's guitar. He pumped one arm in the air, encouraging the applause.

I looked over at Dan. He was beaming.

"This was fun," he said, looking back at me. "Thank you for thinking of me."

"Thanks for helping us," I replied. "Thank you for . . ."

*Being here.* I couldn't finish, but I think Dan knew.

# 62.

SEVERAL PEOPLE ASKED FOR REFUNDS, despite there being absolutely no claims or confirmation of Existential Dead—or any of its living members—performing. Fortunately, among the station and radio broadcasting class members present that night, Mr. Tucker had tapped Sammy to run last-minute ticket sales, and consequently, refunds. "If you really want to take money away from charity," she said, fixing them with that dead-eyed stare. "If that's what you're saying. That you gave money to charity, and now you want to take it back."

A couple of people pressed further. But not most.

Lucas posed for pictures with us, with Dan, with Mr. Tucker and Mr. Tucker's wife, who he had frantically texted before the start of the show, and their seven-year-old daughter, who was too shy to hug Lucas, but gave the biggest smile when he crouched next to her for their picture. The photo ops ended there; Mr. Tucker had the foresight to lock the backstage area down early on during the event, to prevent people from the audience from swarming to meet Lucas afterward.

Regardless, news of Lucas's visit to Meridian North

had gotten out online as soon as the talk began, and a large crowd of fans had formed outside the school by the time it ended. Future Manager Chris had arranged for a private car for Lucas, and asked if they could leave "from the back," which may have worked in a restaurant or nightclub, but was somewhat more complicated in a school.

Mr. Tucker plotted a route to the loading dock on the south side of the building that took us through a series of basement passages I didn't even know existed. The loading dock was near the athletic fields, and if the car could make its way back there, it would be the most discreet exit.

Sure enough, when we wound our way through the school—the *Sounds of the Nineties* team, Dan, Mr. Tucker, Lucas, and Chris—and emerged at the dock, a sleek black car was already waiting outside.

"Thank you guys," Lucas said to us, shaking our hands one last time. "So much. This was awesome."

Chris gave Dan's hand a brisk shake before crossing around to the other side of the car. "We've got all your info. We'll follow up tomorrow, all right?"

Lucas paused, holding the guitar case to his chest. "You're sure you're okay with me taking this now?"

"It's yours," Dan said.

"You're the best. I'm gonna call you next time I'm in town, okay? We can jam."

"Looking forward to it," Dan replied.

With one last wave to us all, one last devastating smile, Lucas from TION was gone.

It was quiet, all of us standing at the open door to

the loading dock watching the car retreat, the night sky clear and dazzling over the athletic fields beyond.

"We did it," Joydeep said eventually, hushed. Stunned. "We actually fucking pulled it off."

A beat, and then he looked toward Mr. Tucker, sheepish. "Sorry."

Mr. Tucker grinned. "You can have that one."

# 63.

**LUCAS POSTED A PICTURE OF** him and Dan the next day.

> *this dude is sicccccck! Nicest guy and great time with @soundsofthe90s!*

We got several thousand followers within hours. Lucas also linked to *The Artful Heart*, and Mr. Paint got even more.

As it turns out, having a pop star randomly show up at your school event makes you into a bit of a viral thing, so viral we went in the days that followed. We were featured on the local news—Mr. Tucker went on to do the interviews—and even got mentioned by some national outlets. We did phone and email interviews with a number of different places—entertainment news sites and the like. An array of headlines followed, accompanied by shaky videos taken by audience members:

*BOY-BANDER LUCAS KIRK SURPRISES HIGH SCHOOL STUDENTS*

*POP STAR DROP-IN SHOCKS STUDENTS
AT SCHOOL RADIO EVENT*

*THIS IS OUR NOW MEMBER CAUSES
FANGIRL FRENZY AT MIDWEST HIGH
SCHOOL*

Joydeep linked that one in particular in our group chat:
*I mean I wouldn't call it a FRENZY
Kind of reductive*

---

While all of this was underway, there was another major event—the middle school play. After months of preparation, Sidney's moment was finally here.

We got seats in the auditorium that were close but not too close to the stage—*I don't want to be able to see you, but I want to know you're there*, Sidney had told my mom.

*So . . . where would that put us? Like center middle?* Mom had replied.

Center middle it was. We had just settled in—Dan had a big bouquet of roses that he managed to tuck under his seat—when there was a tap on my shoulder.

I looked back. Jamie was taking a seat directly behind us, Sasha and Joydeep settling in on either side of him.

"What are you guys doing here?"

"I don't know about the others, but I'm a big supporter of the theatrical arts," Joydeep said.

Jamie smiled. "We thought we'd add to the cheer section for Sidney."

All at once, I was flooded with the same feeling as when I opened the door back in eighth grade at the start of our Kingdom revival and saw Jamie in the hallway dressed in full Hapless garb. Like my heart couldn't fit in my chest. "Thank you."

He nodded.

Sidney was amazing. *Star power* is how Dan described it afterward. Sidney, still done up in her stage makeup, clutched her bouquet and beamed.

# 64.

**MY DAD CALLED ON SUNDAY** night, as always.

He talked to Sidney first, and then to Rose, very briefly. "You guys are all over the internet!" he said, when it was my turn on the phone. "All these people are sending me links to articles and stuff!"

"Yeah, it's pretty amazing."

"Tell me everything."

I told Dad what happened. He exclaimed at all the right moments, asked all the right questions, like a good interviewer should.

"Incredible," he said when I was done. "Seriously. I'm so happy for you guys." It was quiet for a moment. "And . . . I know it sounds like it turned out a million times better than it would have if just plain old me had shown up. But still . . . sorry I couldn't get there for you, kid."

"It's okay."

"No. I said I would, and then . . ."

"It's fine." A beat. "What are you doing right now?" He was never just on the phone—phone conversations were more of an add-on to something else.

"Just stopped for gas. These prices, Christ. Maybe I'll become one of those pricks who go around on racing bikes like they're in the Tour de France. Get one of those head-to-toe spandex outfits. Neon green."

I gave a breath of laughter, and then it was quiet.

"Hey, Dad?"

"Yeah?"

I could see him in my mind, standing at a gas pump while his car filled up. Probably afterward he'd go inside and pick up a pack of spearmint gum and some cigarettes. He tried quitting every couple of years—it never stuck for long.

"Do you remember those bears you got us, with the yellow dresses?"

"You mean Honey Bear? Of course I do."

Irrational tears pricked my eyes. "I can't find mine."

"Yeah, 'cause it's here."

That was it. I remembered. Of course it was.

"Remember you left it when I moved out here? To keep me company? Well, and keep you company too I guess, when you visit, but I will admit I co-opted it. I actually keep it on my desk in my office. Reminds me of my girls."

I swallowed. "I forgot about that."

"Well, that's where it's at. Why do you ask?"

I shook my head, even though he couldn't see me. "Just wondering."

# 65.

MOM WAS SITTING AT THE dining room table a little later that night, laptop open, a thick book titled *GRE PREP PLUS* open next to it. Sidney and Rose were both in our room, working on homework.

I was on the couch, flipping through TV channels. I had homework too, but it was very hard to find the motivation. Instead I went back and forth between a reality show about a pet salon and a sitcom rerun.

We had been to the usual Sunday night dinner at Dan's earlier in the evening, before Dad had called. I had tried to give Dan an envelope containing the Camera Repair Fund. He had long since fixed it, but I figured it was better late than never.

"This is really kind of you," he had said, "but it's not necessary."

"I know that. But . . . I broke it, so it's my responsibility."

Dan had considered this for a moment, and then nodded, taking the envelope. "Thank you, Nina. I really appreciate that."

"You're welcome."

A moment later, a smile teased his lips. "By the way, did I mention I had an early graduation present for you?" he had said, and then handed the envelope back.

I looked over at my mom now. She had her glasses on—green plastic with gold accents. She only used them for reading. Right now she was peering at her computer screen, brows furrowed slightly, eyes searching.

"I found a tape," I said.

"Hm?"

"I found a tape. When I was looking in the storage room."

Mom looked over. The readers magnified her eyes.

"Oh?"

"*Conrad and Mickey: The Supercut*. It was from when you and Dad met, on the radio."

"Ah." A pause. "His producer made that for us, for our wedding. Tracked down a recording of the call."

"Producer Shoebox?"

"The very one. He was your father's best man."

"How was his speech?"

"As terrible as you'd expect."

"Sound effects?"

"Without the soundboard, he resorted to doing them himself."

"Yikes."

Mom took off her glasses, hooked them on the collar of her shirt. "Is that what you've been listening to with that Walkman?"

"Yeah." I flipped channels again, and the sitcom laugh track burst to life. "I liked hearing it. Even if you weren't the lucky caller."

"I was, though."

I looked over. "But you didn't win. That was the whole point, right?"

"No," she said, considering. "I never got tickets. I always called and missed out, that's true. But I got him to pick up the phone. And because of that, and because of that stupid conversation—" She smiled a little, like she was remembering. *I can't give tickets away to every girl whose voice I like.* "Well, we met. And we went out, and everything that happened after . . . everything, all of it, even the bad parts, it led us to you. And that was lucky, Nina. The luckiest thing that ever happened to me."

I thought of what Sasha had said: *It doesn't devalue what you had with them, the stuff you experienced, the time you spent together. That's still valid, even if it wasn't built to last. It's not any less significant.*

I swallowed, and for a second the coffee shop scene on TV went blurry.

"I'm glad you called," I said.

"Me too."

The sitcom guy spilled a cup of coffee on himself, and the audience exploded into hysterics again.

"And I'm glad Dan showed up on your online dating algorithm thing," I continued. "Because he's nice. And I like him."

Mom smiled. "I like him too."

It was quiet for a little while after that.

"What show were you trying to see?" I said eventually.

"Sorry?"

"The tickets. On the radio, when you called Dad. What concert was it?"

"Oh." Mom paused. "Well, I called in a lot, to be honest, but I think that time . . ."

"What?"

"I mean, I was young, keep that in mind."

"What was it?"

"I was, uh, twenty-two at the time?"

"Mom."

"It was tickets to see *NSYNC. The No Strings Attached tour. I was gonna take your aunt with me and we were going to get Joey Fatone to fall in love with one of us."

"Wow." I bit back a smile. "I'm sorry we deprived you of that."

"I can find it in my heart to forgive you," she said with a grin.

# 66.

Joydeep: You're listening to 98.9 The Jam, the voice of the Meridian North Bobcats, and this is *Sounds of the Nineties*.

Sasha: Hello to all the new listeners out there. There are . . . definitely a lot of you, which is very cool.

Joydeep: Very *very* cool. And guess who's definitely not stuck paying for everyone's prom tickets?

Sasha: Who would that be?

Joydeep: This guy. For the benefit of the listeners out there, I'm pointing to myself.

Sasha: Thanks for clearing that up.

Joydeep: You see, I had this bet going with my friends—

Sasha: Should we really be getting into that right now?

Joydeep: No, probably not. But anyway, thanks very much, listeners!

Sasha: So tonight we're going to be playing a recording from our recent live event, with special guests Dr. Dan Hubler and Lucas Kirk from This Is Our Now.

Joydeep: Yeah, so if you missed it, you can hear how it went. I think it went pretty well, personally.

Sasha: I think so too.

Joydeep: You did a great job interviewing.

Sasha: As did you.

Joydeep: You know, this is nice. This is a nice feeling in the studio right now.

Sasha: [laughing] Okay.

Joydeep: I like this for us.

Sasha: Let's just play the recording.

# 67.

JOYDEEP REFERRED TO THAT EVENING'S show as our "victory lap." We filled the remainder of the time with Existential Dead songs, in tribute. It seemed only right.

When we were packing up, I noticed a text from Rose:

*Running late at work! Be there soon!*

So I took my time gathering my stuff. Sasha bid us all goodbye and headed out, but Joydeep lingered, shouldering his backpack and looking between Jamie and me. "Hey, did you guys happen to listen to *Cat Chat* this week?"

I shook my head.

"Oh. It was a pretty good episode. I mean, not *good* good, since it's *Cat Chat* and all, but . . . There was one interesting question. I downloaded it, and uh, you guys should listen to it before you go. I got it all queued up, just have to—" He reached over, tapped a key on the keyboard, and Colby's voice filtered into the room.

"*—so I guess I'd say, it's not the best idea ever, but it's probably worth a try?*"

"See you guys," Joydeep said with an enigmatic smile, and then he headed out.

"*We've got another question here,*" Sammy was saying, "*from someone who calls themselves a longtime listener, longtime question asker. Dear* Cat Chat. *I have two friends—*"

"*Wow, good for you.*"

"*Colby!*"

"*Sorry.*" His voice came close, like his lips were right on the mic as he whispered, "*Not sorry.*"

"*I have two friends,*" Sammy began again, louder, "*who are obviously into each other.*"

Something in my stomach swooped. I locked my eyes on the soundboard.

"*Something happened between them when they were younger—I don't know what. All I know is that one of them is always looking at the other when they think they're not looking. They both think no one else has noticed, but literally everyone around them notices. They get along really well. They both have the same weird sense of humor. Or at least, maybe different weird senses of humor that are compatible with each other.*

"*These days, they look at each other with extra sad eyes, and it's really annoying. I've encouraged each person to talk to the other, but they don't. They talk to me instead, and even though I'm undeniably brilliant—*" She snorted. "*There's only so much I can do. How do I get these two people to admit to each other that they want to—*" Sammy cut off, made a strange noise.

"*You have to say it,*" Colby said.

"*I don't think I can say that on-air.*"

"'*Bone down*,'" Colby said, enunciating very clearly. "*It says 'bone down.*'"

"*Colby!*"

"*It says it!*"

A heavy sigh. "*Signed, Sick of the Lovesick. P.S. Thank you,* Cat Chat, *for providing advice to students and the community at large. Your show is, if I had to say it*"—Sammy's voice flattened—"*not that terrible, or whatever.*" A pause. "*Gee, thanks.*" Another pause. "*So what do you think?*"

Jamie moved abruptly, crossed over to the computer—

"*Well, I think that—*"

He shut off the audio.

"Don't you want to hear the advice?" I said.

"It's . . . No, I mean, it's not . . ." He looked over at me. "Do you want to hear the advice?"

"Yes."

"Why?"

"Because I want to hear what they should do. Like . . . what they think the people should do."

"They shouldn't do anything."

"Why not?"

He looked away. "Because it's not . . ." A beat. "Because . . . maybe one of them feels that way, but they know that it's . . . one-sided. That the other person just wants to be friends. And that's—" He swallowed. "That's totally fine."

I blinked.

I was the person who said, *I'll always be your friend,* and Jamie was the person who said, *Yeah.*

"That's not what they meant," I said. "They didn't meant it like *just* friends, they were saying . . . that's not what they were saying."

One corner of Jamie's mouth lifted. "You seem to know a lot about this random person's intentions."

I let out a breath, almost a laugh but not quite. I looked at him for a moment.

"I have to say something," I said.

"Okay."

I didn't speak.

"Definitely . . . feel free."

I shook my head. "I can't just . . ."

"You said you had to say something!"

"I do, I can, I just . . ." I flapped my hands. "Can you just, like. Not look at me or something?"

Jamie's look of confusion softened slightly, and he turned his gaze to the ceiling.

"Don't look back till I say, okay?"

"Okay."

"And don't say anything. Until I finish saying it. The thing I have to say."

He nodded, face still turned up. I could see the underside of his chin, and something about it was weirdly vulnerable.

"You promise?"

He nodded again.

"I missed you," I said. "So much."

He didn't speak. But that was okay, I had told him not to. I took a breath and went on:

"I . . . didn't realize how much. And it's not that it

went away, like I ever stopped missing you, it's that I got used to it, and once we started . . . all this . . . it was like I remembered how much you . . . like what a big part of everything you were. Are. I don't want it to be weird between us if I say the thing I'm going to say, but you can mean it lots of ways, you know, so just know that when I say it, I mean it all the ways."

Jamie's throat bobbed on a swallow, but his gaze never wavered from the ceiling.

"When I say I love you, Jamie, I mean it as my friend, and I mean it as a *Sounds of the Nineties* team member, and as a neighbor, and as a bagel maker—" He laughed. "And as a coworker, and as a good person, a kind person, as Prince Hapless, as you. When we were little kids, before I even knew what it was, and now. Now I love you how . . . how you love someone that you're in love with. Also. There's also that.

"So when I said that I'd always be your friend, I meant that . . . I always want to be there for you, no matter what. No matter which way. And if you don't feel the same way, that's okay. I understand. I'll just . . . keep on loving you. All those other ways."

He didn't speak, didn't move. Just blinked up at the ceiling. He was the same Prince Hapless who stayed unconscious just because my sister told him to, who didn't break during our final game, even when I was probably the last person in the world he wanted to be around.

"Okay," I said. "That's . . . that's it. That's what I wanted to say. So . . . you can. Talk now. If you want."

He looked at me. I couldn't parse the expression on his face.

"Are you going to say something?"

"Yeah, I mean." He nodded. "Same."

I blinked. "That's it? Same?" I shook my head. "You don't—I mean, if you don't feel the same way that's totally okay, but what do you mean by *same*, what is that, why would you—"

"Because I feel the same," he said, stepping closer, a grin spreading across his face. Radiant, a Lucas Kirk kind of pop-star smile—one that could pin you to the floor from a thousand feet away. "And I thought it would be funny."

I couldn't help but smile back.

"You were right, it was funny," I said. "I would've done the same thing."

"I know. That's why I love you too."

"You do?"

"For lots of reasons, not just that one."

"For real?"

"Why is that shocking?"

"Because you're you."

"And you're you." He shook his head. "I always . . . I've *always* . . ."

I kissed him.

It was *hit the ground running* kind of kissing. *I want every part of me to be touching every part of you* kind of kissing. The singular, fleeting sweetness of the kiss in front of *Acton*, the intensity of that night in my room, this was all that and now a third thing, a new thing, it was enthusiastic, and happy, and relieved, it was joyful as fuck. I broke away just to kiss Jamie's cheeks, and his forehead, and the spot under his ear, and he tightened his grip on me like holding on to each other was the only way to keep us from floating off the ground, the only thing tethering us to the earth.

---

After that, we discovered the true purpose of the couch in the studio. It was for this—precisely this—it was placed here for the sole purpose of making out with each other, for this exact circumstance when we needed to kiss exponentially more and also recline at the same time. It was good work on the part of the universe, and I commended the universe for it, and then thought of nothing but Jamie and how incredibly awesome this felt, until the moment the door opened and Sasha stepped in.

"Agh!" she yelped, and then, face brightening, pointing a finger at us, "Ahh!"

Neither of us moved, but Jamie gave a high-pitched, "Hi! Sorry!"

"I forgot my phone." Sasha looked gleeful. "And I just won the bet."

"What was it?"

"Which one of us would walk in on the two of you"—she waved a hand—"just like this." She stepped in, quickly crossed over to her usual spot, picked up the phone lying to one side of the monitor, and then crossed back. "Have lots of fun!" she called. "Joydeep is gonna flip his shit."

She pulled the door shut behind her.

Jamie just looked at me, eyes wide, and then we both burst out laughing.

# 68.

Colby: Well, I think they're both being ridiculous. Like the whole thing is stupid. I'm not, like, an expert or whatever, but I do know that communication is important. One of them just needs to go to the other one and say, Hey. I like you. If you like me too, let's, you know. Take it to the bone zone.

Sammy: Colby!

Colby: What? It's true! I mean, everyone should take it to the bone zone at their own pace, if that's something they're into. Maybe it's not. The bone zone isn't for everyone. But I'm just saying, they need to tell each other how they feel.

Sammy: Oh my god, you're so embarrassing.

Colby: You like me, though.

Sammy: Questionable.

Colby: Don't act like you've never wanted to take me to the bone zone.

Sammy: COLBY!

Colby: How about another message? Dear *Cat Chat* . . .

# 69.

IT WAS LATE IN THE evening a few days later when my phone buzzed with a message from Jamie:

*Would you rather eat ten whole lemons in one go or give up everything related to lemons forever?*

*Hmm,* I replied. *I'd rather tell you in person*

*Meet downstairs?* He sent back almost instantly. *The crystal room?*

I smiled.

Mom was in her room already. Next to me, Sidney was tucked up under the covers. Only Rose was still up, sitting in bed with her computer in her lap.

"Hey, I'm gonna go . . . run and borrow a book from Jamie," I said quietly, climbing out of bed.

"Uh-huh," Rose said, infused with a heavy dose of skepticism.

"If Mom comes in, just say I'll be right back."

"Okay."

"I've got my phone."

"What about your pictograms?" Rose looked up. "Are they handy, just in case?"

"We're just gonna talk."

"Uh-huh," she said again, just as skeptical, but her gaze shifted back to her computer. "Be safe."

I pulled on my shoes and then paused in the doorway. "What are you working on?"

"Just looking at some classes. I might register for the summer."

"Psychology stuff?"

"Maybe," she replied.

I nodded. "Good."

One of the doors to the Crystal Room—the Mama Bear ballroom's formal name—was open when I got downstairs, and I slipped inside. The streetlamps and the building's exterior lights cast rectangles of orange light across the room. Jamie was already there, standing at one of the windows, and he turned as I approached, looking soft in sleep pants and a hoodie.

"Give up lemons entirely," I said, and then kissed him.

It was the beginning of a long series of kisses that didn't pause until Jamie rested his forehead against mine and murmured, "You could never use anything lemon-scented though. No lemon candy. Lemon meringue pie. You couldn't drink lemonade." His eyes widened. "Or listen to *Lemonade*!"

"You're saying you'd eat the lemons?"

"I would absolutely eat the lemons."

"Hmm," I said, and kissed his ear.

"I just feel like the ramifications of no lemons . . ." His breath hitched. "Could be a lot more . . . widespread . . . than you think . . ."

Nothing was said for a while after that.

But eventually we settled down on the floor, sitting with our backs resting against the wall, and we just talked. Jamie played with my hand absently, running his fingers over mine, as he told me about Gram and Papa, their trip to the doctor's office earlier that day, how Papa was doing really well, all things considered. I told him about the plans for Mom and Dan's ceremony a couple weeks from now; the officiant had been booked. We all had our outfits picked out. I didn't know it then, sitting there in the Mama Bear ballroom with Jamie, but Mom would invite the Russells too, and Gram, Papa, and Jamie would join us on that bright May day, the sky endlessly blue. I'd surprise myself by how emotional I'd get at the ceremony. How happy I'd feel.

Right now I threaded my fingers through Jamie's, squeezed his palm. "We'll be moving," I said. "Over the summer."

Mom and Dan were looking for a house somewhere a little north of the Eastman. They hadn't found anything yet, but Dan was eagerly anticipating some upcoming open houses. *This one right here looks pretty great*, he had said, showing us a real estate listing during our dinner on Sunday. *Room for everyone!*

Jamie's voice was soft: "I didn't know that."

I nodded.

"It'll be weird to not live in the same place anymore," he said.

"You'll still see me all the time."

"Really?"

"Yeah. You're gonna be sick of me."

He shook his head and smiled. "Impossible."

It was quiet for a bit after that, until I looked over at Jamie. "Can I ask you something?"

"Of course."

I felt silly but I couldn't help it: "How did Prince Hapless die?"

"Ah." Jamie considered for a moment. "Well, I guess the short answer is that he didn't."

"What?"

"Funny thing. Remember the tomb? In the wild-flower meadow?"

"Where they have the super dope music festival."

"Exactly. Eventually his people discovered that the tomb was empty. Prince Hapless had faked his death and gone into hiding."

"Why?"

"He was . . . vulnerable, without Aurelie and Iliana and Quad. They were gone, and he didn't know . . . where to look for them, I guess. He didn't know if . . . they needed his help. If they even wanted it. And he knew he would be lost without them, owing to him being just . . . completely hapless, so . . . it seemed like the only way."

"But he's out there somewhere."

"Oh yeah. For sure. He probably . . . got a part-time job someplace. Maybe his wheelhouse was never in being royalty, but he's like really good at customer ser-vice or something."

"He's a banquet server at magical ceremonies."

"I like that."

"Maybe Aurelie will find him one day. When she

drops off some baked goods to the magical catering service."

"I like that too."

I looked over at Jamie. He lifted my hand, rested my fingers over his lips, Kingdom style, and kissed them.

We said good night, eventually, and I fell asleep with that same warmth running through me.

# 70.

OUR FINAL SHOW ARRIVED THE following Thursday.
We were calling it a "nineties freestyle"—hits from the
whole decade.

We were sitting around between links when Jamie
said, "What do you think actually happened to Tyler
Bright though? Like, where is he now?"

There were plenty of theories among the Existential
Dead fandom—the last confirmed Tyler Bright sighting
was in 2001.

We threw our own theories around for a bit. Joydeep
leaned back in his chair eventually and said, "Honestly,
he's so off the grid he could be back on it again and we
wouldn't even know."

Sasha nodded. "Maybe he went totally underground,
changed his name."

"Burned off his fingerprints," Jamie suggested. "Got
reconstructive surgery."

Joydeep raised an eyebrow. "Became a mild-
mannered dentist?"

"What?" I looked over.

"You heard him play guitar," Joydeep said. "And it was *that* guitar. Why would Tyler Bright give his iconic guitar to a random roadie who worked for him for like, three months?"

"It wasn't an *iconic* guitar at the time; it was just a guitar."

Joydeep pivoted: "He wasn't in any of the pictures, though. There was not one single picture of Dan with Existential Dead."

"So? He was probably taking them."

"Unless he was in them already and we just didn't know."

"What do you mean?"

"Tyler Bright had a complete beard and super long hair! There could be anyone under all that hair!"

"You sound like a true Deadnought right now," Sasha said, shaking her head. "Hardcore conspiracy theorist."

"Admit that there's a possibility, though," Joydeep said.

I turned to Jamie. "Are you buying any of this?"

He considered it for a moment. "I could like . . . ninety-eight percent rule it out."

"You seriously think there's a two percent possibility?"

"Yeah, I'd give it two percent."

Jamie smiled at me when the others weren't looking. I was one hundred percent going to kiss his face off later. I had asked Rose to pick us up half an hour late for just that purpose. (I didn't tell Rose that was the purpose, but I think she had her suspicions.)

Joydeep pulled a picture of Existential Dead up on

his phone and held it out to me. "Just look. Look at this and tell me you can honestly say it's *not* him."

That's how it went for our final show. The last *Sounds of the Nineties*. Soon after, classes would wrap up, then there would be finals, then graduation, then . . . everything to come. Whatever that would look like.

The four of us—we weren't built to last, necessarily. Jamie would start at Butler in the fall, and I would be at IUPUI. Sasha would go on to play volleyball for Notre Dame. Joydeep would be at Pomona, Vikrant-adjacent and a comfortable distance from the West Coast Mitras. It didn't devalue what we had or what it was. It wouldn't change the moment in time we all shared together.

And it wouldn't be the last moment we all shared, either. The group chat would still erupt every now and then. Jamie and I would go to Sasha's volleyball matches against IUPUI. We would all meet up when Sasha and Joydeep were back over the holidays.

Jamie and I would spend as much time together as we could amid classes and family stuff. We were an ongoing moment—one I hoped I would never see the end of.

Right now the members of Existential Dead stared up at me from Joydeep's phone, and I focused in on Tyler Bright's bearded face. "He's got sunglasses on," I said. "You can only see, like, one-sixteenth of his facial geography."

"Look at that nose and tell me you can definitively state it's not the nose of our friend and benefactor Dr. Dan Hubler."

"I can't say it's *not* his nose, but I can't say it *is* his nose either."

"Schrödinger's nose," Sasha said, and we debated it until I checked my monitor and caught sight of the time.

"Hey, we got a link coming up."

"Excellent." Joydeep reached for his headphones. "Ready on your cue, Madame Producer."

I watched the counter on the current song, and when the time came, pushed up the volume slider, pressed the button, and we were on-air once more.

# Acknowledgments

I feel amazingly fortunate to have worked alongside an incredible group of people to bring this book into the world. Thank you to Kate Farrell and Bridget Smith, the editor and agent duo of my dreams, for all that you do. Thank you to the folks at Macmillan/Henry Holt, in particular the Fierce Reads team, Brittany Pearlman, and Rachel Murray for all of the hard work and enthusiasm you've brought to every title. Additional thanks to Mallory Grigg for the beautiful cover design, and to Jane Newland for such gorgeous artwork. Thank you as well to Aarthi Dee for the thoughtful commentary and critique.

This book was written during the last year of my PhD, and I absolutely would not have been able to make it happen without the support of my incredible family and friends. Thank you to Mama and Papa, Hannah and Cappy, for all of the love and guidance. To Jiyoon, Pei-Ciao, Rachel and Shawn, Lakshmi, Eshaani, Rochelle, Becky and Doug, thank you for being amazing friends. Thanks too to Lauren James, for first-rate correspondence and for sending me fic recs just when I need them the most!

Thank you to the all the readers, bloggers, booktubers, and bookstagrammers out there for loving books, and for taking the time to share that love with the world.

Thank you librarians, booksellers, and teachers—you are amazing!

Finally, I want to acknowledge my home during the course of my graduate career, Indianapolis, and the local radio stations that have kept me company in transit every day. In particular, thank you to the deejays of the North Central High School student radio station for all of the inspiration, and for adding joy to many a commute.